Home From the War

"Who—are—you?" Cliff said hoarsely.

"My God! Is it possible you cannot *know?*" she cried.

"Know—what?"

"That this is no longer your home."

"But it is—my home," he persisted.

"Oh, why were you not told! Clifton Forrest, it is a pitiful homecoming for you," she wailed, wringing her hands.

"You know—my name?" queried Forrest, astounded.

"I saw it in your book. Oh, if I could only spare you!"

"Spare me? . . . My mother!—My father!" gasped Forrest.

"I know nothing of them. I've been away two years. . . . But before I left they lived—where I used to live."

"Who—are—you?"

"Virginia Lundeen."

"You! . . . Have I lost my mind? . . . But she had red hair!"

"Well, it changed color with my changed fortunes."

"Then—my father—has lost—our old home?"

"Clifton, it is true."

ZANE GREY

THE SHEPHERD OF GUADALOUPE

HarperPaperbacks
A Division of HarperCollinsPublishers

This is a work of fiction. The characters, incidents, and dialogues are products of the author's imagination and are not to be construed as real. Any resemblance to actual events or persons, living or dead, is entirely coincidental.

HarperPaperbacks *A Division of* HarperCollins*Publishers*
10 East 53rd Street, New York, N.Y. 10022

Cover photo courtesy of H. Armstrong Roberts, Inc.

First HarperPaperbacks printing: June 1992

Printed in the United States of America

HarperPaperbacks and colophon are trademarks of HarperCollins*Publishers*

10 9 8 7 6 5 4 3 2

CHAPTER

1

*T*HE sea out there, dark and heaving, somehow reminded Forrest of the rolling rangeland of his beloved West, which he prayed to see once more, before he succumbed to havoc the war had done his body and soul.

He leaned propped against the rail of the great ship, in an obscure place aft, shadowed by the lifeboats. It was the second night out of Cherbourg and the first time for him to be on deck. The ridged and waved Atlantic, but for its turbulence, looked like the desert undulating away to the uneven horizon. The roar of the wind in the rigging bore faint resemblance to the wind in the cottonwoods at home—a sound that had haunted him for all the long years of his absence. There was the same mystery in the black hollows of the sea as from boyhood he had seen and feared in the gloomy gulches of the foothills.

But he hated this restless, unstable, treacherous

sea which seemed a part of the maelstrom in which he had been involved. He yearned for the mountains, the desert, the valley of cottonwoods, home and mother, far across this waste of waters, those dear remembered ties of the past that still survived. The emotion had only come strong during those moments when, ignoring his weakness and pain, he had clung to the rail, gazing into the pale obscurity of the night, out over the boundless ocean, with the consciousness that the dream that had mocked him during nine months on a hospital cot had become a reality. He was on the way home—home to Cottonwoods!

He visualized the winding valley between the silver hills beautiful with the green-gold trees that gave their name to the place; the rocky stream that wound leisurely down, bordered by sage and willow, bringing the blue-tinted snow water from the mountains; the old rambling Spanish ranch house, white-walled, with the vines climbing up to the red tiles.

This retrospect seemed to release him from the vise of the war horrors that had clamped him. It would be best, now he was going home, to live in thought of the brief future allotted him; and his mind clutched at the revivifying memories.

There had been changes at home, his mother's recent letter had intimated—a strange letter coming many months after a long silence, full of thanksgiving and joy that the report of his being among the missing had been erroneous, and evidently stultified over ills she had not the courage to confide. Thinking back, Forrest recalled a letter here, another there, widely separated, the content of which had not augured well for the prosperity of the Forrests. But he had dismissed them with a bitter laugh of recollection at the absurd idea of Clay Forrest, his father, ever losing land or stock enough to matter.

How would he find things at home? The query gave him a pang, for that thought had been seldom in his mind. He hoped now to find his parents well, and surely, in view of his service to his country and the supreme sacrifice he was soon to make, they would forgive the disgrace he had brought upon them. How long ago that expulsion from college! It seemed so trivial now, the cards, the drunkenness, the fight which had ended his school career. He had tramped and worked, now a rolling stone, and again a young man in whom hope could not wholly die. Then 1914 and the war! And now, broken in body and mind, victim of an appalling chaos, like thousands of other young men who had sustained a brutal and terrible affront to faith, honor, patriotism, love, he was voyaging across the ocean, battling the gray specter that hung grimly on his trail, longing for the land of his birth, the wide sweep of the Western ranges, the sage, the cottonwoods—there gladly to lay down the burden.

The huge black ship plowed on through the sullen sea, spreading the inky billows into white, seething, crashing foam, that raced by with spectral glow and phosphorescent gleam, to pale and fade in the darkness. The funnels roared and emitted bulging clouds of smoke that hid the stars. The mighty iron mass drove on masterfully, as if to fling defiance at nature. Forward along the wide deck bright lights shone on women scantily and beautifully gowned, and men in conventional black, not one of whom, it seemed to Forrest, had a thought of the greedy, mystic sea, or the perilously rushing ship, or the precious life so prodigally theirs.

Forrest left his post and walked along the deck, hiding his limp, and the pangs in his wounded side, and the burn in his breast. He walked erect. These were Americans returning home, and many of them were young. He felt no kinship with them. What was a crippled soldier to these idle, luxurious travelers? But once in his stateroom he sagged, and the face he saw in his mirror dropped its mask. Crawling into his berth, he lay in the dark, listening to the rhythmic pulse of the engines, deep in the bowels of the ship. Alone there with his phantoms in attendance he wooed slumber until at last it mercifully came.

On the following day Forrest vacated his stuffy stateroom late in the morning, and sought relief in the open air. The sea had gone down. There was no side roll, only a slow stately pitch, as the ship headed into a moderate southeast swell. Spring was in the air, coming almost balmy on the soft breeze. Passengers were out in force, in sport clothes, making the most of the fine weather. The sea shone bright green without any white crests. Smoke on the horizon attested to the passing of a ship.

Forrest found a steamer chair and made himself as comfortable as his stiff leg would permit. His position was near the wide space on deck where quoits and other games were adding to the amusement of passengers. In the chair next him sat a man whose friendly overtures could not without open rudeness be avoided. So Forrest agreed about the weather and that the halfway point on the journey had been passed and that the passengers were showing themselves this morning.

"I see you've been in the service," remarked the man, after an interval.

Forrest nodded. If his civility invited curiosity, he would have to move, though he was reluctant to do this, because it required effort that was painful.

"My wife and I have been in France," went on the stranger. "We had a boy in the service. Over a year ago he was reported missing. We thought perhaps we might find his grave or get some trace of him."

"Did you?" queried Forrest, in quick sympathy.

"Nothing.—He was just gone."

Forrest turned to eye this father who spoke so calmly of a tragedy. He looked like a small-town merchant, or a farmer who was lost without his overalls and boots. His geniality did not hide the furrows in his face nor did the kindly interest of his eyes conceal their sad depths.

Forrest expressed regret and inquired about the missing son's regiment, thinking that he might have heard something. But the father knew little except the bare facts, and did not seem inclined to talk further about his loss. Forrest liked this plain, simple man, and was quick to feel that such contact was good for him, despite his sensitiveness.

"I was among the 'missing' for over a year," he vouchsafed. "At least that was the belief in my home. I turned up in the hospital, but no report of that was ever sent—and, well, I wasn't in any condition to know what was happening."

"But your people know now?" queried the man, eagerly.

"Yes. They know."

"How good that is! . . . Strange I should meet you. . . . I suppose I'll never cease to hope my boy will turn up alive."

"It might happen."

"I'd like my wife to meet you if she happens along. Would you mind?"

"Not at all."

"Where is your home?"

"New Mexico."

"Way out West! Well, you have a trip ahead of you. . . . And you don't look very strong yet."

"I think I'll make it," replied Forrest, smiling wanly.

"You must! Think of your dad—and your mother," rejoined the man, feelingly. "Maybe I can lend you a hand when we dock?"

"No, thanks. I'll manage. Fact is I feel better this morning than for months."

The little man did not press the point and tactfully changed the subject for a hazard on the ship's run. Then after a desultory conversation peculiar to ocean travel he excused himself and withdrew.

Forrest was left the better for that meeting, though how, he could not define. But he realized that he must not build a wall round himself for everyone. His own father and this kindly stranger would have had much in common a twelvemonth ago.

The sun climbed overhead, making the day pleasant for the passengers at their games or promenading the decks. Forrest, however, felt the slight chill in the air, even under his rug; nevertheless, he was conscious of something that might have been an exhilarating movement of his blood. Not improbably this accounted for a languid interest in the stream of promenaders.

Presently he made the surprising discovery that he was an object of some interest to the feminine contingent. It annoyed him and his first impulse was to retire to the seclusion of his stateroom. Still, it was pleasant there and he was resting more comfortably. What did these women see in him, anyway? To be sure, a half-blind person could read his story from his telltale face. The fact that the interest he roused was sympathetic rather than curious did not allay his irritation. It had rather a contrary effect.

Forrest tried lying back with his eyes closed. This worked fairly well, but as he could not sleep and quite forgot the reason for the pretense, he soon opened them. He found himself staring straight up into the beautiful face of a girl he had noticed before, though not closely enough to observe how really attractive she was. Detected in her scrutiny of his features, she blushed. Then she swiftly averted her face and went on with her companion, a girl of slighter build and less striking appearance.

He stared after them, noting in the taller a supple strong figure and a head of bright chestnut hair, the curls of which tossed in the breeze. Forrest imagined her face perhaps, at least her dark, wide blue eyes, familiar to him. They had been bent upon him with a wondering, penetrating look, for which he was at loss to account.

The incident had about faded from his unquiet mind when he espied the two girls coming back along the deck, arm in arm, rosy with their brisk exercise, walking more swiftly than the other passengers. He watched them approach and pass, which they did this time without apparent notice of him. Both girls were Americans, clad obviously in the latest Parisian styles, of which the short skirts rather jarred upon Forrest. The one with the chestnut hair had the build of a Western girl and the step of a mountaineer. It had been long since Forrest had seen her like, but he had never forgotten.

Upon their next circle of the decks they took up the quoits just abandoned by others, and began to play, with the taller girl at the end nearer Forrest. How gracefully she bent, with long sweep of arm to pitch the quoit! She was an open-air girl, and she had a wrist and hand that could hold a horse. Presently at the conclusion of the game she changed sides with her opponent, and then Forrest had full view of her face. Reluctantly he surrendered to its charm, somehow strangely familiar, as if it were that of a girl of his dreams or of some one he might have known in a far-off happy past.

She was gay, full of fun, and keenly desirous of beating her opponent, who evidently had a shade the more skill. Despite attention to the game, however, while her rival was pitching, she glanced at Forrest. And finally he grasped that it was neither casual nor flirtatious, but an augmentation of her former puzzled and wondering look.

Something of a thrill stirred in Forrest's sad and lonely heart. For six years girls had meant little or nothing to him. Before that he had been sentimental enough, and even up to the age of twenty-two he had suffered divers attachments. In France he had known two girls, both of whom he would have loved if he could have been capable of love. But the war had been hell. He could not become callous. He had not been built to function like a machine. His emotions had destroyed his soul as bullets had his body. Still this young American Diana recalled Christine, a little French girl whom the war had made a waif. She had been petite, with glossy, fine, black hair and eyes to match, that peered roguishly from her pale, pretty face. She had no parents, no home, no friends except chance soldiers; she was a little derelict, yet she somehow embodied the spirit of France, and was unforgettable. Forrest did not quite understand what connection there could be in his mind between her and this girl of his native land. Certainly, there was no physical resemblance.

Again these merry quoit-players changed positions, and presently one of the quoits slid under Forrest's deck chair.

The chestnut-haired girl tripped over, flushed and shy.

"That was a wild pitch. I'm sorry," she apologized.

Forrest suddenly realized what was expected of a gentleman, and he forgot the need of guarding against abrupt movements. As he jerked out of his lounging position, to reach for the quoit, he sustained a tearing agony in his side. But he secured the quoit, and his shaking hand touched hers in awkward contact. No one could have mistaken the caution with which he leaned back in his chair.

"Oh, you hurt yourself?" she asked, in hurried compassion.

"A little. It's nothing," replied Forrest, faintly. Her wide startled eyes denied his assertion.

"You should have let me pick it up," she went on.

"I don't often forget, but you made me," he said, gazing up at her, with a wry smile.

"Ah! You're an American soldier, going home?" she asked.

"All that's left of me."

She did not voice the pity and regret which her face expressed. Evidently confused, if not agitated, by the little incident, she turned to her game, which she rather abruptly terminated.

Forrest lay back in his chair, resenting the angry palpitations of his injured side. How impossible to grow insensible to pain! The tear, the rend, the fiery shock shooting back to the heart, then the quivering raw nerves, and the slow icy sickening settling to normal! He disliked the intrusion of this beautiful, healthy, care-free girl upon his misery; and he overcame some deep unfamiliar warmth within to resent her pity.

Late in the day, when he ventured on deck at the hour most passengers were dressing for dinner, he essayed to walk up and down a little, as he had been instructed to do, at whatever cost to his sensibilities. He really managed very well for a cripple, and in spite of sundry qualms the exercise was good for him.

The sunset lacked warmth and color, yet its pale yellow and turquoise blue, hemmed in by russet clouds, was worth watching, if only to remind him of the West, where the setting sun was a ritual for the Indian, and the best of the day for the hunter, the range man, the rider on his trail, and the rancher on his porch.

Forrest at length had recourse to his chair, and he found pinned to his steamer rug a little packet wrapped in tissue paper. Violets! Who could have placed them there? Only one reply seemed possible. The act touched Forrest deeply, for he took it as an expression which could not have been made in words. He carried them to his stateroom and placed them on his pillow. One of his many tribulations was the fact that he was not permitted to eat more than once a day, and then sparingly. And as he shunned the saloons and was too nervous to read by artificial light, there appeared nothing to do but go to bed.

Soon, in the darkness of his stateroom, he lay with his cheek touching the tiny bunch of fragrant violets, and it was certain that his tears fell upon them. It had been a sweet and compassionate action of the chestnut-haired girl, but it hurt even in its aloof tenderness. For the moment it pierced his bitter armor. In the silence and blackness of the night, with only the faint throb of the engines and the roar of the sea in his ears, he felt what he had missed during these wasted years and now could never have. He held that his sacrifice had been futile. The magnificent glow and inspired fighting fervor with which he had volunteered for the war, had died in the ghastly reality of the truth. Even his belief in God had succumbed.

How strange to feel that there still abided in him depths that stirred to the look in a girl's eyes and the meaning in a gift of violets. She had not known that he should have been beyond the pale of such human sentiments. The worst of it was that he was not. Long indeed were the hours before slumber claimed him.

Next day the donor of the kindly gift might as well not have been on the ship, for all Forrest saw of her. On the ensuing morning he thought he caught a glimpse of wavy chestnut hair disappearing behind a corner of deck, but it did not reappear. And gradually the persuasive force of the incident faded; the fleeting interest that had kept him from morbid retrospection lost its healthy tone, and he drifted back. The little affair, perhaps only a kind thought for her, yet of such incalculable good for him, had been ended. Chestnut-haired girls were not for him.

When in the early rose and gold of sunrise the ship steamed up the Narrows and on past the Statue of Liberty, the hour was one of tremendous moment to Clifton Forrest. His own, his native land! One of his prayers at least had been answered. There was only one left, and he renewed that with a faith incurred by this beautiful answer.

At the docking his ordeal of transfer began. But he kept out of the press of the crowd, and watched the gay fluttering of handkerchiefs, the upturned faces, eager and intent, the hurry of passengers down the gangplank. And looking among them, suddenly he espied her. Had he forgotten? She was clad in white and those around her dimmed in his sight. Yet he saw her welcomed by young men and women, who whisked her away, leaving a blankness over the noisy crowd, the incessant movement and changing color.

After complying with the wearying customs regulations, Forrest sat resting upon his luggage until he could engage a steward who would take him to a taxi. Soon, then, he was dodging the traffic of the streets of New York, the peril of which he thought equal to tank warfare in France.

Uptown, the great canyon streets, with their endless stream of humanity, and in the center the four rows of continuous motors, brought stunningly to him the bewildering fact that he was in New York City. To be sure, a thousand leagues still separated him from his destination, yet this was home. It roused him to a high pitch of gratitude, and of an inexplicable emotion that had long been dormant in his breast.

The stimulus of this grew as he turned into Fifth Avenue, where the wild taxi-driver had to join the right-hand procession and slow up at frequent intervals. Thus Forrest had opportunity to revel in the sidewalks packed with his countrymen. The bitterness of neglect had no place in his full heart then, and the hour was too big for the tragedy of his life to prevail. He had not dreamed it would be like this. Perhaps there was something his misery had blunted or which his intelligence had never divined. Among the thousands of pedestrians he saw women of all degrees, from the elegant lithe-stepping patrician to the overdressed little shopgirl. And it was these his hungry heart seemed to seize. Had he not seen enough men to last ten lifetimes?

At the Grand Central Station he expended about the last of his strength reaching a bench in the waiting-room. The huge domed vault, which he could see through the doorway, seemed dim, and the hurrying people vague in his sight. He leaned back with his coat under his head, and slowly watched the arch clear of dim gloom, of spectral cubistic shapes, like the things of a nightmare; and rays of colored sunlight shine upon the splendor of sculptured walls and the painted dome.

Oddly it struck him then that the clearing of the vast space above might be a symbol of his homecoming. Out of chaos, out of turgid gloom, the beautiful lights on the storied painted windows! But if it were true it must mean out of travail into ease, out of insupportable life to dreamless death.

It took hours sometimes for Forrest to recover from undue exertion. This appeared to be a time when he would just about be rested and free from torture, then be compelled to rouse the fiends of flesh and bone again. It was well that he had to wait for one of the slow trains, upon which no extra fare was charged.

Eventually he once more got pleasure and excitement from the hurrying throngs. Wherever did so many people come from? Whither were they going? Indeed, their paths seemed the pleasanter lanes of life, for few indeed belonged to the lower classes. All well dressed, intent on thought or merry with companions, bright-faced and eager for whatever lay ahead, they impressed Forrest with the singular and monstrous fact of their immeasurable distance from him, from the past that had ruined him, from the bleak ash-strewn shore of the future.

He had given his all for them and they passed him by, blind to his extremity. But for the moment he soared above bitterness and he had clearness of vision. Surely one or more of these handsome girls had a brother under the poppies in the fields of France. Perhaps some of these business-like young men had shared with him the battlefield, but had escaped his misfortunes.

So the hours passed, not tediously for the latter half, until the porter who had carried his bags and purchased his ticket arrived to put him on his train.

"Come, buddy," said the porter, with a grin; "hang on to me and we'll go over the top."

Anyone who ran could read, thought Forrest with resignation. Still his pride would never succumb. Without a falter he followed his guide to Pullman, and once sunk in his seat he sighed and wiped the cold dew from his brow. Only one more like ordeal—the bus ride in Chicago from station to station—and then the Santa Fé Limited! How often from the hills outside Las Vegas had he reined his horse to watch the famous Western train wind like a snake across the desert!

The Palisades above the Hudson, with the sinking sun behind them, appeared to have a faint bursting tinge of spring. At home the cottonwoods would be in leaf, full-foliaged, and green as emerald. He watched the reflection of cliff and hill in the broad river until dusk. Then he ventured boldly for the dining-car. It brought poignant memories. How different his first experience in a diner six years before on his way to college at Lawrence, Kansas!

That night he did not sleep very well, though he rested comfortably. The rushing of the train through the darkness, fearful as it was, seemed welcome because of the miles so swiftly annihilated.

Morning came, and finally Chicago, dark under its cloud of smoke. Forrest naturally was slow in disembarking from the train. All was bustle and confusion. Porters were scarce. And as the connection for the Santa Fé was close he could not risk missing the bus. So he carried his luggage. As a result he had to be helped into the bus, and at Dearborn Street put in a wheel chair and taken out to his Pullman. He was staggering and groping like one in the dark, while the porter led him to his berth and deposited his luggage.

When Forrest sagged into the seat he felt that it was not any too soon. He was glad indeed to lay his head on a pillow the porter brought. Outside, the conductor called all aboard. The train gave a slight jar and started to glide. Forrest heard a passenger exclaim that the Twentieth Century Limited had just made the connection and that was all. Then the train emerged from the shaded station out into the sunlight.

Forrest knew that he had overshot his strength, but if it did not kill him outright, he did not care. He was on the last lap home. And the ecstasy of it counterbalanced the riotous protest of his broken body. Had he not endured as much without any help at all save the brute instinct to survive? He opened his heavy eyelids, and the first person he saw was the chestnut-haired girl he had met on the ship.

CHAPTER

2

"**R**ECKON he's fainted, Miss." The voice probably came from the porter.

"He is very white." This was evidently from a girl. "Are you sure it's the same fellow, Ginia?"

"I know it is." That voice had a rich note that Forrest recognized. It had power to raise him from his lethargy, but he decided he would like staying unconscious a little while longer.

"Miss, he was fetched in a wheel chair," said the porter. "Sho I had all I could do with his luggage, an' I reckoned whoever fetched him would help him aboard. But he got on alone, an' I seen him saggin' here too late."

"Mother," interposed the first girl, "Ginia declares she saw this young man on the *Berengaria*."

"Indeed! Who is he?" queried the mother.

"I don't know," answered the girl Forrest knew. "But I do know he's a wounded soldier."

"Who told you that, my dear?"

"Anyone could have seen. Besides, he told me so. . . . He was alone on the ship. . . . Porter, is there anyone with him now?"

"No, Miss, I's sho there ain't. It was a red-cap who fetched him in."

"Bring me a towel wet with cold water," returned the girl called Ginia. "Ethel, get your mother's smelling-salts, in case I need something stronger."

Forrest felt some one brush his knees and evidently sit down opposite him. Then a soft warm hand touched his cheek, and that gentle contact shot all through him.

"Like ice," she whispered.

"Poor fellow! Wouldn't it be awful if he were dead?" exclaimed the girl who was probably Ethel.

"Hush! Suppose he heard you! . . . Ethel, don't stand there like a ninny. Go back to your mother. . . . Thanks, porter. You might get another pillow."

Then Forrest felt the gentle pressure of a cold wet cloth upon his brow and temples, and the touch of light fingers smoothing back his hair. A most unaccountable sensation assailed him. This was the girl who had given him the tiny bouquet of violets, which he had still in his possession. What chance had brought them together again and now on a train going west?

"He doesn't come to," whispered the girl to some one near. "I wonder if there's a doctor aboard."

Forrest thought it was quite time he was recovering consciousness. Therefore to the best of his ability he imitated a motion-picture actress coming out of a trance, and then opened his eyes. Some one gasped, but it was not the girl bending toward him. She drew back, a little startled. Then the gravity of her face relaxed.

"There! You've come to. We—I had begun to fear you never would. . . . You fainted, you know."

"Very good of you to trouble—about me," he replied, and his unsteadiness was not feigned.

"You must have hurried too fast."

"Yes. You see, I didn't want to miss this train. . . . Another whole day."

A blond head popped up from behind the seat, where manifestly it had been very close indeed. And a pretty girl asked, solicitously:

"Ginia, is he all right?"

"He has recovered, at any rate."

"Thank you. I think the fact that I'm on this train will make me all right—presently," replied Forrest.

"I am very glad," said the girl, soberly, and sat down opposite him.

The porter brought another pillow and slipped it under Forrest's shoulders.

"Anythin' mo' I can get you, boss?"

Forrest shook his head. The girl handed the towel to the porter, and moved as if to rise. But she did not carry out her impulse. Forrest was gazing into her eyes, which evidently confused her, yet held her there for the moment. Her eyes were deep dark violet, wide apart, and somehow they struck a memory chord in Forrest's uncertain mind. Just now they were troubled.

"Was it on the ship—I saw you?" he asked, uncertainly.

"Yes."

"Anywhere else?"

"Not that I know of."

Slipping his hand inside his breast pocket, he drew forth the faded violets and exposed them in his palm.

"I found these pinned to my steamer rug. Did you put them there?"

She blushed rosy red. "I! . . . Why do you imagine I did it?"

"There was only one other person who could have been kind enough. He was an old man and never would have thought of it. . . . Did you?"

"But why do you want to know?"

"I'd like to know truly that you did it, instead of some stranger."

"*I* am a stranger, too."

"You are, yes. But then you are not. I can't explain. I believe, though, I've seen you somewhere. . . . I'd been nine months in a hospital. Missing months before that. God only knows where. . . . The first time my frozen heart seemed to soften was when I saw those violets. . . . I laid them on my pillow—and cried myself to sleep on them. . . . Absurd for a soldier! But the iron in me is gone. . . . Now will you tell me?"

"Something prompted me," she answered, swiftly. "I don't know what. I resisted the impulse. . . . But then I did it. And now I'm very, very glad."

She arose, somewhat confusedly, and backed into the aisle. Forrest felt the intensity of his gaze and that it fascinated her. There seemed nothing more to be said in words.

"I hope you rest and soon feel stronger," she said, and left him.

Forrest thought it would be well to do just that thing, if he were ever to reach Las Vegas. Yet an inner conviction, more stable and determined today, assured him that such hope was no longer vain. He relaxed the tension which had upheld him, and closing his eyes, went back to the old ghastly strife with his pangs. Always he paid for exertion, and that meant of emotion as well as of muscle.

But outworn nature took a hand, and his surrender to reality was only a preamble to sleep. When he awoke the sun was on the other side of the car. Aware at once of relief, Forrest sat up. The flat green country and the wide farms, with their straight fences, told him Illinois was fast passing by.

The blond girl came down the aisle with an elderly woman, presumably her mother, and she smiled at Forrest.

"You had a long nap. I hope you feel better."

"I do, thank you."

"The porter was going to wake you—for lunch, he said—but we drove him off."

"Thank you. I don't need much to eat and it's easy to get. But sleep is difficult. I guess I was just about all in."

"You don't look so—so bad now," she concluded, with naïve encouragement.

The other girl was not in evidence. Forrest leaned on the window-sill and watched the flying landscape, scarcely believing that at last he was on the way home. There had come a break in his bitterness. The broad brown and green acres thrilled him. He had never appreciated his country. If he only could have had everything to do over again! There were horses in the meadows, flocks of blackbirds flying in clouds over the wooded creek bottoms. The lanes, recently muddy, stretched for leagues across the land, empty of vehicles clear to the horizon. How different in France! But America was endless and boundless. Wait till he crossed the Mississippi—then France could have been set down anywhere and lost!

Some one addressed him. Turning, he looked up into the bright face of the girl who had been so kind to him.

"You are better?" she asked, gladly.

"Yes, indeed," he replied, and thanked her for her solicitude.

"Oh, but you had me scared!" she exclaimed. "Are you really as—as ill as you made me believe?"

"How ill was that?" asked Forrest, smiling up at her. The wholesomeness and artlessness of her drew him out of himself.

"When I first asked if you were a wounded soldier you said—'all that's left of me.' "

"Well, isn't it true?"

"I—I can't tell," she returned, the glad light fading. "You don't look ill or weak now—only pale." Here she sat down opposite him and clasped her hands over her knees. She had changed her dark traveling dress to one of lighter hue, and the effect was magical. "Truly, I hoped you were just spoofing—that day on the ship. This morning, indeed, I noticed you were a very sick boy. . . . Still, when I saw you sitting up just now, I hoped again——"

"Boy!—I am twenty-eight," he interrupted, in pain that her kindness made acute. He faced again to the window, biting his lip. "And my doctors give me perhaps a month—to live."

There ensued what Forrest felt to be a very long silence. He could not control remorse. But her youth, her abounding health, stung him into a revolt at he knew not what.

"How dreadful!" she answered, in a hushed voice.

"Only for the thoughtless—and selfish," he returned. "Death is nothing. I have seen a hundred thousand young men like me meet death in every conceivable manner."

"Yes, we *are* thoughtless—selfish, and worse. But how little we know! It takes actual contact."

"Did you have a brother, a friend, or anyone dear —over there?"

"No. Only acquaintances, and I thought that hard to bear. . . . Mr. Soldier, it is courteous of you to confide in me. I can imagine how you hate it. . . . But one question more. You are going home to your mother?"

"Home to mother, thank God!" he whispered, dropping his head. "And dad! —I disgraced them. But this, I feel, has made it up. All I ask is to see them again, to learn all is well with them—and then it can't come too soon for me."

"I say, thank God, too," she murmured. *"Quien sabe?* Home might make you well."

When Forrest recovered from this lapse into agitation, a most irritating and increasing habit that had grown upon him, the girl had gone back to her berth, which was across the aisle and the second down. She faced him, however, and thereafter, whether reading, or talking to the several members of her party, her glance came back frequently to his, as if unaccountably drawn.

The sight of her somehow gladdened him, in a way long foreign to him. Curiosity became added to the attraction he did not try to resist. Who was she?

Where was she going? She certainly did not appear related to the pretty blond girl and her mother, nor to several young men who appeared very attentive. One of these, presently, noted her interest in Forrest, and did not take kindly to it. This byplay assured Forrest that he was not quite yet a disembodied spirit. He was still a flesh-and-blood individual over whom another could show jealousy.

He got out his magazines and a book and pretended to read, when in truth he merely wanted to watch the girl unobtrusively. She was quick to grasp his subterfuge, and adopted it herself, giving him a look and a smile that made his heart beat faster.

Gradually the exchange assumed the proportions of a flirtation, but not the frivolity of one. Her look answered to his, until a consciousness of it perhaps, made her shy. Not for a good while then did she reciprocate, but eventually he won her glance again. This time she laid the magazine in her lap and stared at him with wonderful eyes of sadness, of understanding, and more which Forrest could not define. But it seemed as if she were sending him a message—one which Forrest did not in the least know how to interpret. But as it seemed incumbent upon him to answer her challenge, he turned in his book to a favorite poem, which had in it the elements of his tragedy, and rising he walked down the aisle and handed it to her.

"I'd like you to read that," he said, and went on to hold a little colloquy with the porter about dinner, which he ordered brought to him.

Upon his return one of the young men sat beside her, quite protectively, and he glared at Forrest, as he held out the book.

"Did you like the poem?" asked Forrest of the girl, while he took the book from her companion.

"Thank you. I—I didn't read it," she replied, with what he construed as coldness, and she averted a troubled face.

Forrest resumed his seat more shaken by the incident than he would admit, even to himself. But he was at the mercy of his emotions. Ruefully he opened the book and read the poem he had indicated. Surely there could not be anything in it to offend the most fastidious taste. Perhaps his intimation that her graciousness permitted him to grow sentimental and personal was accountable for the change. He withdrew into his shell and the strange radiancy which had opposed his realistic moods slowly turned to dead ashes. He had made a blunder, for which, however, he did not see the necessity of asking pardon. He did not probe into the nature of his error. Of what avail? How bitter to receive such a lesson amid such new and uplifting thoughts as she had aroused! He had been relegated to his lonely place.

He wondered if the sleek handsome young man beside her—surely an Easterner—had been in any way responsible for the snub. It was quite possible, considering his air of proprietorship. Also he wondered if that languid, prosperous-looking chap had been in the war. A little keen observation convinced Forrest that this fellow had never helped dig a trench.

Nor did Forrest require further observation to insure the fact that the girl with the chestnut hair studiously avoided looking in his direction. His resentment, however, did not augment to the point where he was oblivious to the absence of pride or vanity in her demeanor. Merely she had lost her warmth. Something had blunted her receptiveness. Well, what did it matter? What was one hurt more or less? He had no time to sentimentalize over a woman, however bewilderingly charming she chose to be. He closed the book upon the page where long ago he had written his name. Had she seen that? But the unfortunate circumstance was closed.

The sun set red over the level land; dusk fell to shroud the flying farms and wooded lowlands. He watched the shadows over the fields, the pale gleams of light on ponds and streams, the bright windows of farmhouses that flashed by. Then the waiter brought in Forrest's dinner.

The next event was one of momentous importance—crossing the Mississippi.

Forrest could only faintly see the rolling waters of the great river. But he knew from the sound of the train when it passed off the bridge on to Missouri land. West of the Mississippi!

Forrest lay awake that night while the train passed through Lawrence, Kansas, where five years before his brief college career had ended so ignominiously. What sleep he got was fitful. Next morning when he raised his head to look out of the window he saw the long gray gradual slopes of the plains.

Propping himself on pillows, he lay there watching. The brown ploughed fields, the gray bleached pasturelands, the ranches few and far between, the dry washes, the gradual heave and break of continuity, the absence of trees or green growths, the tumbleweeds before the wind, the dust-devils rising in yellow funnels, the scampering long-legged, long-eared jack rabbits—all these were incense to Forrest's lifting spirit.

The porter roused him. He got up, to find the morning half spent. While he was in the dressing-room, slow and careful about his ablutions, the train crossed into Colorado. The day then went like a dream. Twice that he noted, though he never raised his eyes, the girl across the aisle passed him. She was still on the train. What was it that had happened? But nothing could intrude into his obsession with the mountains. And all the rest of that day he watched the multitudinous aspects of the approach to and the ascent of the great Continental Divide. Such a sunset he had not seen since he had left the West. There was a rare blue sky, deep azure, cut by the white notched peaks, and above, some clouds of amber, purple, and rose, rich as the hearts of flowers and intense with the transparency of smokeless dustless skies.

His dinner he enjoyed. That night he slept and dreamed of his mother. Next morning the sage benches, the boulder-strewn arroyos, the bleached gramma-grassed open slopes rising to cedars and pi-ñons, the black-fringed ranges of New Mexico!

For hours he pored tenderly over the infinite variety of landscape, which yet always held the same elements of rock and grass and timber and range. New Mexico in the spring was somberly gray, monotonously gray over the lowlands, black and white, wild, broken, and grand over the battlements of the heights. He had forgotten all except the color, the loneliness, the far-flung wandering lines, the solitude of the steely peaks. Raton! Lamy! Wagonmound!

There was Old Baldy, the mountain god of his boyhood, lofty, bleak as of old, white-streaked in its high canyons, capped with a crown of black timber, frowning down, unchangeable to the transient present. Forrest trembled and his heart contracted. Almost the little for which he had prayed had been granted. When the train pulled into Las Vegas, stopping before the Castaneda, Forrest sat stockstill, unmindful of the bustling important porter, not even surprised or interested to see that this also was where the girl with the chestnut hair disembarked.

He had to moisten his lips to thank the porter, and then he was almost wordless. There was a dry constriction in his throat. As he stepped down, the last passenger to leave the train, he gazed wildly about, as if he expected to see persons he knew. But there was no one familiar among the many Indians, Mexicans, railroad men, and others present. Forrest stood beside his luggage, seeing, hearing, feeling, though not believing. Almost he wished he had telegraphed his parents to meet him at the station. But he had clung to a reluctance to let them see the wreck of him until the very last unavoidable moment.

A chauffeur accosted him: "Car for hire, sir?"

"Do you know where Cottonwoods is?" asked Forrest, coming to himself eagerly.

"You mean the big ranch out heah?"

"Yes. On the road to Old Baldy, twelve miles out."

"Shore do. Can I take you out?"

"Grab my bags." Forrest followed the driver out to a line of cars. "Put them in the back seat. I'll ride in front."

"Reckon you ain't keen on bumps," returned the chauffeur, with a grin. "Wal, out a ways the road ain't any too good."

"It used to be plumb bad, before the days of autos," said Forrest, as he got in. He had quite forgotten his condition. Indeed, he had no sense of incapacity whatever. He seemed full of pleasant whirling thoughts.

"You ain't no stranger, then?"

"Not exactly. But I don't remember you."

"Wal, I'm new in these parts."

So far as Forrest could see there was not one single change in the business section of Las Vegas. On the outskirts, however, he observed unfamiliar buildings and cottages.

"How's the cattle business?" asked Forrest.

"Ain't any. Thet's why I'm punchin' this heah car."

Forrest concluded he would not ask any more questions. Besides, he wanted to see with all his faculties and all his strength.

The road began to climb. Out there, in front, the gray benches rose. Behind them frowned the mountains, steel-black, forbidding.

Away to the west stretched the magnificent desert, sweeping in noble lines down from the mountains, range after range of ridges that disappeared in the purple distance. Southward, far away, a gate opened in the wall of rock, and well Forrest knew how that led out to the wild country of sage and sand. Straight ahead the mountain blunted the view. It was too close, yet as Forrest remembered, began its foothill rise over forty miles away.

The higher the car got, and it was climbing fairly fast and steeply, the better could Forrest gaze out over that Western land of alternate waste and range. Here began the change of monotonous New Mexican gray to a hint of red and cream and mauve, that gathered strength over the leagues until it burst into the blaze of colorful Arizona.

Forrest could not get his fill of gazing. The car sped on, and soon it entered a zone which gripped Forrest's heart and brought a dimness to his eyes that he had to rub away, and that continually returned. He saw a wide valley, triangular in shape, with the apex closing far ahead, where grand gnarled cottonwood trees, centuries old, brightly glistening in their first green spring dress, stood far apart, as if there were not enough water and sunlight for a closer communion. There were hundreds of them, and it seemed Forrest knew every one. The road wound along a beautiful stream that slid between green and flowered banks on its way to the famous Pecos, historic river of the West. Quail and doves, hawks and ravens, cottontails and jack rabbits, deer and coyotes, gladdened Forrest's absorbing gaze. No change here! Wild and beautiful still! No fences, no fires, no ranches, no progressive improvements! Cottonwood Valley belonged to his father, who held on to the old West.

At last Forrest espied the white-walled, vine-covered, red-roofed rambling house. It had the same beauty against the green and bronze background. Forrest clenched his moist palms. This was home. The unreal and impossible had become a fact. He would soon be in his mother's arms and be gripped by the hand of that great Westerner, his father, whom he had feared and loved, and looked up to with all a boy's admiration for the pioneer, the fighter of early days. Surely they would be home, well, perhaps expecting him some time. For his mother's letter was scarcely more than a month old.

Thus he eased the doubts of a straining heart,

and gave himself over again to the joy of physical sight in beloved things. There, across the valley, where a branch creek ran down, nestled the adobe house that added another sweet thrill to his home-coming. Lundeen lived there, an enemy of his father, a nester who of all those who had squatted on the Forrest broad acres could not be dislodged. Forrest recalled Lundeen's lass, a girl of fourteen, red-haired and pretty, whom he might once have liked but for the enmity of the families. She would be grown now. He wondered. Married to a cow-puncher, probably, and not interested in crippled soldiers!

Forrest lost sight of the picturesque little house, that disappeared behind trees, and likewise the stately home on the knoll which guarded the apex of the triangular valley. It was high, and the driver now swung his car under the blunt, rocky, vine-covered face of the knoll. On the far side, the knoll sloped easily back to the level, and here, spread out across the neck of the valley, where the stream came tearing white and noisy over a rocky bed, were situated barns, sheds, corrals, bunk houses, lime kiln, blacksmith shop, store, and quarters of the Mexicans.

Forrest stared. The picturesque confusion in his memory did not include all of these landmarks. Some were new. Where, too, was the old leisurely atmosphere? What had come over his father, always a stickler for old things and ways? But Forrest scarcely caught a glimpse of the improvements, for the driver whirled him up the gray-walled road, under the flowered arches, out upon the sunlit level, and up to the house, with its many-arched veranda.

What the driver said Forrest did not catch. The moment was insupportably full. He got out, shaking in every limb. A big white automobile was backing down the courtyard. Forrest heard the murmur of gay voices, laughter. His heart lifted, ready to burst. He stepped forward.

Then a girl appeared in the arched doorway. She wore a long coat, and had her arms lifted to remove her hat. As she freed it from her hair she espied Forrest, and suddenly the hat dropped from her hand. Voice and smile froze on her lips. Dark red flooded neck, cheek, temple.

For Clifton Forrest a vague unreality cleared to a sense of calamity. Removing his hat, he bowed and strove to speak. But the whitening face of this girl— her eyes, that were telling him something too stunning to grasp—made his speech difficult and incoherent.

"What—are you—doing here?"

"This is my home," she replied, and horror gathered dark in her eyes.

"Who—are—you?" he went on, hoarsely, and his hand groped for support.

"My God! Is it possible you cannot *know*?" she cried.

"Know—what?"

"That this is no longer your home."

"But it is—my home," he persisted, in bewilderment.

"Oh, why were you not told!" she burst out, in growing distress. Her face had grown a pearly dead white. "I hate—I hate to have to tell you. . . . But this is not your home."

"I've come all the way from France," he said, faintly.

"Clifton Forrest, it is a pitiful homecoming for you," she wailed, wringing her hands.

Forrest no longer saw her distinctly. The murmur of voices had ceased. Another girl came quickly out of the shadow, with startled face.

"You know—my name?" queried Forrest, astounded.

"I saw it in your book. I thought I knew you on the ship, but I couldn't place you. . . . Oh, if I could only spare you!"

"Spare me? . . . My mother!—My father!" gasped Forrest.

"I know nothing of them. I've been away two years. . . . But before I left they lived—where *I* used to live."

"Who—are—you?"

"I am Virginia Lundeen."

"Lundeen?—Lundeen! . . . Not that red-headed kid I used to tease?"

"Yes, the same."

"You! . . . Have I lost my mind? . . . But she had red hair!"

"You remember, indeed. Well, it changed color with my changed fortunes."

"Then—my father—has lost—our old home?"

"Clifton, it is true, I regret to say."

Her face faded then, and her shape dimmed in the archway. A black tide swept away sight and thought.

V IRGINIA, with sudden distress added to her agitation, was not quick-witted enough to keep the young man from falling. He sank at her feet; his hat slipped out of a nerveless hand. For a moment his white face struck her dumb.

"Oh, poor fellow!" cried Ethel. "Ginia, what can we do?"

Virginia's father stepped out from the doorway, followed by others. He was a stalwart man past middle age, whose handsome lined face showed the vicissitudes of a hard life in the open.

"Hello! Who's this?" he queried, in astonishment, espying the prostrate form at Virginia's feet.

"Father!" she replied, recovering with a gasp. "Something dreadful has happened."

"Is he drunk or what? Who is it? . . . Strikes me I've seen him before."

"No, he's not drunk," rejoined Virginia, hurriedly.

"Dad, it's Clifton Forrest, who used to live here. I saw him on the *Berengaria*, but didn't recognize him then. He was returning from France. He must have been badly wounded in the war. He did not know me. . . . He didn't know I lived here . . . that this was not his home. . . . When I told him—he fainted."

Lundeen's features clouded and set. "Young Forrest!—Home from the war! Shore he looks it!"

"Father, let us take him in—and do what we can," suggested Virginia, faltering.

"What? Take a Forrest in my house? I reckon not," returned Lundeen, harshly. He made a sharp gesture, beckoning the chauffeur who had just deposited Forrest's luggage on the flagstones. "Take those bags back to your car, an' pack this fellow out of heah."

"All right, sir, but where'll I pack him?" returned the chauffeur.

"He's a son of Clay Forrest, who lives down the west road. 'Dobe shack. You can't miss it," replied Lundeen, and stamped back upon the porch.

"Ethel, we must think of his mother, too," said Virginia, in a low voice. "Someone must prepare her. Will you go with me?"

The chauffeur laid hold of Forrest, to be checked by Virginia's swift hand.

"Careful! He has been badly wounded," she warned.

"Shore, Miss. . . . Gee! he ain't very heavy."

Virginia did not release her hold on Forrest's arm, as the driver carried him. Ethel ran to open the door of the car.

"You get in first, Ethel. . . . We must avoid any jar. . . . I remember—Oh, driver, be careful! Don't let him slip! . . . There. Now hold him, Ethel, until——"

"You girls needn't bother," spoke up the young man who had followed them from the porch.

"We will bother, thank you, Richard. . . . Driver, is there room for his bags in front?"

"I'll take care of them."

Lundeen appeared again, striding out with manner unmistakable. Virginia saw her mother trying to detain him.

"Virginia, what are you aboot?"

"Dad, I'm going to prepare his mother for—for this."

"You stay out of thet car," he ordered, furiously.

"Why, dad," she protested, keeping her temper, "I must go. It's the very least we can do."

"No. Let Dick go."

"But he might be awkward breaking it to his mother—shock her."

"Wal, I won't have you goin', an' thet's all."

"Dad, I've been away two years, and now I'm over twenty-one. I knew I'd have to tell you, but I didn't think it'd come during the very first ten minutes of my return."

Whereupon Virginia, her ears tingling at her father's profanity, stepped into the car. Ethel was holding Forrest, whose head swayed to and fro. Virginia slipped her arm round his neck.

"Let go, Ethel," she said, and gently drew Forrest to her until his head rested upon her breast. "Now, driver, we're ready. But don't hurry. And stop at the brook."

Virginia did not look out as they entered the driveway, so she did not know or care about what consternation she had left behind. At the moment she was concerned with the strangest sensation she had ever experienced. Had it to do with the pressure of this young man's head upon her bosom? Ethel's eyes were wide as they encountered hers.

"Ginia, isn't it dreadful? Oh, your father was black as a thundercloud. . . . But I'm glad you didn't give in. It just wouldn't have been decent."

"Ethel, my father always hated the Forrests. I remember that all my life."

"But, Ginia, forgive me if I say it's not fair—at least the hate isn't. You have all the Forrests ever had."

"Dear, I know it's not fair. Ever since dad took over this property it has been a thorn in my flesh. . . . But I didn't say I hated the Forrests."

"I'm glad. Poor boy! . . . He's very handsome, Ginia. . . . What will come of it?" And her blue eyes quickened and dilated with all a young girl's mystic sense of romance.

"He's not a boy, Ethel. He's twenty-eight. . . . Even when I was a girl of ten and twelve he seemed a grown-up man."

At the turn below the knoll the chauffeur halted the car where the brook ran clear and swift over gravel bars.

"Wet my handkerchief," said Virginia, handing it to the driver, who leaped out of the car and, complying with her request, hurriedly returned. "Ethel, you bathe his face. . . . Now, driver, take the left-hand road at the forks and go slowly."

Virginia watched Ethel as gently, with trembling hand, she applied the wet handkerchief. She was very serious and grew almost solemn as her efforts of resuscitation appeared fruitless.

"Ginia, when people faint they don't usually stay

under so—so terribly long, do they?" she queried, anxiously.

"I don't know a lot about it, Ethel. But I'd think not. You remember on the train, when he was unconscious so long. That was bad . . . but this is worse."

"Ginia, he—he might be—be dead!" faltered Ethel. "His face is so—so cold."

"Oh, that would be too awful!" cried Virginia, shuddering. Then with right hand, which shook like a leaf, she unbuttoned his vest and felt for his heart. As she found no beat, a slow horror, cold and sickening, consumed her.

"Put your hand up higher," whispered Ethel, equally clamped in dread.

Complying, Virginia felt slow weak heartbeats. "There!—Yes, he's alive, Ethel. . . . Thank Heaven! If he had died—at my feet—I'd never, never have gotten over it."

"Neither would I," murmured Ethel, resuming her task more vigorously.

Virginia leaned her head back and shut her eyes, seeking to free herself from that inward clutch.

"His eyelids fluttered," whispered Ethel, excitedly. "Ginia—he's coming to."

Virginia could not discern any manifestation of this, except through Ethel, who suddenly ceased her task and drew back, with startled eyes riveted upon Forrest.

"Oh, Mr. Forrest, you're all right again!" she said, eager like a pleased and relieved child.

"What happened?" asked Forrest, in a voice which seemed far away, yet pierced through Virginia.

"You fainted. And it took longer to revive you than that time on the train."

"I see. . . . I'm back in the car. . . . Where are you taking me?"

"To your mother. It's not far. We'll be there soon."

"My mother! . . . I thought—I was afraid—when that girl said she knew nothing of . . . where is she?"

"I just told you. Your mother lives down the road a ways."

"I mean that Lundeen girl."

"Oh! She's not very far," replied Ethel, shyly.

Then probably Forrest became aware of the position of his head, and the arm that encircled him.

"Yes," said Ethel, as if answering a mute interrogation. The thing so dear to a woman's heart—the romance inseparable from this situation—shone tenderly and subtly in Ethel's eyes. "It is Virginia who is holding you. She insisted that she should be the one to take you to your mother."

In his slight movement Virginia divined that his position in her arms was vastly distasteful to him, but he had not the strength even to lift his head from her breast. Whatever vague and dreamy sensations of pleasure and pathos had stirred within her were suddenly dispelled. He knew her now as a Lundeen.

At this juncture the driver brought his car to a stop at the vine-covered gateway of a red adobe wall, a wall pregnant with memory for Virginia. She recalled the time when she had sat on that wall, a roguish little girl of twelve, dangling her bare legs, to watch with worshipful eyes Clifton Forrest riding by, calling out: "Hello, little red-head!"—And now, how strange and terrible, after what seemed a changing span of a lifetime, to be bringing him there to his mother, ruined, broken, dying.

"Ethel, you hold him now. Let me go in first."

"I think I can manage, if you steady me," said Forrest to Ethel.

Virginia stifled her own emotions, thinking of the mother to whom this event would at best be staggering, and leaving the car she hurried through the gate and down the shady path she remembered as well as if she had trod it only yesterday. But it was an ordeal. The giant cottonwoods seemed to shadow her in reproach. Almost she wished the red-walled house, picturesquely showing through the trees, was home again, and that magnificent Spanish mansion up on the knoll belonged to the Forrests. How would Clifton's mother receive her? Courteously and kindly as always, she thought, but perhaps with the same fear of Clay Forrest that ever had obstructed friendship. A flower-skirted irrigation ditch, full of murmuring water, further burdened Virginia with poignant associations of childhood and girlhood. The adobe house showed its age, especially in the size of the great vines that climbed its cracked walls, to shade its adobe-tiled roof with spring foliage. The fragrance here was sweet, dry, pregnant with the atmosphere of unhurried time and solitude. Birds sang in the trees and bees hummed in the flowers. Virginia went round to the back of the house from which a trellis, with heavily vined roof, served as a porch. In trepidation Virginia prayed that Clay Forrest would not be in. If she remembered correctly, he was as impossible as her own father. But to her relief it was Clifton's mother who came out, not by any means as aged or changed as Virginia had anticipated.

"Mrs. Forrest, do you remember me?" asked Virginia, earnestly gazing up into the motherly face.

"For the land's sake! Virginia come home!" she ejaculated, mildly, without trace of astonishment, and she leaned off the step to kiss Virginia. "Come in, lass. Well, an' lackaday, it's a woman you are now. Did you fetch home a husband?"

The big living-room smiled at Virginia and seemed to intimate her place was there. Still there were treasures of color and beauty that had not graced it during the Lundeen occupation. Clay Forrest had saved fine rugs and paintings and furniture from the wreck of his fortunes—family belongings too splendid for this adobe house.

"No, indeed, Mrs. Forrest," replied Virginia, "not a husband. But I did bring you some good news of Clifton."

A spasm convulsed the lined face and a quivering hand went to the heart, indications that justified Virginia's decision to break to Mrs. Forrest the news of her soldier son's return.

"Clifton! . . . Oh, my dear, you saw him in France!—How good of you!" The darkening, hungry eyes almost made Virginia falter.

"No, hardly France. We were a whole day out," hurried on Virginia, brightly. "Do you know, Mrs. Forrest, I saw Clifton on the ship several times, and never recognized him. Isn't that just funny?"

"*Ship!*—He was on his way home?"

"Surely. Then by the strangest and duckiest chance he was on my train. Still I didn't know him. I'm so sorry now, because I could have spared him pain."

Mrs. Forrest sat down shakily, but Virginia's wise, kind words had checked the shock of surprise, and now joy was fortifying the revelation that was to come.

"Pain. You mean—he never knew——"

"Poor fellow! Naturally, not knowing, he went direct to his old home. I had to tell him it—it was no longer his. How I hated that! . . . Then I came—down with him—to show him where you lived."

"And he's out there now?" whispered the mother, a glory in her face that struck deep to Virginia's soul.

"Yes, out in the car. You see, the long journey— he must have come right out of a hospital—it weakened him. He's not very strong. He looks pretty thin and—and ill. I wanted to see you first—tell you, so you'd not be frightened."

"Frightened? I am only happy," replied Mrs. Forrest. "Lass, your heart was never that of a Lundeen. . . . Bring my boy in."

"You stay—right there," said Virginia, chokingly. "Else it might be—you'll frighten Clifton—instead of the other way—round."

"You needn't fear. I'm perfectly calm. But hurry, lass."

Virginia ran out with bursting heart, and at the corner of the house she encountered Clifton, one arm over the chauffeur's shoulder and the other over Ethel's.

"Is mother—all right?" he shot at her with a gasp. His eyes seemed to bore into her.

"Yes, she is."

"You prepared her?"

"Clifton, she doesn't dream you—you're so badly off. I didn't dare tell her. But she knows you're sick, weak, all worn out. . . . Now please play up to that. If you do, all will be well. Then, gradually she—it'll be safe to tell her——"

"Where is she?"

"In the living-room, waiting. . . . Oh, Clifton, try to be natural!"

He lifted his arms from his supporters and stood erect, with a light of eye and face which blazed out the havoc that was there. "Virginia Lundeen, I have this to thank you for. . . . I'll go in alone."

Unfaltering, with no hint of his slight stoop and halting step, he went round the house. Virginia kept pace with him, saying she knew not what, while Ethel retained a timid hold on his sleeve, until they crossed the porch. Then he opened the door, as the girls drew back.

"Mother!"

"Cliff! . . . Oh, my son!—my son!"

The door closed on him. Virginia, wiping her blurred eyes, saw that Ethel was crying.

"Wasn't he wonderful? I could just—love him!" sobbed Ethel.

"I'm afraid it might be hard not to—just now, at any rate," replied Virginia, trying to smile at her friend.

"Ginia, I'll wait out in front," went on Ethel. "If I saw his mother—I'd bawl like a baby."

"I'm not so sure of myself. But I'd better stay a few moments. . . . Tell the driver to bring his luggage back."

Virginia was left alone, prey to mingled sorrow and gladness, and a remorse that did not seem as right and natural as the other emotions. She was strong of will, and sternly fought them, as much for Mrs. Forrest's sake as her own. She waited. The driver brought Clifton's several bags and left them. Only silence from within the house! The relaxing of a tension left Virginia nervous. She wanted to get home, to hide in her room, to cry without restraint. And the thought of home roused feelings that were enlightening and dismaying. This adobe house was more her home than that palace above. Virginia had been born in Georgia, her father having been a planter when a young man, but she had only dim recollections of her Southern home. Here, under these spreading cotton-woods, she had slept and played for twelve years. Then she had gone to school in Las Vegas, spent a year in Denver, staying with relatives, and later, when she had reached eighteen, had been sent to a fashion-able school in New York City. The Spanish mansion on the knoll had known her for only few and short inter-vals. Now she had come back to stay, only to find the romance and joy of it ruined perhaps forever.

Here, on this very porch, she used to peel pota-toes, and bend to other chores she hated, when she longed to run and ride, and paddle in the ditch, and play with the Indian children. So marvelous was mem-ory that instinctively she searched for the place in the lattice-work where she used to stick the paring-knife. Then, as memorable and more poignant, was the later time when Cliff Forrest rode across her trail to be-come her hero. She had never had another.

Her sad misgivings were interrupted by the open-ing of the door.

"Come in, Virginia," called Mrs. Forrest, who stood there with traces of tears on her flushed face.

Virginia slipped in with the weight of other years upon her shoulders. Clifton was lying on the couch under the window.

"Mother wants to thank you," he said, clearly, with eyes that would haunt her.

"Please don't," implored Virginia.

"Lass, you made it easy for me," said Mrs. Forrest, quaveringly. "Bless you!"

"Mother, not so long ago this tall dignified young woman was a red-headed tomboy with bare legs," said Clifton.

"Laws—a—me, Cliff, she was indeed," replied his mother, with a sigh. "She's changed like everything."

"My heart hasn't changed," returned Virginia, her cheeks hot.

"Virginia Lundeen, come closer," commanded Clifton, "so I can see in your eyes. . . . Do you know what your father did to my father?"

His query, sharp though it was, had nothing of the confounding quality of his accusing, soul searching gaze.

"Clifton, I know nothing—nothing at all about what happened between my dad and yours," she protested, wildly conscious of her inability to maintain composure. "I've been away most of the time since it happened."

Forrest did not answer for several moments. He appeared to be lost in some mood of introspection. Then he said, quietly, almost matter-of-factly, "We're ruined—penniless—and I've come home to die."

"Oh, don't say that last—don't!" cried Virginia, entreatingly. "Say you will *live*!—You must not—you cannot give up now—and leave them alone, when they most need you. . . . Clifton, you lived to get *home*!"

"My son, prayer and hope and will are mighty," added his mother, fervently.

"Oh, Clifton, that is the spirit!" went on Virginia, eloquently. "You stood it all to get home. Now stand it all and more—to get well. . . . And let me help you. I

—I have more money than I know what to do with. If you will only let me make it easy for you—till you're strong again!"

"Do you imagine I could take money from a girl whose father robbed mine?" demanded Forrest.

"Robbed!—Oh, that's not true," she returned, hotly. "You are unstrung. You speak wildly. My father might have been hard, unforgiving to *your* father, who was hard, too. But dishonest—no. I couldn't believe it —and—and you must apologize."

Heavy footfalls on the porch outside stopped Virginia's lips. The door jarred—opened wide to disclose a tall man with upstanding, grizzled hair like the mane of a lion. Virginia knew him, though four years had passed since her last glimpse of this rugged face, gray like a stone, with eyes of burning jet that transfixed her.

"Mr. Forrest," said Virginia, brave at the sight of him, "I'm Virginia Lundeen. . . . Clifton came up to my—to Cottonwoods by mistake. And as he needed assistance, I—I brought him down."

Forrest inclined his head, as if in forced acknowledgment, and his hand swept toward the open door, dismissing her from a roof that could not harbor a Lundeen.

Virginia fled. And as she reached the porch she heard his booming voice:

"Howdy, prodigal son! So the war drove you home to dad?"

CHAPTER
4

PERHAPS some of Virginia's breathlessness, when she reached the car, was due to haste; however, a little hurry could hardly have been responsible for her scarlet face.

"Ginia, what'd the old devil do?" demanded Ethel, bridling.

"He deigned me—a grand gesture of dismissal," panted Virginia as she flounced into the car. "Take us back, driver."

"Didn't he *say* anything?"

"Not a word. I was dirt—in his house—and his hand swept me out."

"After all your kindness? Mean of him!—Ginia, he was as nice as pie at first. Regular old beau. Not so old, either, and he's sure handsome. I didn't know what to say. But I jollied him along till he asked who was calling. Then I got fussed. I was afraid you'd come out. I spilled the beans all right. He turned as white as a sheet. It was good I wasn't the one to tell Clifton's mother. I felt sorry for him. Then when I got to Clifton's mistake, going to your house, and your bringing him down here—whew! Oh, my! . . . Come to think it over, I don't really believe he meant to curse us. Probably it was the rotten luck of it."

"I wouldn't put him above it."

"But if he loves Clifton? . . . Pretty tough on Clifton, don't you think?"

"Sickening to me. What must it have been to him? . . . But, oh, Ethel, he's game! You should have seen him!"

"Tell me."

"There's not much to tell, really. But what there was of it will do this little lady for a spell. . . . I must have been some time waiting. Ethel, I used to peel potatoes on that very porch. Hated it. And there I stood—and inside there he. . . . Well, his mother asked me in presently. She looked beautiful. And Clifton lay on the couch. His face was wet with tears. I had an insane desire to kiss them away."

"Why didn't you?"

"Ethel! . . . Well, Clifton said they were ruined, penniless, and he'd come home to die. That broke me all up. I—I don't know just what I said, Ethel, but I told him that he *had* to live. And his mother spoke the same way. And by the expression in his face, I guessed the idea was taking hold. . . . I wish I had come away then. But I didn't, and he asked me to come close and he looked through me as if I'd been an inch of crystal water. And he asked me if I knew my father had robbed his. That upset me more, in a different way. I was raving when his father came in. Then my courage went to my boots. He left the door open, bowed to me as if I were a rich duchess and he a poor peasant, with the pride all on his side. And you bet I beat it."

Ethel laid her head on Virginia's shoulder in an eloquent silence. The car was now rolling down into the valley, which spread out fan-shaped, a green, triangularly cut gem in a bold bronze setting. The silver sunlight glanced dazzlingly off the stream. The freshness and beauty of spring took hold of Virginia's senses, but she was conscious of a stultifying change in her reception of them. Something, like a black cloud spreading over a blue sky, had come between her and the joy of her return, the pride in her beautiful home.

"Ginia," murmured Ethel, dreamily, "you'll fall in love with Clifton Forrest."

"I would if it'd help him get well," flashed Virginia, unreckoning. Then she was appalled at a reply which had not emanated from her thoughtful self.

"You've fallen already," went on Ethel, bent on completing her case.

"Ethel, you're a sentimental little idiot," declared Virginia, impatiently.

"Well, darling, if you don't fall in love with Clifton, I will."

"Ethel Wayne! I'll pack you back home to Denver, and never ask you here again."

"You've asked me for two months. You can't go back on that. And, honey, you've likely forgotten how much I can do in little time."

"Do be serious, Ethel. This—this thing has made me unhappy."

"I am serious. And I wouldn't give a hoot for you if you weren't unhappy. But, Ginia, you're as cold as a fish. All our Western boy friends say as much, anyhow. Who'd ever think you were born in the South?

You slip into a Southern accent once in a while—just enough to make me want more, but as for Southern love and passion, why, you're simply not there."

"Ethel, it strikes me you're not paying the Southern girls much of a compliment. And your own mother came from Louisiana."

"I sure am. Love, anyway, is the only thing in the world."

"You speak from a wide experience—that is, deario, if by flirtation you mean love."

"Is that so? You've got a pair of eyes yourself. Don't be a prune, Virginia. Be a good sport, as you always used to be. You've toddled home from the East for good, so you say. You've certainly been away long enough. And you've sure skidded into a rotten mess. Well, there's only one thing you *can* do, if you're a thoroughbred. And Heaven knows that's your middle name."

"Very good, wise little monitor. What is the only thing I *can* do?"

"Help this poor almost destroyed Clifton. Love him back to hope and strength. Give him yourself, for all he's lost."

"Ethel, you sound like a book. But all the same you hurt. . . . If Clifton doesn't despise me now, his father's hate of all Lundeens will soon make him."

"Fiddlesticks! You talk like a ninny! It needs only one to start a love-affair, especially if it's the girl."

"You shameless child!" retorted Virginia, driven to heat. "Would you have me throw myself into Clifton's arms?"

"Sure Mike," coolly replied this tantalizing friend. "Soon as he is strong enough to hold you."

The car stopped, and Virginia looked up to see

they had arrived at Cottonwoods. She gave Ethel a significant little push.

"I'm glad that's over—and your mushy talk, too," she declared. "Here we are home. And I'm reminded I have a house party, worse luck."

Ethel let out a little peal of silvery laughter. "It's coming to you, Ginia, old girl. I always said so. You're too darned pretty and fascinating and good and rich and lucky."

Virginia's mother met the girls as they entered the house. No one else was in evidence, which fact afforded Virginia some ease. She certainly did not want to meet her father just then.

"Dear, you shouldn't have disobeyed your father," said Mrs. Lundeen, reprovingly. She was a woman whose handsome, stately presence failed to hide the travail of earlier years.

"Perhaps I shouldn't," rejoined Virginia, with resignation. "But, mother, I don't always do what I should. . . . Has the baggage come from the station?"

"Yes. And your guests are all settled in their rooms. Ethel is to share yours."

"I'll need a maid."

"You may have Juanita. She speaks English, and is the best of the lot. All our help is Mexican. It doesn't please me any too well. But Malpass runs the ranch."

"Malpass?" echoed Virginia, puzzled.

"Augustine Malpass. You remember him, don't you?"

"The name, but not the man."

"He is your father's partner, formerly superintendent. But he still superintends, as you will see. I advise you to remember him."

There seemed more in her mother's words than a hint not to displease her father. But Virginia made no reply, and led Ethel through the magnificent patio, shaded by the single great cottonwood around which the house had been built. Tinkle of flowing water and fragrance of flowers attested to the luxuriance of this walled-in garden. Virginia's rooms were located in the west wing, overlooking the beautiful valley of cottonwoods and the vast sloping stretches of desert and range, and the purple mountains dim and far away.

Ethel threw off her hat and coat, then flung her arms round Virginia's neck.

"You know I love you, Ginia?" she asked, in manner far removed from the recent tormenting one.

"Why, of course, you goose!" replied Virginia, heartily returning embrace and kiss.

"I'm not serious often, but I am now," went on Ethel. "Ginia, I'm something of a mystic in spells."

"You certainly are mysterious on occasions. Now what's troubling you?"

"I don't know. Maybe it's this tremendous overshadowing Spanish house. But it makes me say I'm no ordinary friend of yours. I don't care a hang for your riches or your favors. I do care, though, for you, very, very much. And if you fell upon evil days—then you'd know me best."

"Evil days? For *me*!"

Ethel nodded her blond head, like a bright-eyed bird: "I've got a queer feeling you might. And it's not in my little toe, either."

Virginia gave her a hug. "You adorable wretch! Don't come any more of your psychic stuff on me. . . . But, Ethel dear, you are my best friend—my only intimate friend. I shall never forget your loyalty.

But let me—help me to forget this—this that happened today. Oh, it goes so deep and so far back. I'm afraid——"

"So am I, but don't forget. Not——"

Virginia stopped her lips with a kiss. "Come, we must unpack. Look at the trunks—and the bags! . . . And here's more in this room. While we unpack, honey, we'll talk. We have a houseful for a week, then, thank goodness, I'll have you alone for a time—till June, when the mob comes. *Then* we will eat and drink and smoke and dance and flirt—and ride, ride, ride. Dad has the finest horses in the West, and he loves to show off and spend money."

"Drink and smoke and flirt?" queried Ethel, with thoughtful softness. "Since when have you acquired these habits?"

"I haven't yet, but I shall. Then we'll ride, ride, ride right into a couple of husbands," replied Virginia, recklessly, and she threw her hat aloft.

"Thanks. But I'll choose mine," said Ethel, demurely. "I've just about picked him. He's pretty young yet and callow. Needs training, which he's getting unknown to himself."

"Ethel Wayne!—You've never told me."

"Well, we never got thick enough until today."

"Tell me who he is. I'll telegraph him to come on," said Virginia, eagerly.

"Indeed not! Do you think I'll risk that precious lad with you? Not now, you lovely, rich, mad creature. Some day, maybe, when I have him corralled. Meanwhile, this riding for husbands, as you so elegantly put it, narrows down to you and——"

"Shut up!" screamed Virginia, "*or I will be a mad creature.*"

The entrance of a maid put an end to possible hostilities.

"Señorita, I come. It is Juanita."

Luncheon brought Virginia's guests together, a merry half dozen, all Western people, among whom was Ethel's mother. Some of these had assembled at the station to welcome Virginia home, and she had whisked them off to Cottonwoods for a weekend.

Virginia noted the absence of her father, and of his partner, Mr. Malpass, who, she understood, shared the hospitality of the house more as one of the family than as a guest. She had tried several times to place this individual in memory, and to establish clearly in her mind why his name had significance.

"If you all don't mind, let's go out to see the horses," suggested Virginia, at the conclusion of luncheon.

A yelp of delight went up from the young people. The Lundeen horses were famous, and Virginia assured her friends that as horseback-riding was a passion with her, they were all invited to choose any mount they liked, and keep up with her, or ride when and where they chose.

"Ha! Ha! Catch her on a horse!" laughed Richard Fenton. "I'd like to see any of you try it. She's a vaquero."

"Virginia, don't, for mercy's sake, lead us after the staghounds," implored Ethel. "That last jack-rabbit chase was a nightmare."

"Fine Westerners you two are! I dare say I'll have to rely on the cow-punchers for company. But you forget. I haven't been in a saddle for over two years. Do you think I'd be leaving you in the dust?"

"I'll bet two bits you would."

On the way down to the stables Fenton contrived by strategy and a little force to draw Virginia behind the others, and he proposed to her.

"Dick Fenton! I've been home just half a day and you begin that again!" exclaimed Virginia, in plaintive consternation.

"Sure," he said, with complacence. "I want to get my bid in first."

"Why the rush?"

"Virginia, your father recently made a crack in the Castaneda that has gone the rounds. He bragged he intended to marry you off quick."

"He did? Well, how funny!" returned Virginia, merrily. But the gossip was more thought-provoking than humorous.

"It's not funny to me. I've found out a number of things. Your father's big money comes from his phosphate mines in the South. Well, August Malpass is in on every deal Lundeen makes. They're as thick as hops. Now, Virginia, you've been away, on and off, since you were sixteen. You don't know things. And I want to tip you off pronto. Malpass was never well thought of. My father knows something shady about him. It's common gossip that Malpass engineered the deals for Lundeen which ruined Clay Forrest. And to come to the point, everybody believes—indeed, I have a jealous lover's certainty of it—that Lundeen intends Malpass to be the lucky man."

"Ridiculous!" burst out Virginia, but her lips were tight. What kind of an intrigue had she come home to? This linked up with her mother's vague intimation. And suddenly she was realizing that since she had come to call Cottonwoods home, for nearly five years she had been packed off here and there to schools, and finally abroad. During that period her father had come to be almost the stranger he now seemed. She had attributed that to success, money, and the power these controlled, which he had always worshiped.

"Virginia, I am most darned glad to hear that," Fenton was saying, fervently. "What's your answer to my offer?"

"No, you wild and sudden Westerner," answered Virginia. "But if you're so serious, I'll be serious. . . . Thank you, Dick, for the honor you do me. I appreciate it, but I must decline. And I have only the same old excuse."

"Reckon I expected it," he said, cheerfully. "But I've started again and I'll soon get in the habit. . . . Hold on now! Just one more word. Suppose it's true. You can't marry Malpass. He calls himself part Spanish, but he's sure half greaser."

"Suppose what's true, Dick?"

"That Lundeen would want you to marry Malpass."

"Why do you always call my father Lundeen?"

"Pardon. Everybody calls him that."

"Well, Dick, in that case, if I couldn't outwit them, I might have to flee to you for protection," she replied, archly.

"Devil!"

Virginia ran on ahead to escape him. "Ethel, hang on to me," she begged with a laugh.

"Heavens!" rejoined Ethel, locking arms with hers. "Dick has gone and done it already. Poor simp!"

They entered the zone of barns and corrals, all new to Virginia, and the place appeared to be overrun by Mexicans.

"Isn't there a cowboy on the place?" queried Virginia, impatiently.

"Virginia I used to be a plumb good one," spoke up Mark Ashbridge, who was escorting Ethel's mother. "Want to hire me?"

"What wages?"

"Let me see. This is pretty swift. Suppose we say sixty a month—and you."

When the laugh subsided Fenton said: "Virginia, I can beat that. Never mind the sixty."

The main barn was a low-roofed enormous structure, with a wide lane running through from one open end to the other. Virginia recognized this as the original barn repaired and greatly improved. It contained twenty stalls on each side, and all but several held horses. What a spirited, glossy-haired, well-groomed lot of thoroughbreds! Not one, however, did Virginia recognize as a favorite of hers. The Mexican vaquero who tended them could not make himself perfectly clear to Virginia. She gathered, however, that there were horses in the pastures. The Mexican said something about Waltrous, which recalled the fine grazing ranch her father owned there.

"Friends, I don't know a thing about these horses," vouchsafed Virginia. "Never rode one of them. I'll find out where mine are. Tomorrow we'll surely ride."

"Gee! but it's funny to visit the most wonderful ranch in the West and not see a single bow-legged, red-faced, winking cowboy," observed Ethel.

"Can't say I love these sloe-eyed vaqueros," added Gwen Barclay. "But they're sure picturesque."

They all finally wound up, even Mrs. Wayne, by

sitting on the top rail of a high corral fence, gayly edified over an impromptu rodeo.

After two hours and more of this kind of entertainment, Virginia's guests, at least the feminine contingent, were glad to bend their steps houseward. And it was when they got back that Virginia met Augustine Malpass. Instantly her memory bridged the gap between the moment and the day some years back when this sleek, dark individual had dared to make bold if not questionable advances toward her. That was before the Lundeen régime at Cottonwoods. Evidently his fortunes, along with Lundeen's, were in the ascendant. Fine riding-garb made fine-looking riders. From his long cruel Mexican spurs and shiny high-top boots to his olive-tan face and magnetic eyes and sleek, black hair he personified the modern Western dandy. He scarcely showed the Spanish-descent rumor attributed to him. But his eyes were black and piercing as the points of daggers. In his speech there was no hint of the foreigner; in fact, he gave the impression of a keen and successful American between thirty and forty.

"August, I'll bet you don't remember Virginia as the kid who used to sit on the counter down at the old tradin'-post," had been Lundeen's introduction of his daughter, with a prideful arm around her.

"Who would?" rejoined Malpass, showing his handsome, white teeth. "If I remember the barelegged kids of those hard days, it's inconceivable that your beautiful daughter could have been one of them."

"Wal, she shore is. . . . Virgie, do you remember August?"

"I didn't by name, but the instant I saw Mr.

Malpass I remembered him very well indeed. I'm quite surprised—if he has forgotten me."

By his reaction to that cool speech Virginia gauged him as a man of depth and resource. These qualities he might always have possessed; however, along with his immaculate riding-garb he had acquired considerable polish. If he had been a little less impenetrable she might have given him the benefit of a doubt. But he masked himself. He was aloof from the man she remembered.

"Father, where are my horses?" asked Virginia. "I took my friends out to the barns, boasting about my neglected pets, and I couldn't find one I knew."

"Shore I supposed they were heah," replied her father. "How aboot it, August?"

"I keep them at the Waltrous ranch. Better grazing pasture there."

"Drive Virginia over tomorrow an' let her see them."

"I want my horses here," declared Virginia, with spirit. "You certainly knew I was coming home. It really isn't like home without my horses."

"I'll take you over tomorrow and you can pick out what you want to ride," said Malpass.

"I want them all. By the way, I suppose my boys, Jake and Con, are in charge?"

"No. I discharged them."

"*You* discharged them!" rejoined Virginia, with undisguised amaze. "By whose authority?"

"Virginia," interposed Lundeen, uneasily, "Malpass has the run of the ranches. My mining interests take all my attention."

"Oh, I see! Very well. But now that I'm home, I shall look after them myself," returned Virginia. These men, if they had considered her at all, had not calculated on possible development. Not improbably they had been so engrossed in their business deals that they had not given her a serious thought. Virginia sensed more than she heard or saw. Her faculties had been shamed and stung acutely by Clifton Forrest's accusation, and later sharpened by Dick Fenton's gossip. Right here, at the outset, she distrusted the situation, and at the risk of being impulsively precipitous she declared herself.

"Mr. Malpass, you need not trouble yourself about my horses—or anything else, for that matter. I have my own allowance and can entertain my friends without drawing more upon father or charging any bills to the ranch."

Malpass bowed politely enough, but the blood thickened under his olive tan. Furthermore, Virginia's keen eyes caught her father biting his cigar. Without more ado she excused herself and went to her rooms.

Ethel was in the bedroom, half undressed, and curled up, fast asleep. Virginia closed the door softly and left her there. She put on her dressing-gown and making herself comfortable on the cushions of the wide window seat, she gazed out over the valley of cottonwoods.

In a vague, easily dismissed way there had always seemed something irregular about the Lundeen household. She could no longer lay it to her father's irresponsible habit of shoving things upon other people's shoulders. Fitting together the few instances that popped out of the past, and what she had heard and seen since her arrival home, she imagined a situation that was very disagreeable, if not worse. Her father had never inspired confidence, let alone love. Her mother was but his echo. It would surely be bad enough for her, even if she did not exaggerate the situation.

She watched the sunset, the first one over a New Mexican landscape, for two years; and the gorgeousness and riot of intense gold, pink, silver, and blue over that far-flung expanse of desert made her ache with the glory of the West. She had had enough of the crowded, sordid, noisy, war-beset East. This was home, and she did not mean the splendid mansion built by the Dons and named Cottonwoods by the Forrests. Home was the open there, the lonely range, and the grand bronze walls from which it sloped, and the ruggedness of the gray-barked cottonwoods, their strength, color, music, and their shade.

Some one tapped on the door. Startled out of her reverie, Virginia called, "Come in." The door opened to admit her father.

"Are you alone?" he asked, coming to the window.

"Ethel is asleep in the bedroom," replied Virginia, studying her father's face.

"May I smoke?"

"I'd prefer you didn't. I hate cigarette smoke in my rooms. There's enough of it outside."

"Shore you're a queer girl," he rejoined, as he sat down, to look at her with amusement and curiosity. "You love money, travel, friends, excitement, horses, don't you?"

"I'm afraid so, especially the last."

"Ethel's mother has been telling me aboot you," went on Lundeen. "She has a high opinion of you. Thinks you ought to get married."

"Yes, she's told me—the old match-maker."

"I'd like to talk to you aboot that presently. . . . We're not very well acquainted, Virginia—that is, like we used to be when we were poor an' you were a kid."

"How could we be? You sent me away to school while I was growing up, and to travel afterward."

"Shore. It's my fault. But there were reasons why I didn't want you heah, outside of my wish to give you a good education."

Virginia did not encourage him to explain those reasons. She feared his candor. He was too cool, too sure of himself, and now, as often in her youth, she divined that she was not a great factor in his life. Still, he did not seem lacking in affection, nor in a complacent pride in her.

"Mrs. Wayne tells me you're home for good. No more rustlin' aboot."

"Did you read my last letter?"

"Wal, if I did I've forgotten."

"Father, you want me to stay home now, don't you?"

"Why, I shore do, Virginia, providin' you're—wal, like your mother. It'd please me to see the ranch over-run by young people. I'm away a good deal. An' the place ought to be kept up."

"I can't be like my mother. I've a mind of my own."

"Wal, that was plain today when you told Malpass where to get off. I wish you hadn't done it, Virginia. He hasn't spoken to me yet, but he shore was riled."

"That is nothing to me. I was annoyed because my horses were not here, and he discharged Jake and Con. The nerve of him! I shall get them back. Why are there nothing but Mexicans on the ranch?"

"He prefers them. Cheaper an' easier to manage.

I'm bound to admit he's right. Cowboys, when you haven't any cattle, are a blamed nuisance."

"Aren't you running any cattle?" asked Virginia, in surprise.

"No. Cattle went to nothin'. Ruined a lot of ranchers. Clay Forrest, for instance. All he had was in cattle. He was cattle poor."

"How did you come into possession of Cottonwoods?" inquired Virginia, casually, but under veiled eyes she watched him keenly.

"Wal, at the beginnin' of the war I sold out, an' for the first time in my life had money. Malpass was the brains of my luck. He advised it. He went in with me an' we lent Forrest money. Malpass saw the break comin' an' knew we'd catch Forrest. Wal, the crux of it came when Malpass struck rich silver in an old mine of Forrest's land. Up in the foothills. Padres in the early days had worked it, an' Malpass had a map. Got it in Mexico. On the strength of that we lent Forrest all the money we had an' could raise. Forrest owed it. He was in a bad fix then, an' it went from bad to worse. Yet the fool had faith in cattle goin' up, so he bought more an' more. But cattle dropped to nothin'. That ruined Forrest. Our deal went into the courts, an' we got Forrest's land an' stock. By land I mean this ranch, which was a Spanish grant. The property below, where Forrest lives now an' which was our home for so long, was not on the grant. It always was Forrest's, an' that was all he saved out of the wreck."

"Father, did you consider that an honest deal?" queried Virginia.

"Wal, it was business, an' that's pretty sharp these days. Clay Forrest an' I clinched from the time we came heah from Georgia. I laid many a hard knock to him. So it didn't grieve me to take over his property. Ha! Ha!"

"But the old mine where Malpass found the silver. How about that?"

"Made our fortune. We got money out of it to develop the phosphate mines in the South. An' there's where our big money comes from."

"Are you and Malpass partners?"

"Yes, in our minin' deals. But this ranch is mine."

"Father, it was crooked," declared Virginia, feelingly.

"Wal, it always was dog eat dog with me an' Forrest. An' I won't split hairs over it, arguin' with you."

"Such a deal might not show Forrest's rights in court, because naturally you'd claim you discovered the silver after you got the land. But morally it *is* dishonest."

"No, not in this heah day an' age. You're a woman, an' you always were sentimental aboot the Forrests."

"But at least you will split the proceeds from the silver mine?"

"I wouldn't give Clay Forrest a dollar to save his life," declared Lundeen, with hate swelling in every word.

"Then I shall," replied Virginia, calmly and coldly.

"Wal, you won't do anythin' of the kind. You haven't it to give. That two hundred thousand I put on interest for you isn't available."

"Where is it?" asked Virginia, aghast.

"Malpass took the principal, or most of it, an' invested it down South. We needed some money quick. Of course you'll gain in the long run. But you can't get hold of it now."

"Then I have no—no income?"

"We'll fix that up, Virginia. I reckon there's ten thousand or so to your credit in bank. By the time you spend it we'll arrange the other."

"Mr. Augustine Malpass! . . . He seems—ahem—quite important in the affairs of the Lundeens."

"Wal, I reckon," returned her father with a short laugh, ignoring her scorn. "An' that brings me to the point. You rode me off the trail. . . . Virginia, as far back as three years ago me an' August talked over a marriage between you an' him, when the proper time came."

"Indeed! How interesting!"

"You needn't be so cuttin'. You shore owe it to August that you got your education an' travel, an' that you're *heah* at Cottonwoods now. It was his brains."

"I have much to thank Mr. Malpass for," returned Virginia, in bitter passion.

"Virginia, I hope you're not mixed up in any love-affair."

"No, I'm not, if that will relieve your extreme anxiety about me."

"Wal, I'm glad. For my heart is set on this. I don't want to rush you, daughter, but in good time, I hope——"

He rose, evidently disconcerted by the sudden turn of her head, to face him with her contempt and shame.

"You are proposing marriage for me—with Mr. Malpass?"

"It amounts to that," he answered, regaining his assurance.

"Thank you. I feel immensely flattered that you'd like to see me the wife of a crook."

"Virginia, he's no more that than I am," protested Lundeen, impatiently.

"Assuredly not. You're both crooks. The meanest of crooks—the kind that can't be apprehended."

"Wal, I'll allow you've reason to be upset," he added, moving toward the door. "Reckon you'll get over that an' think aboot it."

"Father, I don't understand you. I don't *know* you," she ended, passionately. "I refuse—once and for all!"

M ANY a time, years ago it seemed to him, Clifton Forrest had ridden down the shady road along the edge of the cotton- wood valley, to the little town of San Luis, which was populated by Indians and Mexicans. The trading-store there had finally been taken from Lundeen by Clifton's father, who had then run it more to help his many employees than to exact profit from them. The few bits of silver that it now brought in constituted the extent of the Forrest income. Toward San Luis Clifton walked now, and when he fell down, which he did often, he got up and went on.

"Cliff," his mother had said the day of his arrival home, "your father tried to stick in that store. But he couldn't. I hired one Mexican after another. If one was lazy, another was dishonest, and our only income is from that store. Think of that, my son! It used to be one of your father's charities.—What sad pass we have come to!"

"Mother, I'll run the store," Clifton had replied, with cheer and smile that hid his earnestness. And this was why he was trudging along the road, not, despite his mental and physical ills, insensible to the glory of the May morning.

The white snowy cotton seed was floating in the amber air and falling like thistledown on the green grass. Quail ran across the road, leaving tiny tracks in the dust. Birds and colts and calves showed their delight in the balmy air and golden sunshine of spring. Clifton felt the renewal of nature in his own heart and along his veins. He could not help being glad that he had to live instead of die. How he had longed to give up the struggle! Who but one like himself could understand the torture of body, the destruction of faith, the end of hope, the unutterably soothing thought of rest and oblivion?

He could not walk many rods without resting; and he chose the spots where he had halted the day before, and the first day. Some of these he thought he never would reach, yet he did; and there, wet with cold sweat, his internal organs in hideous turmoil, his wounds as cruel as burning hell, he sat awhile, beaten, but unconquerable. Already a marvelous thing had happened to his mind. It had direction and immutability. He had been on his last legs, but now he laughed at the idea. He became conscious of something unquenchable at work within him. So he scouted weakness, misery.

The little adobe store, once a trading-post, was situated off the road, on a bank above the irrigation ditch that supplied water to the natives, whose homes were scattered along the gentle slope above the valley.

The natives had small farms, and a few head of cattle, upon which they subsisted when not working in some capacity on the range. The decline of the cattle business had made them poor and unable to buy much. Therefore the store was fairly well stocked with canned goods, merchandise, tobacco, and all the necessary requirements of horsemen. In addition, there were many blankets and baskets which Forrest had purchased from the Indians.

Clifton had cut the price of everything in the store, but the natives were slow to respond. Outside, by the door, stood an old rustic chair with sheepskin lining, and to Clifton it was the most comfortable one he had ever rested in. Here he passed most of the day, a good deal of which he slept away from sheer exhaustion. The natives, except the wild ragged youngsters, did not pass by often, and they seldom lingered. On the first day Clifton found out that the natives had never overcome the distrust engendered in them during the Lundeen régime of high prices and sharp dealing. Clifton made a present to his informant, and that was his initial act through which he meant to regain confidence.

The view from the old rustic chair could not have been surpassed anywhere in the low country. The whole valley lay in sight, some of it showing between the trees; high on the knoll shone the white-and-red house of Lundeen, rising out of the green like a castle. Across the road and the valley, shallow winding canyons with ridges between sloped up to the mountains, that from this distant vantage-point rose massively in alternate climbing areas of beauty and desolation, forests of green and gold all the more verdant for the contrast of the colossal wrinkled cliffs and crags of rock, and walls of bronze like iron, and peaks of porphyry.

When the Lundeen cars raced down the valley road, raising long trails of dust, Clifton saw them with unconsciously growing hate, like fire that ate slowly under the surface. When he saw the clean-limbed, long-maned horses come leisurely into view with their riders in gay colors, he would hastily turn away from a sight bitter as gall. His precious energy, so meager and so weak, frittered away in agitations he should have restrained. But how impossible to help it yet! These instances began to stir intimations of a driving force that was not wholly due to devotion to his father and mother. But he made no attempt to analyze it.

The day passed like a dream half remembered. Then began the toiling homeward. He told himself this was nothing—nothing. To get his broken bones and lacerated muscles to function!

Dusk caught him stalled at the niche in the adobe wall from which he took a short cut. When his father loomed under the trees, Clifton had survived the worst of his collapse.

"Wal, son, Ma was anxious an' sent me to meet you," he said, and helped Clifton to his feet. He never alluded to Clifton's condition. If it caused him distress, he gave no sign. Clay Forrest had always been a man who considered physical defects things to conceal. But he did not lack gentleness.

"I was stuck here last night."

"Cliff, somethin' happened today," returned Forrest, with perturbation.

"What?"

"I got back early, an' there talkin' to Ma was that Lundeen girl." He made the announcement with suppressed feeling. "I'd showed her the door the other time, an' I did it again. But she wouldn't leave. Shore I couldn't throw her out. An' there I was."

"Well!" ejaculated Clifton. This intelligence made his exhaustion as if it were not.

"Ma said, 'Virginia wants a word with you,' an' it was plain Ma was shore wantin' her to get it. But I swore I'd listen to no Lundeen. She was white an' her eyes were big. I couldn't help thinkin' what a handsome lass! An' brave—she wasn't a darn bit afraid. She said, 'I've come heah to ask you somethin', an' I'm goin' to do it.' Wal, seein' I was out of luck an' couldn't get rid of her quick, I told her to fire away. An' she shore did it, short an' sweet."

"Dad, you could never tell anything. Hurry."

"Cliff, she told me before she went away two years ago she had a couple of hundred thousand dollars in bank. She found, on gettin' home, she had only ten thousand left. Malpass had persuaded her father to let him have the rest. . . . An' by Heaven! Cliff— that girl begged me to take the ten thousand!"

Clifton halted, and even in the dusk he could see his father's ox-like eyes rolling. "She did! What for?"

"I asked her, an' she said she believed we had been wronged, an' she wanted to help right it in what little way she could. Begged me to take the last of her money, an' when I replied I couldn't do it, she tried to persuade me to take half. Then I said we Forrests would starve to death before we'd accept a dollar of Lundeen money. . . . Cliff, she cried out it wasn't Lundeen money, but Forrest money. I was sort of stumped at that. She was actually testifyin' against her father. I could use that when the deal goes to court again, as it shore will."

"You could, but you won't," declared Clifton.

"Cliff, I'm not ashamed to admit she made me soft for a minute, but I soon got over it. I'd use anythin' against Jed Lundeen."

"Dad, you'd never sacrifice the girl, even if she is a Lundeen," protested Clifton.

"Wal, now, why wouldn't I?" demanded Forrest, letting go his hold on Clifton.

"If for no other reason, because I wouldn't let you."

"Hell! Are you in love with that girl?"

"No. I—I hate her, I guess. . . . But I've sense enough to see she's good."

"Wal, Cliff, you shore are. An' so is Ma. Reckon it's aboot the last straw. . . . My stock, my land, my home—an' now my family—gone over to these cursed Lundeens!"

Forrest stalked away under the gloom of the cottonwoods.

"Dad!" cried Clifton, seeing that his father was leaving him. No answer came. The heavy footfalls died away, and not in the direction of the house. Clifton went on, muttering to himself: "Oh, this is getting worse. I'm afraid altogether it's more than I can bear. . . . What a thing for Virginia Lundeen to do!—Wonderful! . . . I knew she was good. It wasn't all pity. She knows her father is a thief. I wish she hadn't given dad that hunch. And this Malpass. I wonder if he can be that greaser-like rider who used to hang round the post, when Lundeen ran it."

Excitement carried him on, and he arrived at the house, breathless, but unconscious of fatigue. The living-room was cheerfully bright and supper ready. Clifton related to his mother the conversation between him and his father.

"He's implacable, Cliff," she said, with a calmness that soothed him. "But for me he'd have shot Lundeen an' Malpass long ago. We have our task, my son."

"Mother, it plumb riled me when he said I—I was in love with Virginia. It sure floored me. And when I denied it he came out more bitter. He even said *you* loved her, too."

"I do, an' I'm afraid he's guessed."

"Mother!"

"Go on with your supper, son," she returned. "As for Virginia—I used to love her when she was a ragged, wild child. An' I reckon it's come back. She's grown beautiful, Cliff, an' spite of it all she's unspoiled. She might spend money like wastin' water, but it means little to her. I think it noble of her to offer what they'd left her."

"Noble, yes. But it's an admission of her father's guilt. I wish she hadn't done that. Dad swears he'll use it in court. We must keep him from it."

"My son, we must keep him from a good deal more," she replied, gravely.

"No one, unless you, could ever turn dad back from anything he wanted to do."

"You can help, Cliff. Your return an' the way you've been have struck him deep. It takes time for a change to work out in Clay. You must be patient. You must persuade. An' if Virginia is anythin' to you—hide it."

"Virginia is nothing to me, mother," he said, after a moment of astonishment at her speech.

"Cliff, I reckon it takes all the heart you have to keep to the task you've set yourself."

"All—and more, I'm afraid, mother dear."

"My son, both your father an' I have taken a new lease on life since you came home. He doesn't know, but I do."

"Then you'll never hear me say anything like that again."

"I must tell you something that ought to be just as helpful," she went on, now in sweet seriousness. "It's about Virginia."

"But, mother, I don't want to hear any more," returned Clifton, dreading he knew not what. It was as if he stood with blinded eyes on the verge of a precipice, which when he saw it would draw him down.

"I reckon it's because you don't want me to that I will. Trust your mother, Cliff. . . . . Do you remember Virginia as a little girl?"

"Not very little. She must have been ten or twelve, anyway. She was a red-headed imp always in sight somewhere. On the wall out here, with her bare legs dangling. She had pretty brown legs. . . . But I remember her best hanging round the post. She was then beginning to be good-looking. But no one would have guessed she'd grow into what she did. I never recognized her on the ship or train."

"As a child she worshiped you. No one but I ever saw it. Then as she grew up, an' her father an' yours became bitter enemies, she visited us less, an' finally never came. Now she's back, an' I think that child worship of you is not dead. Only she's a woman now. Today she told me she had just ridden by the store. You sat outside, asleep. You didn't wake an' she stopped, meaning to speak with you. But she didn't have the courage—you looked so white—so frail—so sad. Then she said to me: 'Oh, Mrs. Forrest, my heart broke. Tell me he is not going to die!' An' I told her I knew you were goin' to live. After that she perked up an' asked me if she an' I could not be good friends. But your father came, interrupting us."

"She is only sorry for me, mother," he replied, with difficulty. "And I'd rather have her hate me, so that I could hate her."

"But hate is terrible, my son. It has ruined your father. If you let anyone hate you, or if you hate anyone, it will poison your blood."

"Mother dear, you are close to the angels." It touched Clifton deeply that his mother should champion Virginia Lundeen, and in her blindness of affection and goodness attach undue sentiment to Virginia's words and actions. Clifton did not dare accept his mother's interpretation.

His father came in, weary and dark, and ate his supper in silence. Soon afterward Clifton went to the little room that had been turned over to him and which once had been Virginia Lundeen's. The very bed upon which he sat in the darkness to undress had been hers, so his mother had assured him, as if there could have been sweetness in the knowledge. There was one window, now open to the gentle wind that was coming down cool off the mountain. Through the great gnarled branches of a cottonwood shone white blinking stars that seemed to have a secret they wanted to share with him. Some fact—true, inevitable, passionless, immutable! He did not want to know it. The frogs were trilling. How this lonesome, solitary melody haunted him! His hands fell idle and he sat there to listen. The wonder of nature, the mystery of life, the sweetness of love, could not be denied. He heard them, felt them out there in the night. What had made him determine to live when all he had longed for was to rest? Assuredly it was the clinging to old ties—love of mother, father. God had failed him, he thought. But there were whispers on the wind, not earthly or physical.

At last, only half undressed, he stretched out on the bed, thankful that he need move no more for hours. The internal strife of blood and nerve, of the very cells of his bones, gradually quieted. In the blackness and solitude, alone with his soul, he could not adhere to doubt, to hate, to mocking bitterness. And the face of Virginia Lundeen with the lovely troubled eyes hung over his pillow. He saw her standing in the archway of the home that had been his, crying out, "My God! is it possible you don't know!" And he pictured her from his mother's words, watching him asleep, helpless, unguarded, with his secret for anyone to read. Clifton repudiated that heart-moving vision of her. It was an illusion. It was his mother's imagining. It was only Virginia's pity. Nevertheless, whatever it might be, out of it welled a melancholy happiness that warred with reason, and survived into his dreams.

Next morning as he plodded out to endure the long walk to his work he espied his father plying a spade in the garden. And the sight was a cheerful one for the beginning of another interminable day. All his father had done was to sit and brood, or walk endlessly under the cottonwoods, unable to shake off the calamity that had befallen him. That, to Clifton and his mother, was more saddening than the calamity itself.

Clifton slipped along, careful not to be seen, and the walk to the store was not so much of a hateful ordeal. A waiting customer furnished another surprise. What a little thing could revive hope and keep it alive a moment! His chair did not see him fall asleep that day. And somehow he got home without fear that he might drop, never to get up again.

Days followed then, slowly dragging, not inspired, and each one sapping his little vitality, which seemed mostly of spirit. And then there came one of the nightmare nights which he had been mercifully free from since his start for home. He did not know what had induced it. But mental depression seized upon him and tightened its grip. He could not get to sleep. The past weighed upon him, phantoms and furies raged, and when he did fall asleep it was to be plunged in a horrible dream, as violent to his physical being as had been the thing it pictured. So when the day came he was already exhausted.

Yet he went to work, and it took all day to recover from the exertion. He remained late, hoping his father would come, as he had several times. But at length he started out alone . . . and by sunset he was crawling on hands and knees, as once he had crawled on the battlefield, badly wounded, yet with less agony.

The sun shone blood red through the cottonwoods. He could see the adobe wall and the break in the corner where the trail went through. Only a little farther on! He believed now that his end was near, and strangled, spent with his effort, and frenzied with the petrifying fear that he might not reach his mother in time, he kept on.

Then he heard the hoofbeats of a horse close behind him in the road. He would be seen. It goaded him to the last remnant of his strength. Inside the break he failed, and sank face down.

Swift, light footsteps pattered in the trail. He heard the swish of brush—a poignant cry. Some one knelt beside him.

"Clifton!—Clifton!" He knew the voice and wished indeed that death had overtaken him. What fate was this? Strong arms lifted him, drew him to a sitting posture. He had one glimpse of Virginia Lundeen's face, terror-stricken, then his head fell upon her breast.

"Oh, Clifton—Clifton!" she cried, holding him tight. "What's happened?"

"I—gave—out," he panted.

"Is it only that? You were dragging yourself along. I thought you an animal. It scared my horse. . . . Oh, you must be terribly ill. You look so—so——"

"I thought I—was dying."

"What shall I do?—What can I do?" she moaned. Clifton felt himself rocked to and fro in her arms. She was kneeling and holding him up. He saw her pull a gauntlet off with her teeth. Then a trembling hand touched his wet forehead, smoothed back his hair, moved warm across his cheek and lips.

"Don't take on so," he whispered. "Maybe I'm—just all in."

"But something should be done," she implored. "I'll run for help—then ride home, get a car, and fetch the doctor."

"Wait until—we see. . . . Maybe it's nothing. . . . I'm such a coward."

"Coward!" she cried, her voice deep and eloquent with scornful denial. He felt his head rise softly with the heave of her breast, and her heart sounded like a muffled drum. She hung over him. Her hair touched his face. She was bareheaded, her sombrero lying where evidently she had flung it. She was bending over him. Hot tears fell upon his cheek. Her touch, that even a half-dead man could not mistake, sharply affected him to the point of uplift. He had not the desire, even if the strength had been granted him, to move out of her arms.

Not for moments did he remember his physical state, and then he guessed it was just the old revolt of outraged nature, driven to the limit this time. As he realized gradual recovery, he dismissed a vague, dreamy thought of how sweet it would be to die in her arms.

"Help me to a seat—there," he said, indicating a low section of the broken wall.

"I am—quite beside myself," she replied, with a confused laugh that told she had at least become conscious of her aberration. She lifted him with ease.

"You're strong," returned Clifton, marveling at her, and he found that with her arm locked in his he could sit up steadily. Her lovely, tear-wet, flushed face would have dispelled all hate. And for the moment her tenderness, her astounding grief at his plight, had dissipated hate, resentment, doubt, all that he had imagined he had ever felt toward her.

"There. You're better. I'm so glad. . . . Oh, Clifton, I was frightened!"

"Why?" he asked, fascinated.

"Even if you'd been a stranger I would have been frightened. But *you*! . . . On the ship, on the train, up at the house that dreadful day you came—and down here, I was frightened for you. But not like this. . . . Oh, my heart is pounding now."

"Even for a stranger? And of course I'm that. I'm glad you said it."

"Yes indeed, Clifton Forrest, you *are* a stranger. For once you liked me—years ago when I was a happy kid—long before the shame of this day to me, and the sorrow to you."

"Virginia, I hardly knew you," he protested.

"You've forgotten. . . . You used to wave to me as you rode by. Then you made eyes at me. And once in the old post you caught me alone—you kissed me."

Clifton awoke to realities, to the void absence and war had made in his memory, to the hot blood that tinged his cheek.

"Did I?—I had indeed forgotten. So much of the past is dark in my mind."

"There! You've made that strange move with your hand," she burst out, impulsively. "You did it on the ship—on the train. And that day up at the house. Now you have done it again. Four times. Clifton, why do you do that?"

"What move? What do you mean?"

"You pass your open hand before your eyes. It's a slow, strange action. You do not touch your eyes. You seem to brush something away. As if a shadow dimmed them and you could remove it."

"It's unconscious. I never knew I did that. It must be to brush away pictures that never fade."

"Of what you've seen and suffered?" she asked, softly.

"Yes, of what I've seen, surely."

"Clifton, you're doing the most wonderful thing I ever knew a man to do. You were a knight of my childish dreams. Now you are a hero. You had made your sacrifice. You came home beaten and broken. You found all changed—your father crushed—your mother sorrowing—both without even the comforts of life. Cheated out of their home—to grow old, poor and miserable! . . . And instead of succumbing you rise like a giant to conquer fate, catastrophe, death itself. Oh, how I honor you for this courage!"

"Virginia, you—you are making strong statements," he faltered. "I can only believe—you're overcome by my—our troubles—and the excitement of finding me on all fours, like a crippled dog."

"Overcome, yes, and I have been overcome ever since you fell at my feet. . . . Clifton, do you hate me because I'm a Lundeen?"

"I'm only human."

"But I had nothing to do with the ruin of your family. If I owned Cottonwoods right now I'd give it back. And if I *ever* own it I will."

"Dad wouldn't take it."

"Would you?"

"Never from you."

"But why? If my father will not right a wrong, why should I be deprived of the happiness of doing it?"

"It would be too late then."

"You wouldn't take *anything* from me?"

"No."

"Clifton Forrest, your nobility does not extend to helping others besides your own people," she said, showing a bitter hurt.

"Don't talk sentimental nonsense," he returned, with passion. "How could *I* ever help you? My God! . . . You—a young, beautiful woman! Healthy, strong, supple, clean-boned, who can ride like the wind! Rich! With home, doting parents, friends by the hundreds. You talk like a fool."

"I do not," she flashed, spiritedly. "I may have good looks. That's a matter of opinion. I am well and strong, thank Heaven, and if I have to work, you bet I can do it. But I haven't any home—any real home. I'd rather be here, where I lived so long. My mother does not side with me in anything. She lives in mortal fear of father. I despise his greedy soul. It's dreadful to confess. But I think I do. And if he keeps on trying to make me marry Malpass I shall hate him. . . . You're not the only one in terrible trouble, Clifton Forrest."

Tears of anger and shame fell unrestrainedly, and reproach darkened her eyes.

"Well, of all things!—Virginia, I'm sorry. I apologize," returned Forrest, aghast. "Malpass! Isn't he the fellow who used to hire the *vaqueros* at San Luis? Dark, slick, fire-eyed Mexican?"

"You know him, Clifton. He is now my father's partner. He's a crook. It is he who hatched the plot that ruined your people. He absolutely dominates father. And he will ruin him, too, if he does not get his way."

"Which means if he does not get you?"

"Precisely. Malpass is too smooth to hint that. But I know it."

"Is he in love with you?" asked Clifton, with an inexplicable curiosity he could not resist.

"He has been for years, since I was sixteen. I didn't believe all father's rant about it. But lately I have found it out. The more I repulse him the madder he gets. I think opposition has fanned his desire. He wants to take me to Mexico City, to Havana, then to Spain. Raves about how he'd show me off in courts—exquisite gowns, diamonds, pearls. Oh, you should hear him!"

"Thanks," returned Clifton, dryly, "but I don't care to. . . . Virginia, how are you going to beat that combination?"

"I don't know. It's maddening. But if he got the best of me I—I'd kill him."

"No. That'd never do for you. I'll tell you, Virginia. Marry some one else pronto."

"Marvelous idea. I've had it myself. But whom?" she returned, with unreadable, dark eyes on his.

"Haven't you lots of—of admirers, among whom there's a fine chap whom you could care for?"

"*You* ask me that!"

"Yes, of course I do."

"Very well, suppose you choose for me."

"But, you child, I don't know your friends," he expostulated.

"You know the one I most want for a friend or—or——"

"Virginia!" he gasped. "Am I crazy or are you?"

"I'm quite sane," she replied. Her rounded cheek was no longer rosy. It shone pearly in the afterglow of sunset. "Suppose I ride down to San Luis tomorrow. Fetch a padre over to your store. . . . We'll keep it secret till the storm breaks. Then I'll laugh in that smiling devil's face!"

"I—I don't quite know how to take you," replied Clifton. "If you're serious—you're out of your head."

"Clifton, I am proposing to you—that *you* save me from their machinations."

"But, my God!—you can't—you mustn't throw yourself away on a shell of a man like me."

"I fail to see the sacrifice. It would save me and might right a cruel wrong some day. And *I* could help you get well even though we kept our secret. Do I understand you to refuse?"

"Yes. What else could—I do?" he replied, faintly.

"Oh, because your father hates the very ground a Lundeen treads on. But I can't help my name. I am asking you to change it for me."

"No, Virginia, not because dad hates your father. But because this would not be right or fair to you. He'd disinherit you. And I would only be a burden."

"You say that for an excuse. You must share your father's hate. . . . Oh, Clifton Forrest! you will never know."

"I tell *you*—I don't hate you," he cried, desperately.

"And I tell you I don't believe you. . . . But this is cruel of me. You've had an awful day. And I, selfish woman, have made it worse for you. . . . Come, let me help you to the house."

"I can go alone. Dad might see you—insult you."

He arose, and she did likewise, still with firm hand on his arm.

"Are you sure you can make it?"

"Yes. I've rested. I'm all right."

"Let me see you walk."

He started off steadily enough.

"Good-by—Clifton," she called, low. The gloom swallowed her before he could muster voice to answer. As he walked on under the whispering cottonwoods he stopped beside one to lean a moment. Then he heard the rapid hoof-beats of a running horse.

BY JUNE the hideous ordeals Clifton had to invite and endure daily, began appreciably to change. He discovered that by imperceptible degrees he had passed the climax of his trial for life.

June brought summer to Cottonwood Valley, and that meant it was hot in the sun, cool in the shade. He was alone one Sunday in the corner by the wall where Virginia had found him that unforgettable day, when he reached the definite conclusion that he would recover. He slipped away from the open, into a shady nook, where vines and brush grew thick under a giant cottonwood, and here he lay down hidden even from the eyes of birds. The sunny drowsy hours of that golden summer day passed by unnoticed. Like an Indian he communed with the visible things about him. There were intervals when the stream of his consciousness seemed suspended and he had no thought at all. He felt, he heard, he saw, he smelled the physical objects of nature about him. The warm brown earth throbbed against his palms; the wind sang softly in the cottonwoods, the white clouds sailed across the azure sky, tipping the gray peaks; the sweet breath of sage filled the air.

That was the spell of enchantment which had transfixed him when intelligence, and not spirit, told him that he had not to bid farewell to the earth. The ghastly cold, mocking thing that had haunted him sleeping and waking folded its gray mantle and stole away. He was not to give up the sweetness of life, the beauty of nature, the strife with obstacles. The joy of nesting birds, the return of the swallows, the swoop of the eagle, the looming, calling mountains, the windswept open range were still to be part of his experience.

But that night, in the dark little room, when the ecstasy of his soul became subdued by thought and reason, he confessed that he had thrown off his burden only to take on another. Virginia Lundeen had won him to hate hate and love love. It had not been joy or hope, but an unabatable fuel that had kept burning the fire of his wasted spirit.

One by one returned the Indians and Mexicans who had visited Clifton's store during the past weeks to get the fair sale for some commodity and the small gift he never failed to hand out. There was no profit in the low price, to say nothing of an additional gift, but Clifton was gaining the confidence of the natives. He would never make a success as a trader, from the point of view of business. They had been cheated long enough. His generosity was not unmixed with the desire to prove the difference between a Forrest and a Lundeen. Every native on the range hated Lundeen for the tight rein he had held on them. Malpass, though he was employing many, was earning a harder repute. Little by little Clifton won his way into the hearts of these simple people.

It was from a vaquero who rode for Malpass that Clifton learned of the arrival of Virginia Lundeen's guests from the East. A fiesta was held to welcome them, and lights burned at Cottonwoods half the night, and strains of music floated down the valley on the soft night wind.

Clifton, thereafter going to and from his work, now happily without resting every few rods, did not want to see, yet could not help seeing the visitors who regaled themselves upon Virginia's bounty.

The huge cars hummed by across the valley, down the road to Las Vegas, or back again, swiftly running from the dust they raised. Horseback-riding appeared to be the chief delight, which was no wonder, considering the magnificent mounts of the Lundeen stables, and the beautiful beckoning range with endless levels and vistas.

Several times each day a party of riders, never less than three couples, passed by Clifton's store, to peer curiously from their saddles. He always contrived to be inside and busy when they rode by. Once he saw Ethel, who waved a gay hand at him; and again he caught a glimpse of Virginia, superb on her shining black. And she looked straight ahead, with clear-cut, cold profile, as if the trading-post of San Luis had ceased to exist.

Clifton knew intuitively that these merry visitors,

keen to absorb all the West possible, would call at his store some day.

But he was wholly unprepared one morning to hear the blowing of bugles and to look out to see a tallyho rolling down the road. It appeared to be loaded with a crowd sportive in both dress and spirit.

"I'm in for it," muttered Clifton, soberly. "But if they want to buy I'll slap the old prices on the goods. I'm no good Samaritan for that outfit."

He hoped the coach would pass by, but it halted opposite the store and a gay company of young people poured out.

The first to enter was Ethel Wayne, very pleasing to the eye in her gay and colorful costume. She tripped in hurriedly, with anxious look, which changed to a bright smile of glad recognition.

"Clifton, I'm just delighted," she said. "You look, oh, so much better."

"Howdy Ethel!" drawled Clifton as he took her proffered hand. "I'd sure been glad to see you—if you'd come alone."

She giggled and squeezed his hand, whispering: "Don't mind. Virginia and I framed this on our Eastern friends. So stick them good. They've got money to burn."

Then the little store became flooded with pretty girls in the latest of sport clothes, and clean-faced young men in golf suits or white flannels. One of the latter said to Clifton, "We want a lot of souvenirs and a wagon load of truck to take on a camping trip."

"Help yourselves," replied Clifton, spreading his hands.

It was pleasant to watch them. Gayly they quarreled over Indian baskets, blankets, beadwork, and silver ornaments. There were eight young women, not including Ethel and Virginia, who, if she had come with them, was still outside. Ethel was the only girl to notice Clifton, much to his relief; and every little while she would give him a bright look and a wink. It became manifest to Clifton that these Easterners had not been informed about him. The young men, except one, paid no attention to him; and presently this one, a rather pale blond fellow of twenty-five, approached Clifton, to offer a hand.

"How are you, Clifton Forrest?" he said. "Miss Lundeen told me to introduce myself. My name is Andrews."

Clifton did not need to be told that this man had been in the service, to his great detriment. Clifton greeted him. With a look and a handclasp they understood one another.

"I'm here on a visit for a few weeks," continued Andrews. "Then I'm going to Tucson. I'm not so well. The doctors want me to try dry warm climate."

"Gassed?" queried Clifton.

"Influenza. Then I had blood-poisoning from shrapnel."

"You'll come around all right out here," said Clifton, reassuringly. "The climate is wonderful."

"Do you know Arizona?"

"I used to. Same as here, only more so. . . . Suppose you ride down alone some day and we'll have a chat."

"Thanks. I'd like to."

"Is Miss Lundeen with you?"

"Yes. She drove us down. Maybe she can't handle the reins! . . . Say, Forrest, do you know this man Malpass?"

"Sure I know Malpass. He used to be a vaquero here in San Luis."

"Vaquero? What's that?"

"He was a Mexican cowboy."

"Is he part Mexican?" asked Andrews, quite surprised.

"It has always been rumored."

"Well! And now he's Mr. Lundeen's partner and a very evident choice for Virginia's hand. . . . I'll tell you, Forrest, that's a funny situation up there. I don't want to gossip about my hostess. But I don't know her, except as a charming, beautiful girl who went to school with my sister. By the way, I must introduce you to Helen. She's the tall blond there, squabbling over that junk."

"She's sure stunning," returned Forrest, admiringly.

"Virginia didn't say so, but I gathered somehow she and you were good friends."

"That was nice of her."

"But evidently Malpass does not share her friendship for you. I heard him objecting to our tallyho trip down here, and Mr. Lundeen sided with him. They had quite a little argument, aside, and to be frank, Virginia just about told them to go where it was hot."

Clifton laughed. "I wouldn't put it beyond her."

Andrews, evidently having caught his sister's eye, beckoned to her, and as she detached herself from the crowd and came forward expectantly, he said to Clifton in lower tone, "Don't spoil this now."

"Helen," he said, as she reached them, a warm-faced, blue-eyed, young goddess, "I want you to meet a buddy of mine in France. Clifton Forrest!—Forrest, allow me to present my sister. You will observe she is one of the reasons we went 'over there.' "

"Oh, Jack—how perfectly lovely! You didn't tell me. Virginia didn't, either. . . . Mr. Forrest, I am most happy to meet you."

No doubt of the open sesame to her regard! Clifton could not restrain embarrassment, but it was certain he thrilled under the clasp of her hand. And just then Virginia entered to approach them, and slipped a gloved hand inside Miss Andrews' arm.

"Howdy, Cliff!" she drawled at Clifton, with the self-possession of intimacy.

"Howdy, Virginia!" returned Clifton, forced to play up to this subterfuge, or whatever was her bent. She seemed unfamiliar, though not in person. It was not the Virginia who had found him exhausted and helpless inside the wall that day. Bright color milled in her cheeks and her eyes burned, which indications of anger were at strange variance with her cool speech.

"Cliff, I thought I'd come in and give you a hunch," she said. "I might have known Helen would try to annex you. Beware of this blond creature, Cliff. She is sure death to convalescent soldiers."

"Virginia, what a thing to say!" expostulated Helen, blushing and reproachful. "Mr. Forrest, pray don't believe her. The truth is that soldiers, especially those who returned ill or injured, have been sure death to me."

Clifton laughed and said, "You look like beautiful life itself."

"Virginia, I've a notion that at the bottom of your wise crack there's a desire to annex Mr. Forrest yourself," returned Helen, with loving, shrewd, arch eyes keen on Virginia.

"Sure. I'm brazen about it."

"Well, you've got in ahead of me, but I'll give you a race, anyway," challenged Miss Andrews, with sweet, speculative glance on Clifton. "You see, he was my brother's buddy in France."

"Helen! You don't say!" exclaimed Virginia, suddenly her sincere self again. "Clifton, is it true? You were friends—over there? . . . Why, how splendid to meet out here!"

"Virginia, I—I don't quite remember Jack," replied Clifton, trying to lie to save Andrews. "But he says so. You know I lost my memory for nine months. And I guess it's not all come back yet."

"You didn't remember *me* on the ship. Or on the train," said Virginia, in a tone that might have meant anything.

"Then perhaps Jack is right. I had a lot of buddies —and some never came back," returned Clifton, dropping his head.

"Girls, you're getting in bad with me, too," interposed Andrews.

"Jack, it might be idle chatter, and then again it mightn't," replied Virginia, enigmatically. "But to be serious, I'd like you to see something of Clifton while you're visiting me. Will you?"

"Delighted. We've already spoken of it."

"And you too, Helen. But it's only square to warn you. In spite of college and—France, Clifton is Western. You remember what you said when you saw my mountains and desert—my cottonwoods?"

"Assuredly I remember. I said 'I love them.' "

"Very well. That is some evidence that you still possess a heart."

"And you don't want me to lose it?" queried Helen.

"On the contrary, I wish you would—to me, to my horses and cottonwoods—to everything Western, especially Clifton. . . . He and I, too, some day may need your friendship."

"Virginia, your devout wish is almost consumated," replied Helen, with a bewildering smile that included Clifton.

They were interrupted by a small whirlwind in the shape of Ethel Wayne.

"Help! Help! These Monday bargain-shoppers are robbing me!" she cried. "I had a lot of stuff laid out, and they're swiping it. Clifton, have you got a big Indian policeman round here?"

"No, but if you can't get your stuff back I've got some more under the counter," rejoined Clifton.

"I had some laid out, too," added Helen. "Come, Jack, help me rescue it. I wouldn't be surprised if Calamity Jane and Deadwood Dick here would like to be alone a little."

The laughing trio moved away toward the mêlée.

"Clifton, is this offensive to you?" asked Virginia, almost timidly, resting a gauntleted hand on his knee, as he sat upon the counter, looking down at her.

"Hardly, Virginia, I'm not exactly a—a boob," protested Clifton.

"But it's so easy to hurt you. Ethel and I put up this job. We're going to clean out your old store. But I didn't intend to come in. Not until I saw Helen Andrews beaming upon you. That wasn't in my program."

"I guess I'm far from being hurt. You're very kind. And they——"

"Clifton, isn't she just lovely?" interrupted Virginia. "Pure blond. You don't see one often that is natural. Men fall for her like—like a lot of tenpins."

"Small wonder."

"Would you?" she flashed, jealously.

"Gee! I did, pronto!"

"Don't talk nonsense!" rejoined Virginia, sharply. "Suppose *she* fell in love with you. . . . Cliff, she's modern, but clean, fine, unspoiled. I'm crazy about her. And rich! Why, her father could buy mine out and call it street-car fare! Besides, some relative left her millions. . . . Suppose *she* were to fall in love with you?"

"Virginia, sure it's you talking nonsense," said Clifton, amazed at her. "You say the queerest things."

"They wouldn't be queer to anyone but a—a—blockhead."

"Humph! I dare say. Well, since you insist on such a ridiculous presumption—if Miss Andrews were to fall in love with *me*, I'd return the compliment most darned pronto. I've been most gratefully content just to live. But in that event I'd pray to grow well and strong again, and handsome, if it were possible, and able to ride a horse like I used to, and everything."

"Clifton Forrest, pretty soon you will tumble off my pedestal," she warned, dubiously.

"Virginia, please don't torment me with your childishness," he said, sadly. "There's no girl like her or you for Clifton Forrest."

"I'm not so sure about that," she retorted, subtly relaxing. "But—how glad I am you're better! Why, you've gained, Clifton! Those pale hollows in your cheeks are gone. You've a little color, too. And your shoulders don't sag. . . . And do you know, only once since I've been watching you here have you made that strange move with your hand across your eyes. Only once! Oh, Clifton, you are going to get well."

Just then Malpass entered, carefully groomed and immaculate as a riding-master. Clifton guessed that he had been watching through the door. He had sloe-black, glittering eyes, a thin lined face expressive of restrained power.

"Virginia, we are wasting time here," he said.

"You might be. We are not," replied Virginia.

"But if we are to go in to town we can't spend hours in this dump."

Apparently Clifton's presence was included in this comprehensive statement; certainly his gesture with his riding-whip was all embracing.

"I informed you one of the objects of this ride was to buy souvenirs and provisions," said Virginia, curtly, with the red spots dancing back in her cheeks.

"You did. I inform you in turn that better souvenirs can be found at Watrous or Las Vegas. As for provisions—I'll order them in town."

"We prefer to buy them here."

"We? You mean *you*. And your object is merely to help this poor beggar of a Forrest."

"Whatever my object, it's none of your business," retorted Virginia, and now the red spots faded.

"Anything you want to do is my business," he replied, showing his white teeth.

"That's what you think. My father has got you walking in your sleep. You'll wake up presently."

Whereupon Virginia, with light pressure of her

hand that still rested on Clifton's knee, vaulted up on the counter, and flipped her skirts comfortably if not modestly. The action, if not her words, penetrated Malpass' courteous impatience, and black lightning leaped from his eyes. But he had control over tremendous passions.

"Virginia, it will be better for you if I continue to slumber," he said, and even his mockery was menace. "But about the provisions. As you persist, and time is precious, I'll buy this rather dingy stock and have it hauled up to the house. What is not fit we can throw to the chickens."

He surveyed the shelves, that indeed were not inspiring to a would-be purchaser. Then he fastened those glittering eyes upon Clifton.

"How much for this stock?"

Clifton stared coolly at Malpass. Dealing with men was something that held no confusion of mind for him.

"Well, señor——"

"Don't call me that," interrupted Malpass, with a flash of passion that showed where he was vulnerable. "You address me as Mr. Malpass."

"Is that so? I'm likely to call you something else pronto."

Clifton felt a slight pressure of Virginia's arm against his, and it had the effect for which it was probably intended.

"How much?" demanded Malpass, his olive skin turning ruddy.

"One thousand dollars—to you," returned Clifton, cool and quick.

Malpass produced new bills, that had seen but little handling, and counting out a number he laid them on the counter. "I'll have this stuff hauled away at once. . . . Virginia, drag your friends out of here before I insult them."

"You couldn't insult my friends," rejoined Virginia with incredible softness.

Malpass strode out.

"Cliff, isn't he the limit?" queried Virginia, turning.

"He's sure a high-class greaser," responded Clifton, in disgust. "Maybe not so high, at that."

"But—I'm tickled pink. We put it over on Mr. Señor Malpass. . . . Say, didn't he flare up at that señor? . . . Clifton, we made *him* pay for the camp grub. That's just fine. Don't you dare say you won't take it."

"Take it? I should smile I will. Why, it's a Godsend. We're getting poorer——" Here he hastily checked himself to go on: "But I'm afraid I cheated him. This supply isn't worth half that much."

Ethel presented herself before them, packing an armful of beaded ornaments and a basketful of belts, buckles, silver buttons.

"How much, Mr. Storekeeper?" she asked, pretending to be a child.

"Nothing to you, Ethel."

"But see here. I want to pay for these."

"Very well. They will cost you a kiss."

"I'll throw that in, after I *pay* for them," she retorted.

"It's a bargain," replied Clifton, in excitement that was not feigned. He produced a pencil and began to enumerate on a paper bag the prices of the different articles.

"Ethel, did you see Malpass bullying me?" asked Virginia.

"You bet I did. But for once he didn't seem to crush you."

"It was because I sat up here beside Clifton. I could have boxed his sleek ears. . . . Ethel, don't you think it horrid and—and cowardly of Clifton to let me be thrown away upon that man?"

"It's a crime. . . . Clifton, you won't stand for that, will you? When you're Ginia's only friend?"

"You girls upset my figuring," replied Clifton, imperturbably.

"Isn't he the cold-blooded brute?" queried Ethel, in good-humored awe. "But I think I see through him."

"Thirty-six dollars—and two bits," summed up Clifton, at last.

"Oh, so cheap? But what's the two bits?"

"Twenty-five cents."

"Here you are," counted out the girl, blithely.

Clifton did not speak of what she had agreed to throw in.

"Help me up. Ginia's so long-legged she could step right up on this awful counter. . . . Aren't we having a jolly time? My kid sister and brother will be tickled with these presents, if I can part with them."

"Ethel, we've bought Clifton's stock of provisions. Never had to pay a dollar!"

"How come? I hope you didn't let him give it to us."

"Malpass bought it. I drove him to it."

"Perfectly grand," trilled Ethel, in ecstasy.

"Ethel, I dare you to call him Señor Malpass, when he comes back."

"You're on. Never took a dare in my life. And that

reminds me." She peered round in front of Clifton, mischievous and daring, to see if the others were watching. They were engrossed in selection and rejection of souvenirs. "Coast's clear." And she raised herself swiftly to kiss Clifton plump on the cheek. "There, my debt is paid. . . . You needn't blush. I don't do that as a general thing."

Virginia bent a little to peer up into Clifton's face.

"Cliff, if I pick out a lot of these souvenirs will you let me pay you *all* in Ethel's good measure?" she asked, alluringly. "You see, I'm about broke, and it would enable me to get a lot of things I really can't afford in cash."

"I will not," declared Clifton, dubiously.

Whereupon Virginia and Ethel left him, with intimate laughter and mysterious backward glances.

The upshot of this visit from Virginia and her friends was that Clifton was cleaned out of all his stores except tobacco and a few odd utensils and harness. In exchange he had a sum approaching two thousand dollars, a really staggering amount, considering that of late he had been grateful even for Mexican pennies. His mother would regard it as manna from heaven, and love Virginia Lundeen as the angel giver. Clifton wished they would hurry away so he could collect his wits.

They filled the tallyho with their purchases and the air with their happy chatter and laughter. Virginia was the only one who did not seem happy. In the confusion attending the transfer of the blankets, baskets, and other articles to the coach she shot Clifton more than one glance, the meaning of which he could not for the life of him interpret.

At last they had everything carried out, and were

vacating to give room to the several Mexican laborers who had arrived. Malpass' familiarity with Spanish became evident. Miss Andrews, her lovely face flushed with the excitement and fun, tripped in, evidently to say good-by. Virginia's impulse to follow manifestly had been prompted by her friend's action.

"Good-by, Mr. Forrest," said Helen, offering her hand. "It has been a pleasure to meet a comrade of Jack's—a real Westerner. He has promised that we shall see more of you."

"It would please me," replied Clifton, heartily.

"We have played havoc with your store. You must load up again for another raid. . . . Good-by."

"Good-by, Helen of Troy. I hope you come back," replied Clifton, as much moved by Virginia's disturbing presence as Helen's graciousness.

"How'd you know I come from Troy?" asked Helen, over her shoulder. "Jack told you, I'll bet. And I wanted you to think me a New Yorker."

"I didn't know. I sure didn't mean Troy, New York."

Helen went out glowing.

"Cliff," spoke up Virginia, just as if she had not had a chance before, "you'd never see me if that girl was around."

"Of course I would, Virginia. I did."

"I believe you learned to flirt in France."

The advent of Malpass saved Clifton a rather tantalizing retort, which was just as well not expressed. He saw at a glance that Malpass' suavity and coolness were only skin deep so far as anything relative to Virginia Lundeen was concerned.

"Go on out, Virginia. Your friends are in the

coach, ready to leave. I'll follow, after I've made sure this storekeeper hands over all the goods I paid for."

"Just what do you mean by that?" asked Clifton.

"Take it any way you like," snapped Malpass.

"Well, I'm sorry, but I'm not quite up to lifting down that heavy canned fruit," returned Forrest, slowly feeling his way.

"You're thick-headed, Forrest," sneered Malpass. "You heard what I said. But if you take it that way, why get a move on and help down with the goods."

"I'm not a peon," retorted Clifton, hotly.

"You're a clerk, and a poor one at that."

"Señor, we understand each other. You *think* I'm a peon and I *know* you're a greaser."

"Clifton!—Mr. Malpass!" cried Virginia, stepping between them.

Malpass swung a riding whip over her shoulder, staggering Clifton with a smart cut across the face, which brought blood. Then thrusting Virginia aside, he struck Clifton, and following up an advantage so surprisingly easy, he knocked Clifton down.

Virginia, in a swift frenzy that was partly fright, gave Malpass a stinging slap across the mouth.

"You yellow dog! To strike a crippled soldier! My God! I despise you!"

Clifton got up, though it was all he could do. "Malpass," he almost whispered, "beat it before I go for my gun."

The threat had the desired effect. Malpass, recovering from ungovernable rage, leaped the counter and went out the back way.

"Go, Virginia, before somebody—comes back after you," whispered Clifton.

"He hurt—you," she returned, with quivering lips, and wiped the blood from the welt on his cheek.

"Not much. I'm all right—only excited and mad. Please go before——"

"Do you suppose I care what they see or think? . . . You're lying to me, Cliff. You're white—you're shaking."

"Well, I reckon that's natural," replied Forrest, pulling himself together. He had been laboring under half a fear that Malpass might return with a gun. More than one shooting scrape had been attributed to this fortune-elevated vaquero.

"Cliff, I'll go, but I must see you soon."

She was clinging to him.

"Virginia, you've lost your head. They'll *see* you! . . . There, Miss Andrews is at the door."

"I'm glad she saw, anyhow," replied Virginia, releasing her hold on him and stepping back. "Cliff, you're a wonderful fellow—but the biggest dunce I ever knew."

CHAPTER

7

VIRGINIA was in camp with her friends, high up in a sylvan glade under the dome of Old Baldy, and for the first time in weeks dared to approach happiness.

It was along toward the end of June, and for that high altitude rather early in the season. The cold nights and frosty mornings, however, made the time ideal for camping.

Climbing up there had been a severe ordeal for most of the Eastern visitors, who, outdoor people though they were, had been unused to strenuous work, let alone miles of perilous, rocky trails where horses had to be led. But once arrived at the beautiful mountain meadow, they said they would not have missed the trip for worlds.

Two green mountains sloped down from the heights, forming at the base a little open valley containing a gem of a lake surrounded by a forest of pines, a fringe of grand monarchs gradually thickening with the rise of ground into the impenetrable timber belt. At the upper end of the oval lake a small peninsula jutted out. Among the scattered pines the tents had been pitched, within sight and hearing of the white cascade that slid down from the green notch above.

At the lower end of the lake the outlet glided swiftly between brown banks, to glance over a fall and tumble with a roar into a purple gorge. Here the mountain slopes sheered away, showing the desert five thousand feet below on the other side of the range.

Of all Western views that Virginia treasured, here was her favorite. To attain it one had to climb to a ledge above the gorge. There were shady nooks under a dwarf pine, mats of brown pine needles and silver-flowered amber moss; and a scene from which no lover of the solitude and beauty and grandeur of nature could turn without regret.

Selfishly Virginia went there alone, desiring humbly to renew her allegiance. This was, she recalled, her sixth trip to this isolated fastness; and the last one, three years in the past, seemed long ago and far away. No longer was she a schoolgirl, but a woman, now, wildly in love, with an abandon that could not have been possible in her romantic teens. Yet the hero of those dreamy, girlish years was still the hero of her womanhood.

She had slipped away from Ethel and Helen, who were the only friends close enough to think of her intimately. Ethel knew her secret and Helen suspected it. Virginia loved them dearly, but she wanted to be alone, here, of all places. For the rest of her friends she was not particularly concerned. Some were exhausted from the arduous climb, and the others were in ecstasies over this ideal spot. Jake and Con, her own cowboys, were in charge, and they had efficient help. Malpass had been left behind. Virginia had not spoken to him since his attack upon Clifton. She absolutely would not consider him in any capacity. A furious quarrel between her and her father, with Malpass present, had ended in the establishment of an armistice until such time as Virginia's guests, all except Ethel, would leave. So this camping trip, planned as a climax in the entertainment of Eastern friends she probably would never see again, bade fair to be a great success.

Virginia was tired, not so much physically as mentally. She threw herself down in the old, comfortable, mossy spot, that had not changed, and invited the spell of loneliness, of murmuring melodious stream, of the purple depths, and lastly the vast silent and illimitable desert far below.

How she had ached to be alone! And here she was far from camp, the white tents only specks above the shining lake, under the spread of the blue heavens, in the sight of marvelously visioned eagles, perhaps, surely of the birds and squirrels that abounded among the crags and trees. It was not only being out of sight of human kind that constituted solitude, it was the fullness of realizing that none of them knew where she was nor how much alone. The fragrant air, the gray crags, the inclines of tufted green, the bold, lofty dome of the bald mountain above, and through the wide gateway below the ribbed sweep, the endless reach, the vanishing of the desert into the dim haze of distance—these things which in that moment she shared with no one, flooded her being, pervaded her spirit, soothed her troubled soul with the ultimate essence of loneliness.

Close at hand, under her, the tips of lacy spruce trees, the downward steps of lichened blocks of granite, led into a purple glen crossed by bars of golden sunlight, by shadows of pines, whence floated upward the muffled murmur of a slow stream, reluctant to take the downward plunges. It glided brown and shallow over the flat ledge, to spread into a white foamy fan that closed again, and took a narrow leap, disappearing in rainbow-chased spray.

These sights and sounds were intimate. But it was the desert, on which at last she spent her reluctant gaze, that forced her into slow-realizing reverence. For she had grown in mind since she had watched there. She had seen great cities, states of endless farms, the gloomy, restless Atlantic, and the plains and mountains of foreign lands. Nothing like this! All so pale in comparison! What was it to see a few miles of tossing green salt waters? Here the desert air was clear, and there wandered two hundred and more miles of rock and sand, of canyon and range, of the dim, red Arizona walls that vanished in haze.

She had come home—home, and she did not see where education and travel had been worth the labor, unless to prepare her the better for appreciation of the West.

It was not then that her favorite Western scene had changed, but that she, bringing incalculably more to it after years of absence, seemed changed herself, a throbbing, aching, dreaming, loving, fighting woman who must find herein the strength and endurance of nature, or perish in all that she held sacred to womanhood.

Virginia knew her father had sunk to the level of a common thief, in her eyes as culpable as the rustlers who used to be hanged on the cottonwoods. Silver mines and lands and mansions did not absolve a thief from the baseness accorded the cattle-stealer. But money had power and it sanctioned crime. Jed Lundeen had more than ruined the Forrests; he had debased their fair repute. Not only had he stolen their property, but also their good name!

Virginia's early training had been one of simple religion. For perhaps ten years back her mother had leaned more and more to her father's path, which, as he prospered by means that would not bear the white light of day, had been away from the church. Virginia's years at school had not been prolific of religious stabilizing, but on the other hand, she had not been greatly influenced by the modern atheism so prevalent in college. What faith she had went into abeyance, through disuse, and now in her extremity she felt the need of it.

So, through the purple depths and the colorful desert, and the infinite nothing of distance, she peered into her own soul. Long she gazed, with wide eyes, and then with eyes tight shut. She saw the same with both. She was now a woman of twenty-two, older really than her exact age in years. She wanted to live her own life, not because of selfishness or egotism, but because of what she regarded as right. She wanted love and children, and if these meant happiness, as well as the nobler state for a woman, she wanted that, too. She could not become the wife of August Malpass, not because she could not sacrifice herself for her father, to save him from the net in which he had entrapped himself, but because such marriage would be a sin. Likewise it would be dishonest, if not actually sinful, for her to shield her father and Malpass, should tangible evidences of their guilt accrue. Lastly, with all her heart and soul, with a growth from childhood, she loved Clifton Forrest, and only through him could the fulfillment of life come to her.

"He doesn't see it," she mused, feeling a satisfaction in breathing her secret to the solitude. "He wouldn't believe it . . . yet how true it is!"

She had the illusion that her brooding, passionate gaze magnified all in its scope. And she saw the desert through her love, her strife with her father, the ordeal of her spirit, all inextricably involved in the single and paramount necessity of finding and adhering to the truth—which was the good, the right, and the faithful.

Space seemed illimitable. Through half-closed eyes Virginia swept in the sheer depths, the expanse of naked earth, the cloud-banked horizon. Again and again she feasted her sight, from the crag and pine-tipped descent to the naked riven earth, and the chaos where desert vanished.

In the end it was out there that her vision lingered. For out there glistened an ineffable and illusive beauty—the plains of silver sand, the beaches of gold bordering seas that were delusions, the islets of red rock ringed around by turbulent surf, the waved dunes ever curving, the dots of sage and cedar areas of acres, yet mere specks on the landscape, the arid washes and flats, proof of the *anno seco* of the Mexicans, the rock country, ribbed and rutted, riven into gorge and ravine, running wild, multiplying its ragged mounds into black buttes, its hollows into canyons, its lines into great walls, and at last to heave and roll and bite at the sky, ebony and beryl and porphyry thrusting into the blue, to end in the nothingness of infinitude.

It was afternoon when Virginia descended the trail, to skirt the lake and made her way back through the pines to camp.

She found Ethel lolling in a hammock, wrapped in a blanket.

"Oh!" she gasped, starting up at sight of Virginia, her pretty eyes expanding, "You look strange, you're ripping! . . . You're the loveliest creature on earth. . . . You've got Helen beat there and back!"

"Why this extravagant mess of words?" inquired Virginia, smiling down upon this volatile bit of femininity.

"Ginia, there's a light on your face—what does the poet say?—never seen on land or sea."

"I've been over to a shrine. Tomorrow I shall take you there. Then you will not wonder. . . . Ethel, I have recovered something that I lost long ago."

"Now—you want to make me sad," responded Ethel, plaintively. "But you can't. I just swear I'll revel in this lovely place. Didn't I use to rave about Colorado? But never again. This beats anything I ever saw, and mind you, honey, I'm no tenderfoot from Noo Yawk. This is heaven. Paradise! . . . If Jack Andrews, or one of his friends—if *any* man made love to me here—or Indian or Mexican—I'd fall like a chunk of lead and be false to the nicest little sweetie in Denver."

"Well, I'm ashamed to hear you confess it. What's happened to you, anyway. . . . Why, you're barefooted! No stockings! . . . Ethel, what would your nice Denver sweetie say to this?"

"He'd be tickled pink," replied Ethel, with a giggle. Then she grew suddenly grave. "What happened to me? I'll tell you, old girl, I darn near drowned. I fell in the lake. Wow! Over my head! And I just froze! Cold? That water was like the way you treat Malpass. Con heard me yell and fished me out. In the nick of time, believe me! My clothes are drying over there by the camp fire. . . . Oh, you needn't look so horrified! I've got on my dressing-gown. And I think you should show some distress."

"Well," ejaculated Virginia, sitting down, "I really want to laugh. You, Ethel Wayne, whom I boasted as an old stager on the trail. What's become of my other tenderfeet?"

"The men are fishing, sure Mike—a lot we'll see of them!—but the girls are lolling around, just too happy for words. Virginia, the consensus of opinion, as I've snookily got it, is that you're the last thing in peaches. Sure I always knew it, but I'm tipping off the Eastern angle. This is a swell outfit you've sprung on me, honey, but I must say they've got something on us Westerners. I like that Jack Andrews and if I wasn't— —There I go. Unstable as water, thou shalt not be true! . . . And I just love Helen Andrews."

"So I have observed."

"Goodness! Ginia, you're not jealous?"

"A little, on your account. A lot on Clifton's. . . . I'm a jealous cat, Ethel."

"Say, why this humility all of a sudden? To stop kidding, I'll say you need never be jealous on my account. I adore you. I'm yours forever. . . . But in the case of Cliff I'm not so darn sure. You're carrying that Lundeen handicap. And believe me, it's something to stagger under."

"Miss Wayne, I am quite aware of that," replied Virginia, in mock hauteur.

"Helen Andrews *likes* Cliff," returned Ethel, seriously, her brows knitted. "We oughtn't wonder at that. He's the most lovable chap, the handsomest, the greatest hero the war sent back to us. You know they've got his number in town now. They've found out what he did. . . . Well, it's quite natural for this rich and lovely lady to be interested in Cliff. I'm glad, even if I am scared. But—if she happened to fall in love with him—good night!"

"Ethel, you mean I wouldn't have a show on earth?" asked Virginia, tragically.

"No, nor in heaven, either," sighed Ethel, sacrilegiously.

"I hope I'm not so—so little that I couldn't be— glad for Cliff's sake," replied Virginia, a little tremulously. This matter-of-fact, down-to-earth talk of Ethel's was rather disconcerting, coming so suddenly after Virginia's vigil at her shrine on the heights.

"Maybe we're borrowing trouble," said Ethel. "Lord knows that's the way of lovers. Don't I know? . . . Helen has seen Cliff three times I know of since we bought out his store."

"Three times? I thought only two."

"Reckon you missed the last, and I sure didn't have the nerve to tell you then. What with your father and that white-toothed Spanish galoot who's crazy about you I thought you had enough to worry along on. . . . Virginia, our fair Helen of Troy rode off alone

Sunday afternoon. Down the valley! You can bet she
went to see Cliff. They had a date. She didn't stay
long, though it was sunset when she came back. . . .
Now, sister, what you've got to grasp to your poor
shuddering heart is this. *Any* man, much less our unfortunate soldier friend, would soon fall in love with
Helen Andrews. Furthermore, she's just as likely to fall
in love with him. The woods are full of such pretty
happenings."

"Ethel darling, I—I could bear it, because I want
Clifton to have some reward for his sacrifices."

"Sure you could. And you're a game sport. But
that is only if it comes to the worst. Helen is no flirt.
She is earnest, fine. There's the danger, though. And
Clifton is slow to like anybody. I'm sure we're safe yet.
They're all leaving on July first. So it'd be just as well
not to break camp here till June twenty-ninth. Perfectly skunky trick, but all's fair—you know. . . . And
while we're up here we'd better plan how to throw a
monkey-wrench into that Malpass threshing machine."

"Ethel, you're a conscienceless, unscrupulous,
terrible young woman, but, oh, what would I do without you?"

Virginia spent seven idle dreaming days at Emerald Lake. Her friends, for the most part, were exceedingly active, appearing never to get enough of the
wonderful sport the camp afforded. So for them the
time fled by.

For Virginia, however, the days spread out long.
Yet she was grateful for it. Affairs at Cottonwoods
were so near a crisis that she was loath to return.
Ethel's spirit and determination to find some loophole

for Virginia was hopeful in itself, but so far nothing had come of it.

The 29th of June arrived all too soon for Virginia's guests. Many and wild were their encomiums. "I'll own this place if I have to buy the whole National Forest," declared Helen Andrews, magnificently. Somehow this remark gave Virginia food for reflection.

The return trip down the winding trail was delight, compared with the toil of the ascent. But few places could not be ridden, though many of the steep steps and the weathered slopes of loose shale brought squeals from the girls. With a happy hour at noon for lunch and rest it took all day to do the eighteen miles down to Cottonwoods.

To Virginia's great satisfaction, and also surprise, both her father and Malpass were absent; where, Mrs. Lundeen did not know. The two men were at loggerheads over mining interests in the south, she said, as if weary of the subject.

Next day Virginia's guests gave far less time to packing than to the outdoor pursuits which had so endeared Cottonwoods to them. It did not surprise Virginia to see Helen and her brother go riding down the valley road toward San Luis. Womanlike, Virginia had to inform Ethel, and from that young lady she got the startling reply, "Sure, you should have beat Helen to it!"

Virginia went about her affairs, which naturally were numerous just then, trying to take refuge in them, when all the time her heart ached.

It was still early in the afternoon when Virginia, opening her door in response to a tap, found herself confronted by Helen in riding-habit, manifestly just from the saddle. A flush like an opal glow showed under her golden tan. Virginia caught her breath at the girl's blond loveliness.

"Hello, old dear! May I come in? I've something to tell you," said Helen.

"Of course. . . . Helen, you look serious."

"It is serious, though not for us. Are you alone? Where's Ethel?"

"She's in the library."

"Virginia, I've some bad news. It has really distressed me," went on Helen, as Virginia led her to the window seat. "Jack and I rode down to see your friend Clifton. We found his store burned down. The interior was gutted, and only a few crumbling walls left standing. We couldn't learn anything at San Luis, so we hurried back to Clifton's home. We went in and found him on the porch with his mother. She's a charming, gracious old lady. . . . Well, Clifton told us that he had restocked his store, spending nearly two thousand dollars, I think it was, for the supplies. That very night some one set fire to the building from the inside. Everything was destroyed."

"Oh, how unfortunate, and worse if some one did it!" burst out Virginia.

"Clifton is sure it could not have been accident. There was nothing to catch fire inside. . . . Virginia, hasn't he enemies here?"

"I'm afraid he has," replied Virginia, bitterly.

"You'll forgive me, old dear, won't you, for appearing inquisitive? I like this Clifton Forrest. Naturally, when I thought he'd been a buddy of Jack's in France, I was interested to get acquainted with him. But now I must confess that even though he and Jack have had no previous acquaintance I'm still keen about him. Surely I don't need to eulogize Clifton to you, but I want you to know that I think him one of the finest chaps I've ever met. . . . Jack offered to lend him money enough to rebuild and restock the little store, which we've learned the Forrests depend on for a living. But Clifton thanked Jack and said he couldn't accept it, because he could never pay it back. Then I made a suggestion. I asked Clifton if he would run the Payne ranch for me if I bought it. He——"

"The Payne ranch! At Watrous?" interposed Virginia. "That enormous place! Why, Helen, the banks hold it at one hundred and eighty thousand dollars."

"I didn't inquire about that," returned the other, "but I was taken with the place and I had a notion to buy it. Of course it'd be a white elephant, like other places I've burdened myself with. But this is really a worthy idea. And I believe I'll go through with it, unless you block the deal."

"I! Why, Helen, I'd be happy to have you out here! It'd be great! And if you were to help Clifton, I—I think I'd like you better than I do, which is a lot."

"Virginia, we've got to do something for that soldier boy."

"Oh, I've tried. He's proud. He won't accept charity. I was afraid he'd be offended when we bought him out that day. It was so barefaced. . . . Hasn't Clifton told you about the Lundeen-Forrest feud?"

"Not a word. But lately, before we left on our camping trip, I picked up things here and there, and put two and two together. Your father and Forrest are deadly enemies. Your Brazilian cavalier, or whatever he is, struck me as a snake in the grass. I know men. He is after your money, Virginia. He made a play for me, which I squelched quick. Imagine that—when it's plain even to strangers he's trying to marry you. He hasn't a chance in the world, has he?"

Virginia laughed her scorn. "Helen, my father is under the thumb of this Malpass. He was led or forced to cheat the Forrests out of this property. He now is trying to persuade me to marry Malpass. Or he was, ten days ago. I imagine when he returns he'll use stronger argument. But I'd die before I'd give in."

"Here's hoping you won't have to go to such extremes! . . . Let's get back to Clifton. You like him, don't you, Virginia? Oh, hang it! why look at me that way? I mean you're fond of him, aren't you?"

"Why do you ask?" queried Virginia, constrainedly.

Helen got up and put her arms round Virginia and kissed her—demonstrative actions very unusual for the Eastern girl. "Old dear, you can't bluff me. And I won't let you be upstage, either. . . . I ask that because Ethel—sly little fox!—put it into my head. . . . Confess, now."

Virginia hung her head, as much from unresisting weakness as shame.

"Confess what—you triumphant goddess, I can't help loving *you*, that's sure."

"You're fond of Clifton?"

"Fond? . . . Good God! Use a Western word!" burst out Virginia, finally won.

Helen's answering embrace and kiss were very warm and sweet.

"So that's it," she whispered. "I'm glad. You'll help Clifton to get well and on his feet. . . . That was what worried me. You jealous child! . . . Virginia, I will return your confidence. My love—my heart are buried in a grave in France!"

VIRGINIA'S father came home drunk, the day
after the departure of her guests, and
Malpass showed a dark sullenness that
boded no good.

She felt like an animal at bay, and she paced her
room, waiting for the approach that she sensed. Nevertheless, it did not come, and she ate her dinner as
silent as her mother, a prey to growing apprehension.
She regretted that Ethel had been called back home to
Denver. A fugitive desire to see Clifton became a real
and persistent one.

The night seemed far removed from the peaceful
and restful ones she had enjoyed up in the mountains.
Morning, however, brought defiance, if not courage.

Malpass presented himself at the breakfast table
as immaculate as usual, and more than unusually self-
contained. He inquired politely about the camping
trip, the departure of her guests, and even expressed

regret not to have seen the beautiful Miss Andrews again. The Mexican servant informed her that her father was having breakfast in his room, where he awaited her convenience.

"Before you see him you may as well listen to me," said Malpass.

"Very well, the sooner the better. What can you have to say to me?"

"Have you reconsidered my proposal?"

"No. I gave it no further thought."

"Then I regret to say I must split with your father."

"That will be most acceptable to me."

"It may not be so when you hear the conditions."

"Mr. Malpass, pray save yourself the trouble of more talk," replied Virginia. "I am weary of the whole business. I don't care anything about conditions."

"But I can take this property away from him as he took it from Forrest."

"Do it and welcome," retorted Virginia, coldly. "Ill-gotten wealth never made any man happy. My father was wicked, but I consider you mostly to blame. I will be glad when he is free of you."

"He's not going to be free of me unless——"

"Unless I become your wife?" put in Virginia, as he hesitated, and her derision broke his studied calm.

"Unless you do he will go to jail for a long term."

"I think you are a liar and a bluff."

"My dealings with Lundeen do not and never did include this Forrest property," went on Malpass, ignoring her words. "Nor did I have any share in the silver mine he stole. We used money from that to gain possession of extensive phosphate mines in the south. The controlling interest was mine. I increased my holdings, raising equal capital for him to do the same. We are now deeply involved and he owes me a sum greater than this ranch could bring. If we settle it out of court, well and good, for all of us. But if I take it to court, I will prove he deliberately stole Forrest's land, fully cognizant of the value of the silver mine. I can prove it because *I* discovered the mineral."

"Yes, and you were the brains of the dishonest deal," rejoined Virginia, hotly.

"To be sure. But at Lundeen's instigation. Never on paper! There's not a word to that effect. If you will pardon my saying it, your father is a sapheaded, greedy old cattleman with a tremendous weakness— his hatred of Clay Forrest. Now if you know your West you will certainly realize what would happen to your father if I betrayed him in court—which means betraying him to Clay Forrest."

"What would happen?" queried Virginia, unable to repress alarm.

"Forrest will kill him!"

"Oh, you are trying to work on my feelings!" cried Virginia. "I don't believe it. You've made this all up to frighten me. . . . Even if it *were* true, Forrest would kill you, too."

"That would not be so easy. And the motive would not be so great."

Virginia veiled her eyes and her own barbed shaft. "Suppose I told Clifton Forrest you burned down his store?"

No guilty man's effrontery and flinty nerve could mask the truth from a woman's love and intuition. The instant Virginia's swift query had passed her lips she divined Malpass had been responsible for the latest misfortune to the Forrests.

"Burned down!—I have been away, you know, and had not heard. . . . Your ridiculous accusation requires no answer."

Virginia laughed in his face.

"If Clifton Forrest found out what I know he would kill you."

Malpass arose to push back his chair. "You drift away from the main issue. I warn you to leave young Forrest out of this. I am aware of your interest in him. It has not enhanced his fortunes."

Virginia sprang up so passionately that her chair fell backward.

"August Malpass, those words betray you, though I never needed words to find out what you are. Do your evilest, señor! This is not old Mexico."

The hard immobility of Malpass' olive face changed swiftly to passion. His eyes became flames. With the spring of a panther he was on her, clasping her in his arms. Crushing her to him he kissed her naked throat, then her face, failing of her lips only when Virginia, overcoming a horror of paralysis, tore clear of him with infuriated strength.

"Señorita, you have—invited violence," he panted, making her an elaborate bow which he had not learned on that range. "I prefer it. Let us be natural. I love a she-cat from hell. . . . Spit! Scratch! Bite! . . . You will be all the sweeter!"

"If you ever touch me again, I'll kill you."

Virginia ran to her room, and locking the door she fell on her bed in an access of rage and hate and fear. When these had worked their will and passed away she rose with a stupendous surprise, and shame the like of which she had never known. Her limbs tottered under her, and the window seat appeared none too close. Could she ever erase the burn and blot of this half-breed's kisses? That she had kept her lips inviolate helped her but little.

In the ensuing hour she learned the appalling gravity of her predicament.

Her father came to her, a changed and broken man, at first neither commanding nor supplicating. He had always been in Malpass' power, though ignorant of it till now. With what fiendish dexterity the weaver had enmeshed him!

Malpass had the proofs to convict, the money to ease his own irregularities, the baseness to betray unless he gained the object he so passionately sought.

"Father, I can't—I can't!" sobbed Virginia. "How can you ask? . . . I'd sooner kill myself."

"It means prison for me—disgrace for you and mother—poverty. . . . Virginia, marry him to save us. You can divorce him later. Give me time to retrieve. Then with money I can fight. Find some way to beat him."

"Not to save even our lives!" flamed Virginia.

"But wait, daughter. You're riled now. Take time. Think. You're not in love with any man. It'd not be so hard. You can leave him—and soon. You can be free."

"What of my soul? . . . I'd feel myself debauched. No! No!"

"Virginia, he'll *make* you give in, sooner or later. He has the very devil's power. It'll be better to have it over. Then we can plan. I swear to God I've realized my crime, an' seek now only to save you an' mother. Daughter, we've gained standin' as a family these last years. We are somebody. If this comes out I'm done— an' you an' mother will hang your heads in shame."

"You beg what is worse than shame," retorted Virginia. "My blood boils and revolts. Not an hour ago Malpass insulted me vilely—beyond forgiveness. He taunted me with the power you think he has."

"I know he has it. You resisted him. Like as not you scorned him. He'll make you suffer more. . . . Daughter, shore the best way—the only way is to give in—fool him. Fool him! If he has to make you marry him—God help you! For he's vain, an' I tell you a half-breed."

"He can't force me. This is not old Mexico. I'll find a way—not only to escape him but to——"

"Drive him to ruin me—or stain my hands with blood," harshly interrupted her father. "Daughter, you've a duty to me an' your mother. We begot you, an' I've sinned to give you comforts, luxuries. Horses! I've spent thousands on your horses. . . . Think before it's too late. I can hold Malpass off. Once he thinks there's a hope of your love he'll melt. Cheat him!—Cheat him! Make him the poor weak fool he's made me!"

After her father had tottered out, spent with passion, Virginia saw the abyss that yawned at her feet. For had she not listened to him? Poor man, he was lost indeed. Yet she, too, was weak, uncertain, torn by love one way, and by self-preservation in another.

At length, out of the chaos of her mind resolved a first and imperative necessity—to insure at least her legal freedom from Malpass. So far as physical freedom was concerned, was she not in peril every hour she lived in that house? In her present state of mind she feared it.

If she married some other man, it would not be

possible for her father and Malpass to persuade or drive or hypnotize her into a marriage that would mean moral and spiritual death. And the world might as well have contained only one man—Clifton Forrest.

She might—she must induce him to marry her. But how? Once before she had broached the subject, only to be repulsed. Still, his reason had been sound, generous, plausible. She could only respect him for it. Why not formulate a plan on the strength of the very reason he gave—that he was a mere shell of a man, probably doomed to a brief and inactive life? Virginia scouted that idea, though it made her shudder inwardly. Clifton would get well and strong again. She was sure of it. But she must pretend she believed him, and that under such circumstances he would be rendering her the great service of giving her his name, secretly, so she would have that moral anchor when the storm broke.

Pride alone was sufficient to conceal her love. Still, would she always be proud? Might not her spirit break? When Malpass hounded her into a corner, and her father thundered her out of his house for marrying a Forrest, would she not creep to Clifton's feet and betray herself? There would be a strange ecstasy in that. But Virginia Lundeen could not quite see herself so prostrate.

Once having made the momentous decision, she would admit no doubts. She would simply have to be strong enough to persuade him. Suddenly she reproached herself. Clifton, learning of her extremity, would offer himself. He had given all for nothing. Never would he begrudge her the stronghold of wifehood.

At her desk, then, she wrote a note urgently requesting Clifton to meet her that evening by the broken corner of wall in his garden. She did not ask for an answer. Sallying forth, singularly strengthened, she strolled down to the barns to get some one to deliver the note.

It would not do to trust one of the Mexicans. Con, the Irish cowboy, would be absolutely reliable.

She found Con and Jake together. In fact, they were always together—a sort of union to combat the horde of Mexicans on the ranch. Jake was a lean, dark, bowlegged cowboy who had been born on the range. Con had been only several years in the West. He was a strong fellow, sandy-haired and freckled. He had big, wide-open, astonished eyes, a light gray in color.

"Mawnin', boys," she drawled. "How are you-all?"

"Tolerable, Miss Lundeen," replied Jake, doffing his sombrero.

"I'm foine, Miss, but when I'm out of worrk I'm out of sorts," said Con, standing bareheaded and respectful.

"There ought to be loads of work," returned Virginia, in surprise.

"Shure was, but the horses are gone."

"Gone! Where?" ejaculated Virginia, with a pang of dismay.

"Back to Watrous."

"Who ordered my horses there?"

"Malpass," replied Jake, shortly. "An' he said we'd not be wanted."

"Well!—Are all my horses gone?"

"Every last hoof, Miss Virginia."

"I was not consulted. Wait till I speak to my father. Meanwhile remember that I hire you and I pay you."

"Shore we know thet. But we're afeared Malpass is gettin' high-handed round here," returned Jake, in worried tones.

"I quite agree with you," laughed Virginia, without mirth. "Jake, if my car is still here, see that it's all right for me to run into town this afternoon. And, Con, I've an errand for you."

When Jake slouched away with jingling spurs Virginia asked Con if he had heard about the fire at San Luis which had burned the Forrest store during their trip up in the mountains.

"Yes, Miss, I've been down an' seen it. Shure tough on young Forrest. He had his all in that store."

"It was too bad. Did you hear any gossip about it?"

"Nuthin'. Mexicans shure ain't sayin' a word. Looks funny to me."

"Well, you take this note down to Mr. Clifton Forrest. Be sure you deliver it today. . . . I'll see you boys tomorrow and we'll talk things over—after I see father."

Upon Virginia's return to the house she encountered her father moodily pacing the porch. After greeting him she asked him why her horses had been ordered away.

"Daughter, it's news to me," he replied, spreading his palms.

"What I'd like to know is this. Are those horses my property?"

"Reckon they are. You're of age. I gave them to you."

"I shall go to Watrous and fetch them back."

"Wal, no one could prevent you. But it'll only make Malpass sorer. An' it's a fact the horses are better off over there. More feed. It costs like sixty heah. An', daughter, money is scarce."

"But my allowance, father?"

"I'll have to cut that off, for the present."

"Oh!—Well, I can go to work at something."

"You! At what?" he snapped.

"I might be a waitress or a clerk—if no better offered," replied Virginia, lightly.

"Nonsense! . . . Reckon you ought to have some money in the bank. Hope you haven't overdrawn your account?"

"I haven't the slightest idea and don't care in the least. You informed me, upon my return from the East, there was ten thousand left out of my—well, what I thought was mine. I paid my New York bills, which were pretty heavy. And it surely cost enough to entertain my friends. I suppose I'm as—as poor as Clifton Forrest."

"Then you're a beggar."

"What a fall for Virginia Lundeen! . . . The humiliation of it has not increased my respect and—affection for you, father mine. . . . Where is mother? I haven't seen her."

"She's sick in bed."

"Oh, I'm sorry. I didn't know. What ails her?"

"Reckon it's this damned mess that's knockin' me," he growled.

"I'll go to mother," said Virginia, soberly, entering the house.

She found Mrs. Lundeen sitting up, quite pale and sick, but evidently not so badly off as her husband had intimated. Nevertheless, Virginia suffered remorse for her neglect of her mother since that first quarrel following her arrival home. It pleased Virginia to grasp that her mother seemed no longer unapproachable.

"Father told me you'd worried yourself sick over this mess here," said Virginia, presently.

"Perhaps. But I wasn't so well before it came to a head," replied Mrs. Lundeen. "I'd like to go to California, if I don't feel better before winter sets in. Your father laughed. Said by that time we couldn't afford to go even to Las Vegas. I can't understand it at all."

"I do, mother. The nigger in the woodpile is Malpass. He has worked father into some kind of a trap. He absolutely runs the place. Father can't call his soul his own. I haven't the least doubt that we'll lose Cottonwoods."

"For my part, I'd not care," returned her mother, wearily. "I'd exchange with the Forrests any day. Down there I had work to do. This is no home. If I were you, Virginia, I'd go away."

"Mother!" exclaimed Virginia. "Only a little while ago you were urging me to marry Malpass."

"Yes, I know. Then I thought you might like the man, and it seemed a solution to our troubles. But I'm convinced now you couldn't save us even if you married Malpass."

"I'm of the same opinion," returned Virginia, in grateful gladness at this unexpected attitude of her mother. "Have you told father that?"

"I have, and got called an old fool for my pains. It's made me think, Virginia, that both Jed and Malpass have gone too far. They think they're a law unto themselves. I do not count. You are only a means to an end, for your father. Malpass seems to want you the more you deny him. Some men are built that way.

Usually they are the kind who tire after they get what they want."

"Mother, I'm awfully glad to hear you say these things. It helps a good deal, believe me," responded Virginia, warmly. "I can take care of myself. So don't worry about me—or anything, for that matter. We'll get along. And we must think of your health. I'm going in to town today and will ask the doctor about you. . . . I'm happy, mother, that this trouble has brought us closer together."

"So am I, dear. But don't make too much of it before your father."

Virginia drove to Las Vegas in a frame of mind somewhat similar to the one she had experienced the first day up at Emerald Lake. This, however, would have as its culmination the rendezvous with Clifton. The nearer Virginia got to that, the less she dared think of it. Could she play the part and deceive him? They would meet in the dark, though, she reflected; there would be a new moon, and he would not be able to see her plainly.

She reached the Las Vegas bank, her first objective, after closing hours, but upon being recognized she was admitted. To her relief she found there was a little money left to her credit, and she cashed a check for this balance. Then she sought audience with Mr. Halstead, who had been connected with the church she used to attend. Once he had been a cattleman, as was evinced by his rugged, weathered countenance. Virginia asked him point-blank what was the condition of her father's finances.

"He is overdrawn here," replied the banker. "That has occurred before, though never to this present extent. I'm sorry to inform you we refused his last request for a loan. Of course his credit is good here, to a reasonable extent. But we couldn't see our way to a loan of a hundred thousand. His Southern holdings are worth a million. But they appear to be involved rather deeply with his partner's."

"Has Mr. Malpass any dealings with your bank?"

"No. He has not even a checking account."

"Where does he bank?"

"Albuquerque, so I've been informed, but only in small amounts. He must have extensive bank dealings elsewhere."

"Who pays my father's Mexican help?"

"No checks have been presented here since Malpass' connection with your father. The presumption is that they are paid in cash."

"Will you tell me frankly, Mr. Halstead, what you think of Malpass' connection with my father?"

"Well, the connection has not inspired greater confidence in your father," replied Halstead, evasively. "May I ask, Miss Lundeen, if there is any truth in the rumor that you are to marry Malpass?"

"None whatever," returned Virginia, decisively. "My father wished it, but I refused absolutely."

"No doubt your many Las Vegas friends will be glad to hear that."

"You are at liberty to tell them. . . . Thank you, Mr. Halstead, and good afternoon."

Virginia deduced from this interview that Malpass had little if any reputable standing with Las Vegas men of affairs, and she was equally certain that her father was fast losing their confidence, if not more.

From the bank she went to the family physician, whom she had known as a little girl. He had been called to attend her mother during Virginia's absence in the mountains. Like most doctors, he would not speak openly. Virginia left his office convinced that her mother had some organic ailment, which, though not serious at present, might eventually become so.

Virginia invented excuses to call at the county clerk's office and upon the new minister, a Western man with a charming wife. In both cases she extended herself to be gracious and winning. Upon leaving, she thought of Ethel, and giggled in imitation of that young lady bent upon some deep scheme. Virginia had a plot of her own, which she believed transcended any Ethel had ever concocted.

Following these errands she shopped for an hour, then went to the Castaneda for dinner, a procedure that evidently invited conjecture from a party of townspeople present.

Dusk was gathering when she drove out of Las Vegas, taking a road that skirted the lower spread of Cottonwood Valley, and then turned north under the bank to San Luis. A few pin-points of light flickered out of the lonesome darkness of the little town. From this point she drove slowly, and in due time arrived at a level spot near the Forrest garden. How much more familiar were these surroundings than those where she lived! Driving off the road against a thicket of young cottonwoods, she extinguished the car lights and got out.

The night was warm and sultry, with a slow wind off the desert. Frogs trilled and crickets chirped out of the deep low hum of insects. Thousands of bright stars seemed to watch her, winking out of a deep blue sky. A thin crescent moon shone weirdly, low down through the cottonwoods.

She glided silently along the trail, knowing her way in the gloom under the trees. A small animal rustled away into the brush. Coming to a fallen tree, she sat down, conscious of suspense and dammed emotion. Whatever her motive or deceit, she knew in her heart that the truth which made this tryst unutterably sweet and fearful was her love for Clifton Forrest. And listening to the merciless voice that was her conscience, she confessed her motive was not only to save herself from Malpass. Somehow she justified it. Yet what a monstrous thing she had to pretend! If his actual presence did not still her mounting agitation she would be lost. Then she put a hand to her breast. How it swelled! How her heart beat, beat, beat! Her blood was throbbing and thrilling through her veins.

The giant cottonwood that she knew so well stood near the corner of the wall. She had hidden in its capacious hollow as a child. Its dark spreading foliage gave forth a low rustle of many leaves. Beyond, other cottonwoods stood spectrally.

It seemed simple and inevitable that the crowning adventure of her life should begin here, in the familiar solitude of this old home and in the lonely gloaming hour. The wind off the desert fanned her moist brow. Black and bold loomed the great mountains. This was her West. No arch plotter could drive her from it or kill her joy in it. Riches were superficial and, if ill-gotten, wholly destructive to such happiness as appealed to her.

Presently she moved on, though reluctantly. The little wait had only accelerated her thrills and starts. She gained the break in the old wall. Again she paused, and leaned against the corner, to peer into the vague shadows. She quivered as if she had expected to meet a lover and leap into his arms. She was mad. *Quien sabe?* In making her his wife, Clifton might be getting back the fortunes of the Forrests.

She went on, feeling her way. How black the garden corner! She peered on all sides. Nothing moved except the gentle leaves. The section of wall where she had talked with Clifton was vacant. She whispered his name. No answer! Suddenly she sank down on the wall. He had not come.

CHAPTER
9

"*CLIFF*, I'm damn good an' glad they burned you out," Clay Forrest averred to his son as they sat in the shade of the cottonwoods. It was a day in July, hot and still. The cicadas were in shrill blast.

"Dad, you make me tired," returned Clifton, with good-humored patience. "Why do you always say that? I think the store just caught on fire. Spontaneous combustion, or something."

"Huh! Somethin'. You bet. An' that somethin' was a greaser in the pay of Jed Lundeen."

"Oh no, dad! You're hipped on the Lundeen stuff. You lay everything to the Lundeens. If it were anyone it might have been Malpass. I didn't tell you before. He was in my store the day that Eastern crowd of young folks bought me out. And, well, we had some sharp words."

"What'd it lead to?"

"Nothing on my part. He struck me. Knocked me over. . . . It was just as well I didn't have a gun handy. I've got sort of used to one."

"Cliff Forrest! You never told me. . . . I'll beat that Malpass half to death."

"Dad, I'd rather you waited till I get strong enough to do it myself," replied Clifton, grimly.

"Humph! An' how soon will that be?"

"Not so very long. I'm gaining pretty fast now. Mother says I'll eat her out of house and home. Besides, it wouldn't take much of a man to lick Malpass."

"That greaser will have a knife about him somewhere. Wal, I'll tell you, son. You an' Ma have kept my hands off that Lundeen outfit too long. An' the longer I wait the harder it'll go with them."

"Revenge is natural, dad. But is it anything to give in to here? Suppose you went to horsewhip Lundeen and Malpass? You know how hate works if you give in to it. You might end in killing one or both of them. You'd go to prison. Then what of mother?"

"Hell, son, your arguments are unanswerable. Long ago I seen that. . . . A fight would end in blood-spillin'. All the same I don't believe any court in New Mexico would convict me."

"Don't you fool yourself," retorted Clifton. "What did that Las Vegas court do to you? It was fixed, no doubt. Well, Lundeen could fix it again."

"He couldn't hang any jury if he was dead. An' neither could Malpass," returned Forrest, thoughtfully.

"On the level now, dad, you've had it in your mind to do these two men?"

"Why, son, I was brought up in the West!" replied his father, as if apologizing for Clifton.

"You've been brooding over this wrong for years. That's why you've quit. You could have begun life all over again. You're only fifty-odd. But you putter around the garden. You idle and feed that hate in your heart. You're breaking mother's heart. She never minded the loss of Cottonwoods. That's all you think of. You are making yourself old. Worse, you're not helping me very much to take care of mother."

Forrest dropped his head a moment. "Wal, it does seem that way, son," he replied, resignedly. "An' that's the hell of it. I know just as well as you if I keep on mullin' over this trouble much longer I'm done for."

"Dad, if you do keep it up I'm done for, too."

"What you mean?"

"I mean a lot. . . . I've had more of a fight here than I had in France. To fight the hate you've given in to! And to fight my tired, tortured body into carrying on! I've got an even break now. If I can keep it up I'll get well. But I'd just as lief chuck the chance and beat you to Lundeen and Malpass."

"You'd forestall me! Kill that outfit!" burst out Forrest, dreadfully.

"If you don't give up that idea right now, for good and all, I'll go after them," declared Clifton, in cold ruthlessness. This was not a bluff, though he actually hoped he could intimidate his father. In his dark hours that ghastly desire had often abided with him.

"But, my Gawd! son, think of your mother!" ejaculated Forrest, appealing with his huge outstretched hands. "It nearly killed her when you were over there. An' now that she's got you back. . . . Aw, Cliff, it's not to be thought of for you!"

"Sure it isn't," rejoined Clifton, eagerly seizing

upon victory. "That's why I say you can't think of it, either. One or the other of us—it's all the same to mother."

"All right, son, I crawl," said Forrest, huskily, and covered his face with his hands.

A step on the leaves and a clink of spurs arrested Clifton's thankful response to his father's surrender. It was a victorious, happy moment. Clifton turned to see the red-faced cowboy from Cottonwoods.

"Howdy!" he said, genially, and handed Clifton a note. It was a square white envelope upon which was inscribed his name in a clear handwriting Clifton had never seen. But instantly he recognized the faint fragrance that came with the missive. Clifton felt the hot blood leap to his face. He did not want to open the letter, but as the cowboy stood expectantly he had to do so. And he read it.

Clifton's head seemed to swim. He tried to appear unconcerned, but if his confusion showed outwardly he must be making a sorry mess of it.

"All right. No answer," he said to the cowboy. "How are things up on the hill?"

"Shure slow now with the hosses gone an' no worrk."

"Gone?"

"Shure. Malpass was afther sindin' thim over to Wathrous."

Whereupon Clifton's father evinced signs not wholly lost upon the cowboy.

"I sympathize with you," said Clifton, with an understanding laugh. "I'm looking for a job myself."

"Shure they're scarce. Good day, sor," replied the other, and strode away.

"Cliff, who was that?" queried Forrest, a peculiar glint coming to his big eyes.

"Con something or other. He used to come into the store for cigarettes."

"But he's employed by Malpass!" exclaimed the father.

"I think not, dad. It runs in my mind the young lady up there is his boss."

"Lundeen's girl! Was that letter from her?" asked Forrest, in a tragic voice.

"Yes, dad."

"Hand it over. Let me read it."

"See here, dad, it's not polite to ask. And sure I wouldn't let anyone read a private note. At that it doesn't amount to much."

"Cliff, you're carryin' on with Lundeen's girl."

"I am not."

"You're a liar! I can see it in your face. You got red as a beet. You acted queer. Now you're white. . . . By Gawd! if this ain't the last straw!"

"Father! . . . I'm not a liar," retorted Clifton, both hurt and angered. "There's nothing between Virginia Lundeen and me. I can't help it—if she asks me to do something for her. Believe me, that girl has her troubles."

Forrest lumbered to his feet, his face blotched, his eyes like burned holes in a blanket.

"Wal, if all you came back home for was to get sweet on Lundeen's girl—I wish you'd never come."

He stalked away under the cottonwoods. Clifton was so stricken with mortification and fury that he could not call his father back. Little good that would have done! What a bull-headed old fool he was, anyhow! The mere mention of the name Lundeen made him see red.

Clifton reread the note and that was sufficient to relegate his father, and everybody else except Virginia, to oblivion. He guessed her trouble. But what could she want of him? Clifton felt suddenly weak. If she broached again the persecution to which Malpass and her father had subjected her, Clifton would ask her to marry him. Never could he resist that insidious, beautiful, terrible temptation again. To know that Virginia Lundeen was his wife! Even the conviction that she would only be using him as a checkmate against an unscrupulous wooer could not deprive the idea of its allurement.

The afternoon passed with Clifton in a trance. Every now and then, when a practical flash illumined his dreamy mind, he was amused at the romantic trend of his thoughts. He built a little drama in which he was the central figure. But he soon discovered that Virginia Lundeen played no small part in his imagined destiny. What a foolish dreamer he was!

When darkness came he went to his room, apparently to go to bed. He did not trust his father's surly observance. Then he had to climb out of his window, no slight task for him, as the casement was narrow, and the distance to the ground considerable. But with the aid of a vine, and by careful labored work he accomplished it.

The hum of a motor car down the road had ceased. It had not occurred to Clifton that Virginia would come any other way than on horseback. He had forgotten about her horses being taken away. Another of Malpass' scurvy tricks! Clifton hurried noiselessly under the cottonwoods. It was some distance to the corner of the wall.

Clifton did not want to be discovered by his father, for Virginia's sake as well as his own. So he stopped to listen and look back. All was dark and still in the direction of the house. But he waited a moment longer to insure safety. What a wonderful summer night! The stars blazed, the breeze sighed, the insects hummed, the frogs sent high trills tremulously out into the drowsy air.

Hurrying on again, Clifton soon began to draw close to the corner. His footsteps made no sound. Under the cottonwoods the shadow was impenetrable, but in the open a new moon and the starlight painted a pale silver against the black background. When he reached the spot he was out of breath, but his exertion was not responsible for the throbbing of his heart in his throat.

"Virginia," he called, very low, trying to pierce the strange shadows.

"Oh—Cliff!" she cried, in almost a gasp. "I was afraid—you weren't coming."

He could almost have touched her, and in two more steps his groping hand found her.

"Sorry I'm late," he whispered. "But I was afraid of dad. He was with me when the cowboy brought your note. . . . I had to climb out of my window like a girl sneaking to meet her lover."

"You did? How funny! Yet it's great," she replied, thrillingly, and she squeezed his hand. "Which room is yours? Oh, maybe I don't remember that old house!"

"I sleep in the little room you used to have."

"Oh, Cliff—how strange!" she murmured, after a

pause. "But how did you ever get out of that little window and down?"

"I managed somehow, but it was a squeeze."

"You might have hurt yourself!"

"Well, I didn't."

"How many, many times I stole out of that little room!"

"Not to meet boys, I hope?"

"No, never that. But just to get out—to be free and wild in the moonlight under the cottonwoods."

"Virginia, let's get away from this trail," he said. "I can't imagine anything worse than to have my dad catch us."

"Except to have *my* dad do it," she returned. Her laugh was rich and deep, with a note of defiance.

Clifton led her away from the corner, under the giant hollow cottonwood to the wall, where he had to feel his way to a seat he well knew.

"Here we're safe, at least from our dads," he said, responding to her mood. "Sit down, Virginia. It's dry and soft. You can lean against the wall."

She complied, but she was significantly slow about letting go of his hand; and after that she was silent so long that he wondered. But he had no desire to break the silence.

"Cliff, how would it be if our fathers did not hate each other?"

"How would what be?"

"You are surely unromantic, Cliff Forrest," she retorted.

"I dare say. I had it knocked out of me. But if you mean our—our queer friendship—I'd say it wouldn't have any kick."

"Has *this* a kick for you?" she asked, challengingly.

"It will have, darn pronto, if dad catches us," he laughed.

"No! Would that great hulking brute dare kick you?"

"I should smile. . . . Virginia, would your nice, loving, angel dad dare—well, let us say, spank you?"

"He would not," she retorted, and there the levity ended.

Clifton's eyes had become used to the darkness and could see her clearly, though mystically softened and paled by the moonlight. She removed her hat.

"Were you surprised to get my note?" she added, presently.

"I'd have been surprised in any case, but with dad there watching me read it I was sure flabbergasted."

"First, Cliff, I want to tell you that I know Malpass burned your store, or had it done."

"How do you know?"

"I accused him—sprung it on him by surprise. And he might just as well have confessed it."

"You don't say! Virginia, you don't lack nerve. . . . Well, I had a hunch myself that Malpass put some greaser at that job."

"Was your loss considerable?" asked Virginia, sympathetically.

"For me, it surely was. Do you know, Virginia, I'd have made good in that store. Of course the big sale I made to your friends and Malpass would have been responsible. I invested all the money in new stock; filled the store, and had a lot of grub left over, which fortunately I stored here in the house. I'll bet it'll come handy this winter."

"Cliff, I'm broke, except for a few dollars, and at the end of my rope," announced Virginia.

"Good Lord! You broke? Why, I heard in town that you spent barrels of money."

"I did, and now I wish I'd hid some of it in a barrel. . . . Cliff, father and Malpass together have made away with my fortune. They've taken my horses back to Watrous. I learned only recently that the ranch over there belongs to Malpass. It wouldn't surprise me to find I couldn't recover my horses."

"Well, the dirty crooks!" replied Clifton, coolly. "I reckon they're trying to break you to Malpass' harness."

"Indeed they are. Father is desperate. Swears he'll have to kill Malpass unless I give in. And Malpass —well, he has insulted me outrageously."

"How?" queried Clifton, feeling the hot blood rush to his head.

"We were alone at breakfast. This was after his return with dad from town. Malpass must have put on the screws during this absence. Anyway, when I cut him short he showed the cloven hoof. He could throw dad in jail and would do it. I think among other things I called him a greaser. . . . It ended in his seizing me. Oh, he was a beast. I was paralyzed with disgust and surprise. He kissed me a number of times before I could break loose."

"My God! Virginia, that's terrible! Somebody ought to kill him. Your father should——"

"Father has lost every semblance to manhood."

"Virginia, what are you going to do?" queried Clifton, anxiously.

"I don't know. I told you I'd reached the end of my rope."

"Well, suppose you marry me?" broke out Cliff, almost involuntarily. "If he touches you again I'll horsewhip him. And if that doesn't stop his greaser tricks I'll kill him."

After a penetrating quiet, Virginia asked, in changed tone, "Cliff, do you really mean it?"

"Of course I do, Virginia. Reckon I'd have done it before if I'd known you were in such straits. . . . That'll give me the right to protect you. . . . If you can keep it secret from your father the—the marriage need not be anything but a safeguard. Knowing it— that you can block their schemes any minute—will help you through it. At least you won't be in such fear of being dragged into a hateful marriage. . . . Something will happen sooner or later. All you need is time. Malpass will hang himself sure. He's not the kind of a man who can play a game long. . . . Then, you have only to get your freedom. As to that, Virginia, I may not last very long——"

"Hush!" she whispered, putting a soft palm to his lips. Presently she sank back against the wall, and even in the deceiving light Clifton could see her suppressed emotion.

"Virginia, I dare say there are weak spots in my argument. But I make the offer."

"You are my dearest—my only friend," she said. "I accept—Clifton."

"You will marry me?"

"Yes."

Clifton tried to fill aching lungs that appeared empty. "Very well. How can we arrange it?"

She seemed buried in deep thought that he could feel.

"I have it," she cried, suddenly, with an exultant note in her excited voice. "I'll drive to town tomorrow. I'll get the marriage license from the county clerk. I know I can persuade him to keep our secret. Then I'll go to the new minister. I can persuade him, too. You meet me here tomorrow night at about this time. Perhaps a little earlier. And perhaps you'd better walk down the road from the corner. I'll drive back to town with you. . . . We'll be married. And I'll get you home without anyone being the wiser. . . . What do you think of that plan?"

"Fine, if you can pull it off," he replied, trying in vain to speak lightly.

"Then it's—settled." She rose rather hurriedly. "I'd better go now. . . . Tomorrow night it won't matter if I am late.—Nothing will matter."

"Virginia," he replied, gravely, as he stood up, "I'm bound to advise you that if we're caught it will matter."

"We won't be caught—and if we were I'd laugh."

"I wouldn't. . . . How far is your car?"

"Just a step. I'll go alone."

"No, I'd rather you didn't."

He followed her out through the break in the wall and up the dark trail until she halted in the gloom of a thicket along the road. Then he saw the car. She looked up and down the road, listened a moment, then stepped into the automobile.

"Good night, Cliff. Tomorrow!" she said, turning on the lights.

"Yes, tomorrow," he replied, thickly. How abruptly she had ended the interview! It seemed to him she avoided his outstretched hand. Then the engine whizzed, the car lurched, and he stood alone, watching a swiftly vanishing red light. He faced about to enter the trail and plod homeward, now aware of the dark melancholy Western night.

CHAPTER
10

*C*LIFTON secured work at Watrous, in the Landis General Merchandise store, which, during the heydey of the cattle industry, had done a large business, but now had fallen into the hands of a creditor who was hard put to it to make ends meet.

His job as accountant was a trying one for Clifton. He did not shine at figures and to be chained to a desk indoors seemed no less than purgatory. But he had to work and was grateful for anything.

Watrous lay out on the range at some distance from San Luis. Clifton, however, preferred to go and come each day. To this purpose he had bargained with a Mexican for a rickety Ford, which he had genius and persistence enough to make reach its destination twice daily.

The very first day at Watrous, at the noon hour of which Clifton took advantage to get out into the open air, he saw Virginia and her cowboys driving a bunch of beautiful horses through town on the way to Cottonwoods. Virginia certainly did her share of the driving. She looked the part of a cowgirl and rode it. Clifton watched her out of sight, and deep within him his secret glowed like the heart of an opal. She was his wife and he wanted to cry it out to the range.

No doubt that secret was the spring of the resistance with which he kept at his task. In his store at San Luis he could rest and sleep and dream the hours away, and thereby he had very gradually gained strength. But this was a different kind of a job. The books were behind and in a state that engaged his energy to the limit. At the end of a week he was on the down grade, and knew it. He was not, however, in the least discouraged. He would stick it out as long as he could.

August passed. He did not see Virginia again nor hear from her, both of which circumstances apparently indicated a favorable condition. At first Clifton had feared that the fact of their marriage would leak out; and he both dreaded it and gloried in it. But no hint of its being suspected ever came to him. The condition of his father and mother had gradually improved; and though happiness held aloof, it did not seem that this would be so forever. Clay Forrest brooded less and harvested the garden he had planted. And he stayed away from Las Vegas. This was a most welcome fact to Clifton. In town Forrest drank and harangued with other old cattlemen who had seen better days, and when he came home he was dark, moody.

Clifton feared he would not be able to carry on much longer. In the mornings he would feel fresh and equal to several hours' work, but by noon he was working on his will-power, and by night he was "shot to pieces," as he called it. Still he refused to give up, and began his second month at Watrous.

One morning, as Clifton bent over his desk, he heard Mr. Hartwell, his employer, enter the office with some one whom he very volubly made welcome. They passed close to Clifton, who, without raising his eyes, caught a glimpse of shiny high-top boots and tight, immaculate riding-breeches that gave him a sharp start. It was not necessary to look up to recognize Malpass, even before the suave voice, a moment later, told him doubly who this visitor was.

"It's a particular job, Hartwell," Malpass was saying, and he slapped his boot-tops with his whip. "Expect to be married to my partner's daughter soon, and spend the winter in the South. I'd want to start building here upon my return in early spring. You will have ample time to get all the materials here. I'm giving you this large order because, as I expect to live in Watrous, I want to patronize men who'll be my neighbors."

"I appreciate it, Mr. Malpass," replied Hartwell, deferentially, almost with gratitude. "I'll go over these orders very carefully, an' guarantee delivery in time, at lower figures than you could get in Las Vegas."

"Later I'll mail you orders for lumber to build barns, corrals, and——"

Malpass ceased abruptly, and Clifton awakened to the fact that his ears were tingling.

"Who is that?" spoke up Malpass, in a lower, changed voice.

"Where?"

"There—at the desk."

"That's my bookkeeper," replied Hartwell, also in

lower tone. "Fine young man. Shot up bad in France. Name's Forrest."

"Aha! I thought so. Used to live at Cottonwoods."

"I don't know. You see, I'm a newcomer here. His father's name is Clay Forrest."

"Well, you can fire him right now, or consider my order canceled," returned Malpass, peremptorily.

"Why—Mr. Malpass! Do you know anything to his discredit?"

"I do."

"Indeed! I'm very sorry. We got along fine. But, of course, I'll discharge him. I wish to serve you, an' I wouldn't keep any help you disapproved of."

"If Lundeen should happen to come in here to see you employed a Forrest he'd walk out and never enter your place again. He's in town, too. Rode over with me. You'd better get rid of this wounded soldier here."

"Reckon I will, at once," replied Hartwell, hurriedly.

Clifton leaped up with a bursting gush of hot blood.

"Save your breath, Mr. Hartwell. I quit," he declared, passionately.

"I'm sorry, Forrest. I'd have had to let you go. Mr. Malpass assures me he knows somethin' to your discredit, an' I——"

"He's a damned liar," interrupted Clifton, stalking to the rack for his hat and coat. "And you will live to regret the day you listened to him."

Malpass carried off his part exceedingly well. Manifestly his last encounter with Clifton was uppermost in his mind, and he looked cool, contemptuous.

There shone, however, a deep hot gleam in his sloe-black eyes.

"Forrest, if you weren't a poor empty sack of a soldier I'd slap your face," he said, and he spoke loudly, not averse to being heard by listening clerks and customers.

But for this, Clifton might have controlled his fury in time and gotten out.

"It'd be a sorry slap for you, Señor Malpass. . . . Of all the rotten tricks I ever heard of, this is the rottenest. To have me thrown out of a two-bit job! It wasn't enough for you to hire one of your greasers to burn up my store at San Luis. You've got to hound me here and put Hartwell against me."

"Ha!—Hartwell, you can easily see what the war did to Forrest," laughed Malpass. "He's gone mentally, too."

Hartwell came slowly forward, plainly perturbed. Clifton had gotten outside of the office rail, into the store proper.

"Young man, you're making a plumb wild statement," said Hartwell.

"Not so wild, when you know Señor Malpass. He's a liar and I'm not. That's all, and I'll live to prove it."

Then Clifton realized he was in for battle. Remembering Malpass' reaction in their former encounter, he saw that he did not intend to let this pass, unless Clifton fled. That indeed was the last thing Clifton would think of. He backed against a counter littered with leather accouterments for horsemen, and his quick eye caught sight of a long black whip, the kind used by teamsters. Clifton would far rather have had a gun within reach, but this weapon would serve.

"You take that back, you white-faced beggar!" ordered Malpass. He snarled, but he did not yet give way to undue anger. His play was to impress the bystanders, and whatever he intended to do, he showed confidence.

"Make me take it back, you yellow-faced greaser millionaire," retorted Clifton, feeling the surge of released restraint. "You burned up my little store—all I had to make a living. Now you bully Hartwell to fire me! You'd like to see me and my poor old robbed father and mother starve. I said *robbed*. Do you get that? I said it and you know it. What's more, Virginia Lundeen——"

"Shut up!" hissed Malpass, and he struck Clifton across the mouth. "I beat you once . . . I'll do it again, if you dare speak my sweetheart's name."

The blow made Clifton cold and steady with a realization that something terrible was about to happen.

"Sweetheart?" he laughed, jeeringly. "You poor conceited ass! Money has gone to your head. . . . Virginia Lundeen despises you. How could she be your sweetheart—you damned half-breed? . . . How, I say—when she's my *wife*?"

Malpass was lunging when the word, more astonishing and stunning than a blow, halted him almost off his balance.

"Wife!" he choked out.

"Yes, my wife."

"You're crazy."

Clifton, appalled at what passion had led him to, realized he was driven to prove his statement. With a sense of fatality—a feeling that he was betraying Virginia—he whipped out his marriage certificate and shoved it under Malpass' nose.

"Forgery!" gasped Malpass, his lips white.

"Who wrote that? . . . Don't you recognize the handwriting? . . . Virginia Lundeen!"

Malpass indeed read his defeat in that quivering paper. He seemed staggered by an incredible, insupportable catastrophe. His eyes of black fire followed the certificate as Clifton folded it and replaced it in his pocket. Then they blazed at Clifton, comprehending that a gigantic hoax had been perpetrated upon him. And suddenly the rest of his features kept pace with the hell in his eyes. Calling Virginia a vile name, he cut Clifton across the face with his riding-crop.

Clifton had his right hand behind him gripping the handle of the teamster's whip. With all his might he swung it. Like a pistol report it cracked and like a black snake it curled round Malpass' neck. The man let out a strangled yell. Clifton jerked so hard on the whip that he threw Malpass to his knees. Up he sprang nimbly, to ply his crop upon Clifton's head, in short, hard strokes, the last of which knocked Clifton flat and also broke the bone handle of the crop.

Panting and malignant, Malpass put his right hand to his hip pocket. Hartwell shouted in affright. The other onlookers, exclaiming incoherently, scattered from behind Clifton, who again swung the whip viciously. It streaked out, snakelike, to crack across Malpass' face. As if by magic a red stripe leaped out. Malpass screamed, true to the stronger half of his blood.

"Shoot, you greaser!" yelled Clifton. There was a fierce joy in this encounter. It liberated passion that must slowly have dammed up. He began to dance around Malpass, suddenly to attack with his whip.

Malpass drew a small automatic gun and hurriedly shot. Clifton ducked at the flash. The bullet hit a man behind, who fell, yelling: "My God! I'm shot! . . . Help! Help!"

Instead of going to his assistance, the others broke pellmell and ran. Hartwell dodged behind a counter. None of them could escape from the store because at the moment Clifton was dodging back and forth across the doorway that led into the street. The place was in an uproar. Men came running from outside.

Clifton spoiled Malpass' aim by swift blows with his whip. But Malpass kept on shooting, breaking windows, scattering bullets into the wall. His eyes protruded, horrible with murderous intent. Then another slash of the whip appeared to obliterate those eyes, as if a purple band had crossed them. Malpass was momentarily blinded. He screamed maledictions in Spanish, and shot again. Clifton felt a light shock, as from a puff of air. The long blacksnake whip darted out and the end curled round Malpass' extended hand that held the gun. It held fast as if it had been knotted. Malpass was shooting at random. Clifton pulled with both hands on the whip, swinging Malpass helplessly, to stumble over an obstruction and fall heavily. The gun flew out of his grip. Clifton got the whip loose, and swung it aloft with both hands, and brought it down hissing hot. Malpass shrieked, and flopped over on his face, to huddle against the floor.

Clifton beat him until the whip dropped from his spent hands. Then he staggered out of the store to the sidewalk. Men and boys, whom he saw but indistinctly, spread before him. Some one, whose voice he recognized, took his arm and steadied him along the street a few rods to where his car was parked. Clifton stumbled in and hung over the wheel.

But he did not lose consciousness, though his sight was dim and his hearing imperfect. Still it became obvious to him that a crowd was collecting, and this goaded his fainting spirit. With shuddering, desperate effort he wiped away the blood that flowed from a cut on his forehead into his eyes, and then started the car. Soon he had left Watrous behind, and once out in the open country he ran off the road into a clump of cedars, to rest and recover.

He came near to collapse, yet the effort had carried him over that point, and gradually he approached something like physical normality. Then he became aware of painful welts upon his face, and his right hand and wrist, where Malpass' crop had fallen. His shirt was wet and at first he thought it came from sweat. But it was blood. Malpass had shot him, after all.

A bullet wound meant little to Forrest. He did not even search for this one, nor care whether or not it might be fatal. He was not conscious of any pain. At length he felt blood trickling down inside his shirt, both front and back, on his right side. As it did not appear to be a copious flow, he concluded the wound was high up on his shoulder, cutting through the fleshy part on top. Already his handkerchief was soaked, so he did not have anything to serve as a pad over the hole.

He rested over his wheel, and by degrees thought impinged upon his sensorial perceptions. He knew he had been in a fight, but what was the cause and what had happened? Virginia had wanted to keep their marriage a secret until she could use the fact of it as a last resource. Clifton had promised not to reveal it under any circumstances. He had failed utterly. He had not counted on unbearable provocation nor the unknown quantity of jealousy. Almost he wished Malpass' bullet had finished him at once.

What would come of this, he wondered, as his mind quickened. He had accused Malpass of burning his store. He had flaunted the fact of his marriage. He had passionately resented the vile name the mad Malpass had called Virginia, and he had beaten him into unconsciousness. If that whip had been a gun Malpass would never wake in this world.

Clifton plodded on in his deductions. Hartwell and others besides Malpass had heard his assertion about Virginia being his wife. Likewise they had seen the marriage certificate. He had betrayed Virginia. That fight would become range gossip before the day had passed. And if Malpass had killed a man with the random shot there would be court proceedings. Alas! to what a pass his passions had brought him!

Presently he raised his head, and starting the Ford, he drove out of the cedars, back onto the road. It was about all he could do to hang to the wheel. But for its support he would have fallen over. The few miles to San Luis seemed vast and hateful distance, never to be surmounted.

Upon reaching the village he stopped at the hut of an old Indian whom he knew, and who was a medicine-man of local note.

Clifton's wound was a deep furrow in the shoulder muscle, and not serious. When bandaged with a soothing ointment he forgot it. The stripes on his face, however, were brands that could not be concealed. Nevertheless, with the blood washed off, and his coat well buttoned over his shirt, he did not, at least, present a frightful appearance.

He wanted to get home, if possible, without encountering his father, and to get in without distressing his mother. And luck was with him, so far as those two were concerned, for he reached the house and got in unobserved. He was lying down in the shaded living-room when his mother came in. Her anxiety was easy to allay. But his father presented a different proposition, and Clifton welcomed the fact that delayed a meeting between them. He rested until the betraying faintness of his voice had gone.

Toward sundown, when his mother went out to prepare supper, his father came in, evidently having been informed that Clifton was home early and that all was not so well with him as it might have been.

"Howdy, son! an' what ails you?" queried Forrest, gruffly, as his big eyes ran curiously over Clifton lying quietly on the couch.

"Why do you ask that?" returned Clifton, to try out his voice. It was pretty weak.

"Wal, you're pale, except for them long marks, an' I reckon I can smell blood," replied his father, drawing a chair close up to Clifton. He was troubled and suspicious, but cool. There seemed to be little use trying to deceive him, especially as the gossip of his encounter would spread like wildfire in dry prairie grass.

"Dad, let's keep all we can from mother?"

"Shore."

"Well, to begin with, I've lost my job."

Forrest nodded his shaggy head.

"Hartwell fired me."

"What for?"

"Because my name happened to be Forrest. . . .

Malpass dropped in the store. He talked over orders for lumber, etc., for building he expects to do in the spring. Big job. All of a sudden he saw me, and he hit the roof."

Forrest bent over Clifton with sudden intensity, his great eyes beginning to flare.

"He told Hartwell to fire me or he'd cancel the order."

"Wal, if that wasn't low-down!—An' Hartwell did?"

"No. When he showed yellow I just quit. . . . I made a couple of remarks to Malpass, but at that, dad, I meant to get out of the store to avoid trouble. I started out, backing out, in fact, and of course I kept shooting off my chin. Malpass backed me up against a harness counter. . . . Well, he hit me first, with one of those bone-handled crops. I grabbed up a black-snake whip and took after him. He pulled a gun. His first shot hit somebody who went down with a yell. Might have killed him, for all I know. Then I kept dodging and cracking him with the whip. And he kept shooting. Finally I whipped the gun out of his hand. He fell, and I beat him till I gave out. . . . Somebody helped me to my car."

"An' how often an' where did he shoot you?" asked Forrest, without emotion.

"One bullet nicked my shoulder. It's nothing. But I'd rather mother doesn't know."

Forrest let out a rolling curse. "Hasn't this Malpass got it in for you?"

"Sort of looks that way."

"Why? He's no Lundeen, an' he's never made any target of me. What's he pick on you for?"

That happened to be the very thing Clifton dared not explain to his father, wherefore he lied.

"Looks damn queer to me," replied Forrest, dubiously, with his ox-eyes piercing his son. "Reckon you didn't kill him?"

"No. But I'll bet he'll have a little dose of what I've had so much."

"Wal, if he killed somebody it sure strengthens our side. In any case it will stew up the Lundeen-Forrest deal good an' hot. I'll go to law."

"I wouldn't, dad. We haven't any money, and we'd only get the worst of it," advised Clifton.

"Wal, I don't need any money. There's a new lawyer come to Albuquerque. He's young an' he's keen. Came out West for his health. I've had two conferences with him. An' he said if I was tellin' facts he could get my property back."

"But, dad, how can you prove these facts?" expostulated Clifton.

"Wal, that's the rub. But this last trick of Malpass' will help. I'll go to law."

"I don't think you've a ghost of a show. Suppose Lundeen did cheat? You were in deals with him. An' you owed him money. Even a gambling debt is a debt. He got your property. And afterwards they struck silver. It's as plain as the nose on your face."

Forrest shook his head with dogged stubbornness. "Reckon you'll never see it from my side of the fence. An' I ain't doubtin' the reason."

"What reason, dad? I've got a mind of my own."

"Yes, an' so has Virginia Lundeen," returned Forrest, enigmatically. "I'll bet I live to see the day somethin' hatches between you two. But I hope I die before."

"Dad, I've done the best I could do in a rotten situation," said Clifton, resignedly.

The hum of a swift-running motor car came in at the open window, and what made Clifton note it was that it ceased abruptly. It had stopped outside. He groaned inwardly, sensing calamity. His father got up uneasily, and began to pace the room.

Soon quick footsteps struck Clifton's ears. Then they sounded heavily on the porch. A powerful hand assailed the door. It swung in, as if irresistibly impelled.

Jed Lundeen stood on the threshold, his dark face and somber eyes indicative of mighty passions all but spent. Stamping in, he closed the door, and seemed to fill the room with his presence.

Clifton sat up. He knew what was coming. His father paled with more than amaze.

"Forrest, there's shore hell to pay," he announced, stridently.

"Wal, I'm lookin' at you," returned Forrest, in cold, sullen expectation. The mere sight of his old enemy had unleashed his passions.

"Forrest, I didn't come heah to fight. But I'm packin' somethin' that'll hit you harder'n any bullet."

"Is Malpass dead?"

"No. But shore he's darn near it. That war-crazy son of yours jumped him with a bull-whacker's whip."

"Lundeen, it was a plumb good job. An' I wish it'd been better. Reckon you ain't acquainted with facts. Malpass started the fight, an' when it got too hot he throwed a gun. Shot Cliff, as you can see for yourself."

Obviously that was astounding to Lundeen, and he required the confirmation of his own penetrating eyes. His regard, however, was one of icy indifference to the established fact. He had no word for Clifton.

"I'm inquirin' if the other man Malpass shot is dead?" continued Forrest.

"Did he shoot some one else?" demanded Lundeen, hotly.

"Yes, by accident," interposed Clifton. "He was aiming at me."

"Fine chance that half-breed would have if a Westerner threw a gun on him instead of a whip," added the older Forrest, scornfully.

"Malpass was aboot out of his haid. Maybe that accounts for his omissions. He raved an' cursed."

"Wal, Lundeen, if that's all you've butted in here to say——"

"I came sayin' there was hell to pay, didn't I?" interrupted Lundeen, harshly. "An' there shore is. This slick son of yours, with his crippled-soldier sympathy bluff, is goin' to pay it, too."

"Leave out what you think my son *is*. It ain't safe. . . . What more has he done?"

"He married my girl, by God! That's what!"

Forrest turned a dead white. "Say, you're drunk, or crazier'n your crooked pardner. No son of mine would give the name Forrest to a Lundeen."

"Ha! But he did, an' though my Virginia takes the blame, the disgrace of it is just that. My lass has become a Forrest."

"It's a lie. Another of your plots," shouted Forrest, his neck bulging purple. "An' if it was so I'd swear the disgrace was suffered by the Forrests. But it's an infernal lie."

"Ask him."

Forrest whirled a distorted face toward his son. "You hear him. Why don't you nail his lyin' talk?"

"Dad, it's true," replied Clifton.

Sudden death could scarcely have caused a ghastlier change in a strong man's features and body. This was the last straw. The end of pride! The conclusive stab to bleeding vanity. Forrest fell into a chair, so abject, so beaten, that Clifton could look no more at him.

"Forrest, that's why I'm heah," said Lundeen, acidly. "Because it's true, an' I can't change it. My daughter is of age. It couldn't be kept secret an' Virginia refused to hear of a divorce. She took the blame. She led your son on. Marriage with him was an escape from Malpass. I wanted a match between him an' her. But she'd have none of him, an' to keep out of it she aboot asked your son to marry. She knew he wasn't long for this world, but long enough, maybe, to scrve her turn. . . . He's dirt under her feet! She cared nothin' on earth for him! You understand?"

"Lundeen, I reckon I do," returned Forrest, hoarsely. "But I wouldn't believe your oath on your knees before God. . . . Clifton, is that last true?"

"Is what true?" echoed Clifton, his voice failing huskily.

"That this Lundeen woman thinks you're dirt under her feet."

"Dad, I don't believe that. She's too big for hate. She's kind. But I think she cared nothing for me."

"You think!" returned Lundeen, dark in passion. "You need to be damn shore you know, young man. I'm tellin' you. I choked it out of her. If she'd confessed to love of *you* I'd have killed her with my own hands."

Clifton slowly sank back against the wall. And the brutal speech that crushed his tired heart had an opposite effect upon his father, who rose in a single upheaval, and towered erect.

"Tell this man Lundeen you had no use for his daughter! You did a manly act to save her from a schemin' half-breed! No more. Tell him quick!"

Clifton had seen his mother open the door part way, to disclose a terrified face. It steadied him. He must prevent bloodshed here, and if the quarrel between these blinded foes went farther it would end in tragedy. He would have perjured his soul to save his mother any more agony.

"Dad is right, Mr. Lundeen, I just wanted—to help Virginia."

"That's good, then, on both sides, if any good could come out of an impossible relation," replied Lundeen, a visible break in his relentlessness. "Forrest, I gave my daughter a choice: either to divorce your son or get out of my house."

"Ahuh," muttered Forrest.

"She chose to get out," concluded Lundeen, thickly.

"Wal, they never fooled me," rejoined Forrest, in an acrid melancholy tone. "An' I'm not givin' my son *any* choice."

"Shore you're not," retorted his enemy, with strong sarcasm. "You're bankin' on him gettin' money through Virginia. An' you'll die hopin'."

"Lundeen, you always was low-down white trash from the South. You couldn't savvy a Westerner. My son gets no choice. He gets out."

Both fathers, gray with passion, implacable,

clutched in the vise of their hate, turned a haggard gaze upon Clifton.

He rose to take his father's pronouncement.

"Young man, you're no more son of mine. Get out!" thundered Forrest, and the gray shaded black.

"*Dad!*" cried Clifton.

But the outcry was involuntary. And an instant afterward Clifton had a revulsion of emotion. His sluggish blood regurgitated to his cold veins.

"You're a couple of fine fathers," he lashed out, pitilessly on fire. "If you had any guts you'd play the game like men. You fight, and impose your hate upon two innocent young people who have the misfortune to be of your blood. . . . Lundeen, it's no wonder Virginia sought the protection of even a poor, crippled, and now homeless man. You're no father. You're no better than the greaser dog you'd give her to. For money and greed! . . . Now I've one more word. You and Malpass stay clear of me."

Then Clifton vented the climax of his accumulated wrath upon his ashen-faced parent.

"I'll get out. And I'll never come back. You're not only wicked, but a doddering old idiot. Locked in your insane hate of anything Lundeen! If you ever were a Forrest you've lost the thing that made you one. You, not I, have brought the name down."

Clifton stalked to the door of the hall leading to his room, and stepped up. But the white heat of his anger demanded more. He faced them again.

"I lied to you. I love Virginia with all my heart and soul. And it'd be retribution for you both if she came to love me the same way. I pray to God she will. . . . I'll not die! I'll *live* so that she may! . . . Now, you cowards, go out and kill yourselves!"

*T*HE fortification of secret marriage far exceeded Virginia's vacillating hopes. For while making up her mind to this grave and uncertain step, she had been both inspired and frightened. It turned out, however, that in her most sanguine moments she had not realized its true portent. She was saved from the peril of a despicable alliance. She had only to safeguard herself from being shamed again by physical violence.

Therefore she gained a tranquillity of mind she had not experienced since her arrival home. She laid clever plans to avoid Malpass and adhered to them, while waiting for the end of August, at which time she was to visit Ethel in Denver. She took her meals to suit the convenience of her mother. When she went to Watrous to get her horses, and on rides thereafter, she made sure to be accompanied by Con and Jake. She avoided the living-room and the porch except when her father or mother was present. She was always careful to lock herself in her rooms.

Thus, when Malpass approached, she had him at a disadvantage. He knew it was intentional and chafed under the restrictions. Sometimes, even before her father, he would attempt to further his suit, but Virginia found countering these advances interesting if not stimulating. She mystified the vain courtier, whose Latin blood boiled at restraint. On several occasions she amused her father, who gradually grew less hearty in his championship of Malpass. She deceived both men, in that she did not seem to be absolutely unattainable. Evidently Lundeen had wearily retrenched to a wearing down process. But Malpass labored under not only the hot impatience of a lover, but also the growing doubts of a man whose intelligence had begun to operate against his vanity. Now and then Virginia caught a veiled gleam in his eyes that caused her to bless Clifton Forrest and to renew her unending vigilance. Malpass was capable of resorting to anything.

Several weeks went by. Mrs. Lundeen's health did not improve, and plans were effected to send her to Atlanta for the winter, to visit her old home and relatives. Virginia approved of this, but it meant that she must prolong her own absence from Cottonwoods. Still, the immediate present was all that she could meet adroitly. The future would take care of itself.

Her attitude of mind toward Clifton was something over which she had no control. The meeting with him that night, her monstrous deceit, the calm, barefaced carrying-out of an apparent marriage of convenience when she loved him more every moment —these thrilling things could not be barred from consciousness, never by day and seldom by night. She resisted numberless temptations to drive here or there in the hope of accidentally seeing him. Her woman's heart told her that he was big and fine and good, that he would win his battle against any odds of health or fortune, that when the differences of the Lundeens and Forrests were settled—as some day they must be—she might find his love.

One morning Virginia, with her cowboy escorts, started out to see the silver mine which had played such an important and mystifying part in the affairs of Forrest, Lundeen, and Malpass.

Virginia had ridden up there often, especially in early years when it was merely an abandoned mine, picturesquely located and romantically significant with Spanish legend. Con had seen it. But Jake, range-rider though he was, had never been there since the rediscovery of silver.

Now it chanced that Jake, according to his own version, was something of an authority on minerals. He had prospected, on and off, while riding the range, all over that section of the country. This information had come in answer to Virginia's queries, which had been instigated by a thought-provoking remark of Jake's. "Wal, I'm from Missouri an' I gotta be showed. Never took much stock in thet Padre Mine."

Added to this was the significance of the fact that Malpass had lately ceased to have the Padre worked. Once more it had become an abandoned mine. Any move whatever of Malpass' roused distrust in Virginia. Her father had been considerably upset by the assurance that the mine had "petered out," as Malpass called it. After the first large profit, the several others had been considerably smaller, and dwindling. Virginia was interested to get the keen range-rider's opinion of the late operations at Padre.

The morning was glorious. Early fall on the slope of New Mexico was a time to conjure with. High up, the frost had tinted the vines in the hollows, the brush along the gray rocky defiles, the aspens at timber line above. Against these, and the bleached white of the old grass, the cedars and piñons stood out in their straggling isolation. Above it all loomed the great black-belted bulk of rock, raggedly sharp against the sky.

Virginia, as she rode up the trail, did not look back. Time enough for that heart-stirring risk on the return trip! Cottonwood Valley must already be exposed from this height, a glowing, multi-colored level set down amid the range slopes; and the rambling Spanish house, with its white and red, its trellises and arches, must be looking up at her, reminding her that she dare not love it more; and then, far down to the west, along the fringed line where the yellowing cottonwoods met the gray sage rise of ground, her old adobe home which now sheltered one grown strangely precious.

She was riding Dusk, not one of her spirited racers, but treasured because of his easy gait and sure foot and gentle disposition. Virginia was not running wildly over the range these days. Getting thrown upon her head might have meant a swift and merciful termination of her troubles, but for reasons she did not confess to herself life had become suddenly unfamiliarly sweet, full, marvelous, all-pervading.

In due time they arrived at Padre Mine, to find, to Virginia's disappointment, that its former picturesque charm had given place to sordid ugliness. A hideous slash had been cut in the beautiful grove of juniper, piñon, and cedar. High up the slope the brook had been choked into a rough chute, now broken and down in places. The willows that once had graced the little pool, where legend recorded the padres were wont to drink, were gone along with the glancing water. Flowers and sage were not. Tracks and trestles, dumps of clay and rock, seepings of russet-colored water from denuded banks, bleak sheds with galvanized iron roofs, and rusting machinery littered around, and piles of tar-coated pipe attested to the approach and desertion of destructive men.

"Wal, wouldn't the old padres turn over in their graves?" asked Jake, with a mirthless grin, as he surveyed the scene.

"They surely would," returned Virginia, ruefully. "Now, Jake, we'll play that I am a prospective buyer with very little cash and you are an expert adviser."

"Shure it looks loike a dump outside of Noo Yoark," put in Con.

"Miss Virginia, I reckon you'd better find a shady place an' wait," advised Jake.

"But I want to poke around," she replied, dismounting. "You boys needn't bother about me. I'll not crawl in any holes or walk out on a trestle."

"Con, bring your flashlight," directed Jake. "It'll be dark in the tunnel."

"If you don't moind, I'll sthay out," returned Con as he clambered down after the business-like Jake.

Virginia was left to her own resources. On previous occasions she had ridden up by the trail, merely casting curious and disgusted glances at the jumble of wood, iron, and earth, trying to piece them together into the idea of silver production. This time she followed an intuitive prompting which seemed at once both strong and illusive. She was on a tour of inspection. Her father had informed her lately that the failure of this mine had killed extravagant hopes. Her own large income had formerly come from this source. Virginia's opinion was that Lundeen, after running cattle all his life, was no judge of mining ventures.

She inspected every place she could get at, and did not mind exertion or rust or dirt. And after she had thoroughly tired herself she concluded this mine, once famous in legend if never in productiveness, was nothing but a conglomeration of clapboards, old iron, tracks and trestles, and various shades of drab naked earth. She repaired to the only shade tree on the bench, and there sat down to rest. From here the valley below was not in sight, but the distant range spread out to the dim mountains, compelling and beautiful.

Her reverie and gaze might have been more pleasant if she had been far removed from this spot desecrated and despoiled by Malpass. She could not quite forget it and that an insistent and insatiable distrust of the man had led her there. She was glad when she espied the cowboys emerge from under the brow of a slanting bank of clay and climb back to the horses. Their faces were hot and their clothes, especially their knees, had come in contact with something like chalk, and their boots were splashed with red mud. Seeing Virginia under the tree, they led the horses up to her.

"Wal, Miss Virginia, shore an Irishman is scared more of the dark than a nigger," observed Jake, complacently, as he dropped the bridles and sat down to remove his sombrero.

"Oi'm sayin' no nigger would ever have follered you where I went," responded Con.

"You both look spooky," laughed Virginia.

"Miss, I'm plumb curious," went on Jake, now serious. "Did Mr. Lundeen ever employ any white men on this minin' job?"

"Father never employed anybody. Malpass did all that. I remember there used to be complaints on father's part. Malpass hired none but Mexicans. And as I understood it, the work suffered for this reason. Inefficient boys running engines, and—oh, I can't recall much. I do remember that no consistent work was carried on, much to father's annoyance."

"Wal, between you an' me an' Con here I don't believe there ever was *any* work carried on."

"What!" ejaculated Virginia, sitting up with a jerk. "Why, Jake, it appears to me endless work went on here! Look! At the sheds, the tracks, the old cars, the trestles, the piles of pipe, the flumes, and hills after hills of rock, gravel, clay, all dug out of the ground."

"Shore it took work to do thet, an' a mighty sight of it, but what I'm alludin' to is miners' work. All this packin' an' buildin' an' diggin' was done for nothin'."

"But, Jake, many thousands of dollars came out of that hole," asserted Virginia, emphatically.

"Then, by gosh! it was shore planted there beforehand," returned Jake, bluntly.

"What an extraordinary statement!" ejaculated Virginia, her receptive mind whirling with conjectures and imaginings.

"It is—sort of," admitted Jake, scratching his close-cropped head. "But doggone me—thet's my idee. . . . Miss Virginia, I've seen a heap of mines. I spent some years over around Silver City. An' I've been in Colorado. I know how mines are worked. I'd bet a million there was never an ounce of silver came out of this hole."

"Jake, on what do you base that positive opinion?"

"Because I couldn't find a single trace of silver. But look here!"

He opened his huge palm, in which had been crumpled a bit of paper. When he carefully unfolded and smoothed it out Virginia's astonished sight recorded a number of grains and specks of gold.

"Gold!—Where on earth did they come from?" demanded Virginia, much mystified.

"Where! Haw! Haw! Wal, they came out of the earth an' not from on it."

"Jake, I know I'm stupid, but please explain."

"Wal, back in the mine there are holes thet were made by blasts. Some heavy ones shore. I'll bet no miners were inside when they shot them. Must have clogged up the shaft. I ought to have told you how a number of shafts run off from the main tunnel. No sense or reason in them, accordin' to my figgerin', except to make more shafts. . . . Wal, I thought of somethin', an' I crawled into one of the biggest blast holes, higher'n my head an' wide as a room. I filled an old pan I found with loose earth an' shale. Fetchin' it out to the light, I shook an' blew the heavy parts away. We used to call this dry pannin'. When I got out of wind Con took a turn, an' shore he's windy enough to be a glass-blower. Result was we got down to these few grains of gold."

"And what does all this prove?" queried Virginia, in breathless interest.

"Wal, when all's said it proves nothin' thet I can prove," returned Jake, in perplexity. "I know what I think. We shore found this little trace of loose gold. There it is in your hand. But I'd bet a lot nature never put this gold in thet hillside."

"You mean you believe gold like this—in large quantity, perhaps, was taken into the mine from outside?" asked Virginia, her mind quickening with many scintillating thoughts.

"Planted in there, Miss Virginia," said Jake, very soberly. "Thousands of dollars in gold, mebbe. An' then blasted! That would blow the gold fragments into the dirt an' gravel an' shale. It's an old trick. But I never heerd of it in these parts."

"An old trick! . . . To deceive? To raise greedy hopes? To blind? To give false and tremendous value to a worthless hole in the ground?"

"Miss Virginia, you've hit it plumb center. . . . But I'm bound to tell you I may be wrong. Thet's the hell—pardon, Miss, I'm some excited—but thet's the wurst of it. The gold might have been there of its own an' nature's accord. I don't believe so. It looks fishy to me. But I might be wrong."

"Jake, could a mining expert prove positively whether this gold was planted there to defraud, or belonged there along with the other natural deposits?"

"He shore could," asserted Jake, emphatically nodding his head. "But I'm weak on mineraloogy. Thet's the weak point in most prospectors. They don't know enough about the earth—geooloogy, they call it. They don't know what to look for, or what they've found, unless they pick into the real shiny yellow stuff."

"Boys, this is a very singular thing," concluded Virginia, gravely. "It may mean nothing and then again it may mean a great deal. . . . I'm asking you both on your word of honor to keep this secret with me?"

They solemnly promised in unison, and Virginia felt that she could trust them. With trembling fingers she carefully tied up the telltale grains of gold in a corner of her handkerchief and stowed it safely away, thinking the while of the strange result of a chance remark. But then, how alertly distrustful she was to anything pertaining to Malpass' activities!

With this disturbance in her mind, she was ill prepared to face the downward journey, where all she loved eloquently intrigued her, from the green-gold blaze of the cottonwoods, from the white-walled, black-arched ranch house, from the little red adobe place she had always called home.

She feared Dusk found her loath to let him choose his leisurely way. And once down on the long bench above the ranch she put him to his best speed, making the delighted cowboys ride to keep up with her. There was something poignant in the cut of the cool, sweet wind.

Her habit of late had been to ride up the road, under the arched gates and through the court, to dismount at the porch, and turn her horse over to one of the cowboys.

This day she trotted Dusk in abruptly upon a scene of disorder and confusion. The court appeared full of strange cars and strange people. Virginia spurred Dusk clattering over the stones, and she leaped off at the porch landing. Jake, with a warning call, had just caught up to her and reached for her bridle.

Her father and a young man and Mr. Hartwell were lifting some one out of the car.

"Father, what has happened?" she cried out.

But no one heard her. They were all talking excitedly, and the Mexicans crowding about were exclaiming to their saints. Then Virginia saw Malpass' boots, his white riding-breeches, and lastly his face—that she did not recognize. It appeared webbed with bloody stripes.

She clapped a hand to her lips too late to stifle a scream. Then, "My God!—is he dead?"

"Go into the house," shouted her father.

Virginia had no idea of obeying, even had she been capable of moving. Her feet might as well have been cased in lead boots. A horrible chill attacked her within and froze pulse and vein. Her mind had flashed upon one appalling thought and there had congealed.

"Lundeen—drive them—away!" shrieked Malpass, and then he cursed and raved in Spanish.

Virginia nearly dropped with the instant release of her faculties from an icy compress. Suddenly she had a sensation not unlike the worst of seasickness.

Lundeen bellowed at the gaping employees of the house, at the drivers and occupants of the other cars.

"Hell's fire! Get me—inside!" Malpass could not stand without the aid of the men who locked arms under his. He could not walk at all. They slid and dragged him. His thin coat and shirt were cut into ribbons. The olive tan of his neck showed a broad welt like a band of red velvet.

Following them, quaking and thrilling alternately, Virginia entered the wide hall, and then the living-room, where they laid Malpass back in an armchair. He called faintly for whisky. The chauffeur ran out. Lundeen rushed to the cabinet where he kept liquors. Hartwell endeavored to ease the stiff posture of the recumbent man. Virginia stood fascinated and horrified.

"Oh, father! What happened?"

"How the hell—do I know?" he quavered, his jaw wabbling.

"Miss Lundeen, there's been a terrible fight," said Hartwell.

"Between whom?" queried Virginia, her hand on her bursting heart. She did not need to ask. That heart told her what her fears wanted confirmed.

"Leave the room," ordered Lundeen, hurrying with a glass full of red liquor that spilled over his shaking hand.

"No! She stays to hear this—by God!" hissed Malpass.

When he had gulped the whisky his head fell back, his eyes closed. And Virginia engaged all her forces in an effort to look clearly at him.

He presented a spectacle like a beaten beast. His stripped shirt was red with blood, whether from cuts on face and neck, or a wound not visible. The sleeves of coat and shirt were ripped back to the elbow, showing a wrist that looked as if it had been burned to the bone.

"Hartwell, who'n'll's to blame?" burst out Lundeen, throwing the empty glass back to crash on the cabinet.

"Cliff Forrest," returned Hartwell, explosively.

"So help me Heaven! I reckoned so. . . . How'd he do it?"

"Beat him with a bull-whacker's whip. Beat him unconscious, Lundeen, an' if Forrest hadn't give out he'd have beat him to death."

"For Gawd's sake, why?"

Malpass stirred as if he had been pricked. His eyes opened. Under the swollen lids and the brand across his forehead they gleamed with most baleful luster.

"Hartwell, get out of here," he ordered, in a stronger voice. "And keep your mouth shut—if you want my favors."

"But if Mason dies, sir, they'll make me talk. An' he's bad hurt," replied Hartwell, nervously wringing his hands. "Besides, there were others present."

"Wait then. Keep me posted."

Hartwell mumbled a few incoherent words and beat a hasty retreat.

"August, hadn't I better send to town for a doctor?" queried Lundeen, anxiously.

"No. . . . I'm in agony, but only beaten, burned. . . . It was a whip. Forrest jumped me with a whip."

"He'll go to jail," boomed Lundeen.

"——! I'll cut his heart out!"

Weakly, with strength infinitely less than his passion, he stretched the lacerated arm, and pointed a bloody hand and quivering finger at Virginia.

"You brazen hussy!"

Not the frenzied insult of his words but their connotation left Virginia stricken and mute.

"Heah!" shouted Lundeen, his paleness vanishing. "Have a care. You've shore cause to rave, but not——"

"Lundeen, you'll—kill her!" panted Malpass, his breast alternately lifting and sinking.

"Me! You're wild, man. She's my own flesh an' blood."

"That's why. . . . If you don't kill her—you'll curse her—throw her out. . . . Then, by God! I'll drag her down!"

Virginia flamed out of her petrifaction.

"Mr. Malpass, I make allowance for your condition. But you're not quite insane. I tell you nothing you have done, or can do or say, will move me in the slightest."

"*I'll drag you through mud!*" he hissed, with a fiendish malignity.

Lundeen intervened, at least with semblance of self-control.

"Shut up, Virginia!" he ordered. "An' you, Malpass, do the same or talk sense. What's this all aboot?"

"Your loyal daughter is the wife of young Forrest."

"WHAT!" yelled Lundeen, leaping up as if at the sting of a lash.

"She's married to Clifton Forrest. I saw the marriage certificate. He stuck it before my eyes! . . . Laughed in my face, the——!"

Lundeen sagged under the blow, though mind and body seemed to repudiate it. Slowly he turned to Virginia, his dry lips failing, his eyes strained in terrible question.

"Yes, I am Clifton's wife," answered Virginia, her voice ringing, her head lifting erect. The dénouement had been staggering, but she could recover to glory in it.

"Wife! . . . Lundeen-Forrest! . . . Married! . . . All the—time—you've been—married?"

"All the time lately—yes. All the time Mr. Malpass has been courting me so assiduously."

"You she-devil!" Malpass screamed it, but his voice did not carry beyond the room.

Lundeen lifted a nerveless hand. His face was bloodless.

"Malpass, you fought Forrest aboot this—this marriage?"

In his agitation Malpass leaned forward, and though he spoke for Lundeen his snaky eyes scorched Virginia.

"It happened at Watrous. I went in to see Hartwell. Talked over building supplies. Mentioned my coming marriage with your daughter. Ha! Ha! . . . Then I espied young Forrest at a desk. Hartwell said he worked there. I asked to have him fired. . . . Forrest got up and addressed me in a way no man can talk to me. If he hadn't been a crippled soldier, I'd have shot him. But I tried to get past him. Then he shoved his marriage certificate under my nose— bragged of Virginia being *his* wife. She could never marry a half-breed! . . . I accused him of forgery. He made me read. I saw—recognized Virginia's handwriting. Then I knew we'd been tricked. . . . Damn you, Lundeen, for a doting old fool! You're to blame for this. . . . Forrest was red in the face. He swelled up like a toad before the clerks in the store—and others who came in. He wasn't missing a chance to spread the news that Virginia Lundeen was his wife. That *he* would some day lord it over Cottonwoods!"

Lundeen made an implacable gesture of denial, more significant than any words.

"I struck Forrest—with my crop," went on Malpass, hurriedly, now breaking from faintness, or fury. "He snatched a whip—off the counter—and—and beat me down."

"Ahuh. An' how aboot Mason, who's bad hurt," Hartwell said. "Where'd he come in?"

"I forgot. Before I went under—thinking Forrest would beat me to death—I pulled my gun. But I couldn't shoot straight. He kept—slashing me with that infernal whip. . . . I missed him—shot some other man—I saw him drop. It must—have been Mason."

Malpass, clammy and haggard, sank limply back in the chair. Lundeen moved laboriously, as one under too great a strain for swift action, and lunging at Virginia he seized her with ruthless hands.

"Girl, you've ruined me."

"Oh no, father. Don't rave. Don't be guided longer by this snake."

"You're the snake. I reckon I'll kill you." His big hands slipped up to her neck, and choking her convulsively he forced her to her knees. Limp and terror-stricken, unable to struggle, Virginia thought this must be the end. But he loosed his grip.

"She's no Lundeen!" he snarled, evidently fighting some restraining voice.

"For God's sake—father—don't murder me!" entreated Virginia, gasping for breath. "You are beside yourself. Think of mother!"

"What'd you marry that hellion for?" he demanded, pierced by her supplication.

"To protect myself. Malpass and you—somehow would have forced me to marry him. I'd rather have died. . . . It wasn't a regular elopement. . . . I was to blame. I almost begged Clifton to save me. He didn't —he doesn't care for me. He believes he'll not live long. . . . I thought—it seemed—oh, father, it was a mad thing to do. But I was desperate."

He let her get up, and breathing like an ox, lowering at her, he stood there freed at least from murderous instincts. Virginia drew away on uncertain feet. With deliverance from terror her wits returned.

"Choose. Divorce this heah Forrest or leave my house," said Lundeen, with dark and gloomy finality.

"In any case, I'll leave," she replied, and with that ultimatum, and safe distance between her and this ruffian parent, the hot blood of courage and insupportable outrage flooded over her. "You are no father. You're a brute and a coward. You're the tool of this thief—this low hounder of a woman. . . . I rejoice to see him thus—a beaten dog!"

"No more. Get out!" roared Lundeen, black in the face, goaded past endurance.

"May I pack some things—and say good-by to mother?"

"Take your belongings. But you're through with the Lundeens. Go!"

Virginia fled.

CHAPTER
12

THE only unhappiness and mortification affecting Virginia on the moment shuddered round the fact that Clifton Forrest had broken faith with her. To be sure, Malpass was an atrocious liar. But from Clifton alone could have come the knowledge of her marriage. That was enough to condemn him. No other part of Malpass' raving story need be considered. She was bitterly shocked and alienated.

Freed now from the ever-present fear of being way-laid by Malpass in and around every corner of the house, Virginia hurried first down to the barns. Jake and Con espied her coming and hastened to meet her.

"Boys, I want you to take all my horses away from Cottonwoods," she informed them, abruptly, without wasting time or explanations. "Do you know where you can take care of them for the winter?"

"Shore do," replied Jake, cheerfully. "I was thinking about winter range. Used to ride for Jeff Sneed. His ranch is south. Good water an' feed. An' Jeff will be glad to have us."

"That relieves me. Here's some money, all I can spare. But don't worry. The horses are worth ten thousand."

"Wal, you needn't worry, either," responded Jake, with a loyal smile.

"Where shall I write you?"

"Las Vegas, I reckon. Course we couldn't never get in town, but mail would come out now an' then."

"Very well. Pack up, and start as quickly as possible. Don't excite suspicion of your intentions. But don't let anybody stop you. These horses are my property."

"Reckon there ain't anybody round who could stop us, Miss," replied Jake, nonchalantly.

"Good-by then. I'm very happy to have you boys to rely on."

They bade her good-by, haltingly, full of wonder, and sympathy they dared not speak.

Virginia rushed back up to the house. Before she reached her rooms she had decided upon a plan of action. She would pack her belongings, drive to Las Vegas with her bags and send a truck back for her trunks. Then she would wire to Ethel and take the night train for Denver.

Whereupon she plunged into the packing—no slight task—and before very long she discovered that ever and anon she would stop a moment to do nothing but stare at the wall. When she realized this and divined why, she was angered with herself. Her natural instinct was to fly to Clifton. How wonderful if only she could have yielded to it! But he had failed her—he would not welcome her; and besides, that would ag-

gravate a situation already grave. She must dismiss
Clifton from mind for the present. The effort seemed
to rend her. Poor boy! The war had ruined him, and
his home-coming had been forlorn, miserable, unbearable. Small wonder if he had transgressed loyalty! Still,
she could not conceive of him boasting about her being his wife. Some day she would get at the bottom of
what really had been said and done. A thrilling idea
began to form and would not be denied—Clifton had
beaten Malpass for her sake. She simply had to be
cold and unreceptive to that incalculably far-reaching
possibility. By Malpass' own lips—swollen and discol-
ored—she had learned that he had been beaten by
Forrest, and it was enough.

As luck would have it, Virginia's mother came in
to see her, unsuspecting, and quite surprised to find
her in the midst of packing.

"Mother, I'm going to Denver a little ahead of my
invitation," she explained, relieved that Mrs. Lundeen
manifestly did not yet know of the upheaval.

"Dear me! Always on the go! Will you never settle
down?" she complained, mildly.

"I guess I'm about settled now, mother," said Virginia, "if you only knew it."

"It would please me to see you married."

"To the same individual father picked out for
me?"

"No. I wouldn't want you to tell it, but I don't
believe Malpass could make you happy."

"You're an angel to say that, mother. I promise
you I'll get a husband—pretty quick," returned Virginia, gleefully.

"I wish you would be serious. . . . Virginia, I

came in to tell you I'd like to go to Atlanta soon. And if you are leaving I think I'll go."

"Mother, I approve of that. And I might run down to Atlanta to see you this winter."

This delighted Mrs. Lundeen, and finally Virginia made the visit a certainty, providing her mother kept it a secret, and furthermore would not be distressed or influenced by any circumstance that might arise on Virginia's account in the meantime.

"You're mysterious, dear," smiled her mother. "But I'm so glad you will come that I'll agree to anything."

Virginia experienced a rush of unusual tenderness for her mother. She was tempted to tell her everything, but decided that there might be the chance that her mother would get away to Atlanta without being the wiser, and would therefore have a quieter mind. Mrs. Lundeen lingered talking for some time, and bade her good-by without being any the wiser as to the catastrophe of the day.

Spurred on and cheered, Virginia finished her packing. Then hurriedly dressing, she was soon ready for departure, and as she had seen her mother, she felt that she could leave without overpowering regrets. But a perverse devil of self tempted her to drive down on the Forrest side of the valley. She was proof against weakness. Nevertheless, as she passed a point opposite the little red adobe house, she could not refrain from looking across. "Well, Cliff, my soldier man," she soliloquized, "wonder what *your* dad said about your marrying a Lundeen?"

Arriving in town, she left her luggage at the station, and sent the car back, and also a truck with express order to fetch her trunks speedily. Then, after securing her railroad accommodations and telegraphing Ethel, she decided she would wait in the station, as at that hour some of her town acquaintances would probably be at the Castaneda. She wanted to think.

Three hours later Virginia was aboard the train. While in the dining-car she had a last glimpse of the slope above Cottonwoods, and the dark spot that was the Padre Mine.

Strange now to consider the events of the day. Not the gratifying downfall of Malpass, not her father's rage and her expulsion from home, not the crystallizing sense of melancholy in Clifton's disloyalty, but the astounding developments at Padre Mine dominated her thought.

Virginia went back to her Pullman, and leaning at her window she watched the end of that eventful day darken over the ranges.

The more she pondered over Jake's discovery at the mine, the stronger grew her conviction that deception and dishonesty on a large scale had been perpetrated there. Padre Mine bore the earmarks of having been the keystone of some gigantic plot of Malpass', through which he had made a fortune. Virginia was interested only in the deception. The question hammered at her—if she could prove Jake's contention would she not have power to break the hold of Malpass upon her father?

Doubts and misgivings faded like misty clouds before the sun. The matter clarified with analysis. Once upon coming back home from school, four years and more ago, she had been elated by the wonderful development of the mine. Her father was soaring to the clouds. She rode up to the mine, to find there hordes of Mexican laborers, dust, noise, and confusion, every indication of a marvelous strike. Money appeared to be as abundant as the sage. This was the period when her father had bought her all the fine horses available.

Two years later, upon another of her infrequent visits home, she was astounded to hear that the Padre Mine had failed. It was a subject about which no one risked speaking to her father. Virginia knew him well enough to be sure that he had suffered poignant disappointment, the more as he had allowed himself to become obsessed and confident. His reaction had not been to questionable dealing. Jed Lundeen might be deceived once by one man, but never again. No matter what his subjection to a shrewder intellect, and notwithstanding the fact that he had driven hard bargains himself, he would never stand to be cheated.

Hope of reinstating herself in her father's regard came as an afterthought, following the first and passionate desire to circumvent Malpass, and then it was more for her mother's than her own sake.

Presently the porter brought her a telegram, which he informed her had been given the conductor as the train pulled out of Las Vegas. It was from Ethel. She said she would be "piflicated with joy" to see Virginia, that she should have her baggage put off at Colorado Springs, and meet her at the station there. This appeared to be more good fortune for Virginia. The quiet of the resort would be preferable to Denver. Virginia had her berth made up, and went to bed dreaming before she fell asleep.

Next day the hours grew tedious. Virginia had to change trains at La Junta, and at length arrived at Colorado Springs. As the train pulled in, Virginia espied Ethel through the window. How the bright eager little face warmed her! True friends were rare. She had come to a juncture of her life when she could appreciate their value.

Then presently the porter was handing her down the step to the platform. Ethel let out a squeal of rapture and rushed to embrace her. Certain it was that Virginia returned it in full measure.

"You darling—lovely, gorgeous thing!" cried Ethel, between kisses.

"Oh, Ethel—I never was so glad to see you," returned Virginia, fervently. She was released at last, and Ethel condescended to remember baggage, trunk checks, cars, and other practical necessities. And soon they were speeding to the hotel where Ethel explained she had brought her mother for a rest.

"Ginia dearest, you look strange—now I can *see* you," said Ethel.

"Do I? How so? I surely feel strange," laughed Virginia.

Ethel studied her face with the keenness of loving, remembering eyes from which nothing could escape. "You've lost your bloom and your round schoolgirl cheeks. You're pale, honey. There's something dark in your eyes. It's not my old roguish Virginia. . . . Yes, you're older. You've changed, and oh, how it becomes you! . . . You used to be handsome. But good night! Now you're a sweet, sad, lovely woman."

"I shore reckon I needed you," murmured Virginia, fighting a perfectly silly and almost irresistible longing to cry.

But before she dared yield to the luxury and wholesomeness of such relaxation there was the hotel to reach, and the gauntlet to run of idle guests to whom a newcomer was an event, and the gracious

Mrs. Wayne and her friends to meet, and moment after moment to endure.

Ethel's room at last! Cozy, comfortable, light, and colorful, looking out upon the green-sloped, gray-cliffed, white-peaked Rockies, it seemed haven for Virginia.

"Lock the door—savior," cried Virginia, her voice rich and full and breaking. She threw her gloves, her coat, she tossed her hat, and all the while she avoided the wondering, dreading eyes of her friend.

"Virginia! You scare me stiff. What has happened?"

"I am—an outcast," sobbed Virginia, but with Ethel's arm around her.

At length the paroxysm was over, and Virginia felt the better for it.

"When have I cried like that?" she asked, raising her flushed and wet face from Ethel's shoulder.

"Never since I knew you," replied Ethel, still awed and shaken. "It broke my heart, Virginia. But how happy it makes me to know you've come to me in your trouble! . . . Now, tell it, darling. I'm a punk fair-weather friend, but try me in storm."

"I'm an outcast," replied Virginia, mournfully, and wiping her tear-splashed eyes she faced Ethel bravely and yet with shame.

"Outcast!" ejaculated her friend, bewildered.

"Yes. My father turned me out. I have no home and very little money. I sent my horses away to try to save them. I've got my clothes and jewels. And here I am, Ethel."

"Tell me—a little at a time," rejoined Ethel, gasping. "Turned you out!—The damned old hard-shelled crab!—Because you wouldn't marry Malpass?"

"No. Because I—I married some one else," whispered Virginia, hanging her head. It was not easy to confess, even to gentle, worshipful Ethel.

"Virginia!" And Ethel plumped down to her knees, rapt and wild, her eyes starting, her hands clasping Virginia's, her whole being shot through and through with vitalizing current.

"Married!—Married to whom? . . . I'd die if it were anyone but Clifton!"

"It was Clifton, dear."

"Oh, thank Heaven! I liked that boy as if—as if he were ten brothers of mine all in one. . . . Dear old sad-eyed, silent suffering Cliff! He was a hero. . . . And to think you've been and gone and done what I prayed for! It's just marvelous. You're the most satisfactory girl in all the world. You keep romance alive. What's all this bunk about modern girls and money, luxury, jazz, and loveless marriage? . . . And that old buzzard father of yours threw you out?"

"Almost. He said the Lundeens were through with me."

"Humph! And what did Mr. Slick-haired, goofy-eyed Malpass say to your marrying Cliff? I'll bet *he* threw a fit."

"It was he who told father. He raved. He foamed at the mouth. Oh, he was not human! . . . Ethel, he had to be brought home—carried in. Cliff had beaten him with a whip. His clothes were slashed to ribbons. Bloody! Black and blue! Ugh!—Cliff beat him nearly to death."

"Virginia Lundeen! You *tell* me!" screamed Ethel, frantically.

Thus inspired and impelled, Virginia, without realizing it in the least, fell to a Homeric recital of her story. She was to learn quickly, however, that her powers of narrative were supreme. Ethel quivered and shivered and wept over that rendezvous with Clifton in the garden; she went into ecstasies over the secret marriage; and when the sordid sequel ended—the passionate, vivid description of Malpass' denunciation—*he would drag her through the mud!* and her father's brutal hands at her throat, to prove which Virginia had but to show the discolorations on her neck, Ethel became a clenching-fisted, blazing-eyed little fury.

She launched out into an incoherent tirade that did not lose force until she lost her breath. And then she burst into tears. Virginia in turn ministered gentle consolation.

"And now what?" queried Ethel, recovering belligerently.

"Well, as I said before, here I am," replied Virginia, smiling.

"Of course, for the present. And it's great for me. But what are you going to do?"

"Ethel, I haven't any idea. Except I intend to investigate the Padre Mine failure," rejoined Virginia, and she gave Ethel minute details of her trip to the mine with the cowboys, and Jake's discovery.

"You bet!" exclaimed Ethel, her eyes wide and shining. "When we get to Denver you must consult a mining engineer. And if he gives you any encouragement, take him back to Las Vegas. I'll come with you. We'll put it over on Mr. Malpass. Gee! wouldn't it be great if we could prove he's crooked? In court, I mean. Wouldn't we make your father crawl?"

"I don't care about that, though it would be a satisfaction," continued Virginia. "I just want to free him from Malpass."

"Strikes me one's as bad as the other," said Ethel, bluntly. "What you want is to see justice done. To yourself and your mother—and the Forrests."

"Father has been led or forced into dishonest dealing. But even if he gets out of the clutches of Malpass, I doubt that he would ever square up with the Forrests."

"That'll be left for you, Virginia. And I should think you'd get much joy out of it."

"I would indeed. But you know Clifton refused assistance from me."

"That's different. He couldn't refuse *now*."

"Couldn't he? Much you know Cliff!"

"But you're his wife."

"Yes," mused Virginia.

"Don't you love him?" went on this indefatigable and relentless romancer.

"Terribly."

"Well then, it's perfect. Cottonwoods will belong to both of you. And I shall spend half my time there."

"Ethel, come down to earth. . . . Clifton doesn't care for me."

"Bunk!"

"But I tell you he doesn't. He sympathized with me. Was sorry. Wanted to help me out of my plight. I'm sure he doesn't believe he'll live long. It didn't matter to him. So he asked me to marry him."

"Listen to her! . . . So he was very kind and practical. No sentiment. Just made himself convenient for a damsel in distress. Jollied you a little about dying soon, huh? . . . And you let him get away with it?"

Virginia stared at her volatile friend, on the verge of both shock and anger.

Ethel laughed at her. "Couldn't you see poor, proud Cliff was madly in love with you?"

"No, you incorrigible little match-maker, I couldn't."

"You were as blind as a bat. Cliff didn't want you to know. Why, I'll bet right now he's hugging you to his breast—figuratively speaking."

"Ethel! You're a crazy, lovesick schoolgirl!" cried Virginia, in desperation.

"You bet your life I am. That's why I know things. . . . Didn't I see Clifton Forrest looking at you when you didn't know it?"

"I don't dare believe you," protested Virginia.

"Suit yourself. But I could save you a lot of agony."

"You'll only make agony for me. Suppose I listened to you—believed you, and then it turned out you were mistaken?"

"You'd never be. I'm sure death on these affairs of the heart. Have seen so many, then had one of my own. But for the sake of argument, to salve your wounded feelings, we'll assume I am wrong. We'll assume a lot of rot. Clifton home, broken in body and spirit. Haunted by the war. Penniless and unable to do a man's work. Occupied with his pangs and his lonely soul. Turgid ebb and flow of misery stuff. Too sick to be lovesick! . . . Do you follow me, darling?"

"I—I think so, though it is a bewildering process."

"Very well. The rest is simple. You'll stay with me

in Colorado for a while, until that scandal blows over. Then go back home and waylay Cliff at every turn."

"Waylay him? But I couldn't. . . . Even if I could what use would it be?"

"O Lord! . . . Well, maybe that's why I love you so.—Virginia, you don't have to do anything to make people love you. All that is necessary is for you to happen across their horizon. Once ought to be enough. If not once, then twice. Three times would be an avalanche. And after that we'd only have burials."

"You might help me if you could be serious," returned Virginia, plaintively.

"I may be slangy, honey, but I'm in dead earnest."

"You're very blind and loyal, Ethel. It's well for me that I can keep my head. . . . Now let's forget my troubles and plan to have a good time."

Virginia spent three weeks with Ethel at Colorado Springs and did not know where the days fled.

There were few social exactions. They passed most of the daylight hours outdoors, hiking, motoring, climbing the foothills, playing golf. Saddle horses were to be had for the asking, but Virginia could not be induced to ride.

She enjoyed most an afternoon in the Garden of the Gods. A motor car was not available at the hour, so the girls, bent on a lark, hired an old relic of a Westerner, a driver of a dilapidated open vehicle with a horse that matched both man and hack. He took them for tourists and proceeded to acquaint them with himself.

"My name air Josh Smith an' I hail from Indianer. Fust come West in 'sixty-eight. Was a lad then an' the redskins made me an orphan. Reckon thet everythin' the West could give I got—'cept six feet of ground, an' I near got thet a hundred times. I be'n teamster on the plains, helped to build the Santa Fé, freighter, scout, cowboy, miner, gambler, an' 'most everythin'."

"My, Mr. Smith, but you've seen a lot!" said Ethel, with a mischievous wink at Virginia.

"Right smart, though I've knowed fellars who'd seen more."

"And how old are you?"

"Reckon I don't know. But I'm over eighty."

"Were you ever married?"

"Haw! Haw! Lots of times, on an' off," he replied, plying his whip to the almost motionless horse.

"Well, that's fine. Then you didn't find marriage a failure, like so many people of today?"

"No, indeedee. Marriage is all right, if you kin change often enough."

"That's an original idea," went on Ethel, unmindful of a dig from Virginia's elbow.

"Air you married?"

"Oh dear, yes! At least I was. And I've four children. My husband deserted us, and now I have to—to travel around and write for newspapers to make a living."

"You're purty young-lookin'. No one would guess thet. . . . An' your quiet friend hyar—is she married, too?"

"Oh dear, no! She's deaf and dumb and doesn't care much for men. She's very rich. I'm her traveling companion. She pays me for it."

"Wal, by golly! Deaf an' dumb? I'll never grow too old to get a stumper. Who'd have thunk it?"

"Isn't she handsome?" went on this incorrigible little devil, despite sundry covert kicks and cuffs.

"Oh, you can say what you like about her. She can't hear and I won't tell."

"Handsomest gal I've seen this summer, an' thar's some peaches hyar durin' July an' August. I ain't seen one, though, with the shape your friend's got. Te-he, te-he, te-he! She'd drive any young buck to drink. I shore wish I was young again."

Ethel by this time was bursting with glee, and Virginia, too, could scarcely contain herself; but their arrival in the Garden of the Gods changed the direction of the old Westerner's mind to the natural spectacles of the wondrous rock formation out of which he made his living.

"See thet rock?" he queried, becoming professional. "Thet's the Elephant. Thar's the bulk of the body, haid an' ears, an' the trunk. One tusk missin'."

"Oh, it's a perfect elephant!" declared Ethel, clapping her hands. As a matter of fact it did not resemble an elephant more than any other of the many rocks near at hand.

Next came the Tomcat, and close to him the Mud Turtle. Following them in succession was a remarkable assortment of animals, evidently, to this old man, admirable stone statues of the creatures he named.

"An' thar's Apollonaris Belvedeerie," he announced, grandly, waving his whip at a huge red crag, fluted and draped, and, without a distorting name, a beautiful thing to gaze upon.

"But last summer you told me that one was Ajax defying the Lightning," rejoined Ethel, in demure amaze.

"What? Was you out hyar with me last summer?" he queried, sharply.

"To be sure I was. I'd never forget you."

"Wal, mebbe 'tis Ajax. I see these doggone gods so doggone much."

They rode on, and he seemed a little less declamatory about the significance of cliffs and stones. Nevertheless, he had a label for each and every one. Virginia had been there before, and of course the Garden was like an old book to Ethel.

"Now looka thar," suddenly spoke up their guide, once more animated. "Thar's the Wild Stallion. Thet one fetches all my patrons. It's shore the beautifulest picture of a great wild hoss turned into a stone god. See his noble haid an' his flyin' mane, an' thet wind hole which is his eye."

This was too much for Virginia. The rock designated resembled nothing alive, let alone the wondrous beauty of a wild horse.

"That?" she burst out. "It's a dumpy red rock. No more."

In his amazement the imaginative guide dropped his whip. His lean jaw dropped, too.

"Hey, wasn't you deaf an' dumb?" he ejaculated.

Ethel vented a silvery peal of laughter and leaped gaily out to the ground. Virginia followed, though less actively.

"No, I wasn't deaf and dumb," she retorted. "And I'm no tourist, either. I live on a ranch so big you could lose your old Garden in it. . . . Aren't you ashamed, trying to fool people about these rocks?"

"Wal, by gum!"

"Wait for us, driver," said Ethel. "And think up some more fakes. You sure are the bunk."

"Reckon I be'n buncoed, too," he returned, grinning. "I'll bet four bits them four kids of yours is bunk. . . . Haw! Haw!"

Ethel mumbled something, what Virginia was unable to distinguish.

"Come, you kid," she called to Virginia. "I'll beat you to the top of the slide."

Next day they went to Denver. And Virginia was once again in contact with the theater, the motion-picture, the department stores and restaurants of a city. While there she ascertained the name of a well-known mining engineer and contractor, with whom she made an appointment.

She found Mr. Jarvis a middle-aged man, a Westerner, shrewd and plain, and one inclined to inspire confidence.

"My errand may be absurd," she explained, "but then again it may be important. That is for you to say."

"I'm at your service, Miss Lundeen," he replied, with interest.

Thereupon Virginia related as briefly as possible the circumstances connected with her last visit to Padre Mine.

"Now what I want to know," she concluded, "is whether or not you suspect there might have been something queer about that mine."

"Queer indeed," he returned, almost with amusement. "If the facts you have told so clearly can be substantiated, it will lay bare something more than queer."

"And what may that be?"

"Nothing more nor less than a plain crooked mining deal."

"As I suspected," returned Virginia, breathing quickly. "The gold was brought to the mine—planted there—and then blown up, so that it'd be scattered everywhere. All to deceive my father into believing it was a rich mine."

"Exactly. May I ask, did he sell the mine?"

"No."

"Then he invested money in the operating of it?"

"Yes. I have no idea how much. But altogether I imagine several hundred thousand went into that mine."

The engineer lifted his brows in surprise. "So much! Well, this is worth digging into. Of course the mine is abandoned now?"

"Yes, for two years and more. Now, Mr. Jarvis, if you will give me reasonable assurance that you can prove whether or not this was a crooked deal, I will engage you to investigate."

"If the mine is as accessible to me as to your cowboy prospector, I can absolutely give you proof."

"Can it be done quickly?"

"How far from town is this mine?"

"I can take you there in less than two hours from Las Vegas."

"Then half a day will be ample."

"Very well. Consider it settled," rejoined Virginia, rising. "I'll be going home soon. I'll choose an opportune time—for I want it to be secret, so we are not intercepted—wire you to come on, meet you upon your arrival and take you directly to the mine."

13

*T*HE sheep were grazing south. Every day they made a few leisurely miles, keeping to the grass and sage benches, never straying far from the water-courses.

November heralded the beginning of winter in that latitude, but only toward the high slopes was the weather severe. Old Baldy had put on his white cap, and there were patches of snow along the black-fringed rims of the battlements. The wind whipped down from the heights, bitter cold and mournful at night, keen across the bright steely desert at dawn, and lulling and tempering through the noon hours.

The sheep route, over which the Mexicans had driven their herds for a hundred years and more, gradually drew down and away from the mountains, southward toward the vast open, with dim purple ranges in the distance.

At sunset the shepherds with their dogs rounded

the flocks into a natural corral, a protective corner of canyon, or under the lee of a ledge, and there passed the night, to leisurely move on again at sunrise. Since the failure of cattle on the range there was grazing in abundance, but the sheep had to be worked down into lower and warmer country. This old custom had worn a rut in the commerce of the state, as it had worn broad trails up and down the desert.

The last of these widely separated bands of sheep to leave the uplands of San Luis halted late one afternoon at Gray Rocks, far out on the windy plain.

The shepherd was a white man, and he had a Mexican lad as assistant, and four dogs. He moved with extreme weariness, this man, as he unpacked the two burros and turned them loose. The lad was active, and with the dogs drove the pattering, baaing flock into the wide notch of a low gray broken cliff.

A few scraggy cedars marked this camp site, old trees devoid of sheaths of gray bark and gnarled dead branches so characteristic of the species. This stripping attested to past camp fires, and yet to the regard with which the lonely shepherds held trees on the desert.

The shepherd threw the rope of his little peak tent over a limb and pulled it up, and tied the rope to the trunk. Then he rested a moment, dark face lowered, a hand on his breast. Next he unrolled his bed, consisting of some sheepskins and a blanket, which he spread inside the tent. After that he opened the other pack and spread its contents of utensils and bags upon a canvas.

Meanwhile the Mexican lad returned with an armload of bits of dead sage, and weed roots, and sticks of cottonwood. He whistled while he lighted a fire, but he did not talk. Next he picked up a little black bucket and pot, and went off down the slope for water, with one of the dogs at his heels. Soon he returned, whistling the few notes of a Spanish tune.

It was evident that the white shepherd was about at the end of his tether, for that day at least. The lad saw it and was quick to help prepare the meal, where he was permitted. Presently the coffee-pot steamed and the sheep meat sizzled in the pan. There were also dried fruit heated in water, and hard biscuits which were warmed on a rock beside the fire. Soon, then, the shepherds sat to their frugal meal, generous only in supply of meat. And they ate hungrily and drank thirstily, while the lean shaggy dogs stood around with shining eyes to beg for bones. They were not neglected. When the meal ended the man washed the utensils and the boy wiped them dry.

Meanwhile the sun had set stormily amid dusky and dull red clouds far down in the west. The weird lights of the desert began to darken, and far behind, the mountain range stood up black as ebony, sharp and bold against the cold sky. One by one pale stars shone out, blinking, obscure, aloof. The sheep bleated, and the cold wind tore through the cedars.

The lad spread his sheepskins under the tree, and rolled in his blanket upon them. One of the dogs, evidently young, curled close to him. The others had gone out to guard the flock.

The white shepherd sat by the fire and fed bits of sage and dead sticks to the glowing bed of coals. His hands were dark and lean like his face, that a month's growth of beard did not hide. The flickering blaze lighted somber hollow eyes that found ghosts in the opal embers, and ever and anon gazed out over the melancholy desert to see nothing there. He had a racking cough and it appeared he could not warm his palms enough.

Night fell, growing colder, and the desert lay black under the hazy sky and wan stars. Coyotes raised their hue and cry, and the wary dogs yelped their menace. A lonesome owl hooted from the recesses of the rocks; faint rustlings came from the sage; a rush of wings overhead attested to the passage of an invisible bird of the night.

These sounds mitigated the pressure of the solitude, which lay like a thick mantle over the earth. They made it bearable to the man who was scarcely conscious of any save physical agonies. At last all the sticks were burned. The fire died down. Still he lingered over the ruddy embers, from which sparks flew away on the wind, to die out in the blackness.

When the red faded out of the fire he crawled into the little tent, and wearily stretched his aching body upon the sheepskins, and covered himself with the blanket. He did not remove even his hat, which perhaps he had forgotten. And he groaned: "O God—O God!"

The sleep of exhaustion ended his tortures. And inside his tent the desert night increased its somber mystery, its weird voice on the wind, its staccato alarms of prowling coyotes, its bleak and ruthless solitude.

Clifton Forrest had been a month on the desert. Sunset of that day in which he had horsewhipped Malpass, and had been made an outcast by his father, found him at the hacienda of Don Lopez, a rancher outside of San Luis. There he spent the night, grateful for succor he felt would be denied him by people of his own color. And the next day he became the shepherd of a Mexican's flock, at a wage of a few cents a day.

The world had about come to an end for Clifton. But the beating he had given Malpass had no place in his remorse. His heart was weighed down because his natural and unfortunate subjection to passion had been a betrayal of the woman he loved, who owed to him the loss of parents and home. She had trusted him—she had appealed to him alone of all her friends —she might one day, if he had proved worthy, have reciprocated in some degree his love. And he had failed her. What avail to blame endlessly that cursed Malpass and his own hot jealousy? He had been weak. His manhood was gone. And, perhaps as reprehensible, he had added to his mother's burden of sorrow.

So he had taken to the lonely reaches of the desert, as a winter shepherd. The constant movement and the labor of this job were beyond his strength. Three days after leaving San Luis his remorse and grief had been overshadowed by the horror of old bodily pangs, which soon augmented into agonies. Cottonwoods and Virginia Lundeen and his mother became dim phantoms back in a past that was gone. Before him stretched the naked shingles of the desert, the brutal destroying ruthlessness of which he welcomed, but which brought back the rend of nerve, the ache of bone, the torture of muscle, the hell of physical suffering without making an end of him. He would lie for half the night in misery, but at dawn he would get up and go on. He fell in the trails, but he rose and stumbled on. Then at the worst of his collapse he lay for days on his back, tended by the faithful Mexican lad. But he did not die and he could not surrender. He crawled out to plod on behind the sheep for a half day, and the next he went farther, until as the days passed he reached a full one in travel again—ten terrible hours that brought him to Gray Rocks, a resting and grazing point for the sheep on the southern drive.

November dawn on the desert came reluctantly, gray and slowly brightening, to diffuse a pale rose along the eastern skyline, and turn to the yellow flare of sunrise.

Clifton saw it through the open flap of his tent. Another day! He had never moved during the night and his feet were like clods of cold lead. To start to arise was a horrible wrench—on one elbow, then his hand, a lift of back that had to be accomplished with gritted teeth, a turn of body which was the worst, then on hands and knees, and at last up, though bowed like an old man.

Yet this morning he proved something that had haunted him with mocking insistence—there had come an appreciable difference in the length of time, the terror of effort, the reflux of pain that it cost him to arise.

He had not prayed for that. He had hardly wanted it. But as he faced the cold gray monotonous waste, stretching and rolling and breaking away, lonely, barren, lifeless, magnificent in its isolation, appalling in its desolation, stupendous in its distances and beautiful with all the strange somber mystery of the desert, he felt the link between his unquenchable instinct to survive and a spiritual consciousness stronger than anything in primal nature. While there was life there was hope, good, truth, joy, and God. It came to him.

He could not deny it. His bitterness was of no avail. The pagan specter that had hovered like a shadow on his trail faded away.

Clifton began the tasks of the day, lighter here by reason of the fact that there was to be a break in the drive south, a two-day stop at Gray Rocks.

"Buenos días, señor," said the Mexican lad, in his soft liquid accents, as he came with his arms full of firewood.

Clifton discarded his limited Spanish and spoke to the boy in his own tongue. A subtle change affected him. Nevertheless, he went at his camp tasks with slow guarded movements. The lean dogs came down to sit on their haunches and watch him. They were ragged, thin mongrel canines, bred by the Indians and trained by Mexicans, antagonistic to white men. It had been the province of Julio to govern these shepherd dogs, so that Clifton had made no attempt to lessen their animosity. Julio was a son of Don Lopez, and had been brought up with the dogs and the sheep.

Clifton saw them all less aloofly this morning. They had accepted him. Why had he not accepted them? He spoke to the dogs. How clear-eyed, watchful, knowing! Were they only hungry beasts?

The camp fire was a comfort. It sent up a thin column of fragrant smoke—the scent of burning sage. It crackled and blazed, and burned red. It warmed Clifton's cold feet and took the sting out of his fingers. The water left in the pan had become solid ice. All around, the sage and brittle-bush and creeping vines glistened with silvery frost. What would the desert have been without fire? The earliest man-creatures must have developed in a tropic clime.

After breakfast the bleating, restless sheep were

released. With a tiny trampling roar they poured in a woolly stream down out of the rocky fastness, to spread out over the shallow wash. They nipped the grass, the weeds, the brush, and the sage.

In number the flock approached three thousand, a very large one, especially to belong to a Mexican. But as food and water were abundant, two shepherds with trained dogs could easily care for the flock, their main duty being vigilance. Straggling sheep sometimes got lost in the brush, to become prey for coyotes, and wildcats and cougars that occasionally stole down from the cliffs, and a wolf now and then that came from out the desert.

Julio carried a light rifle and always ranged out at the fore of the grazing flock, accompanied by the young dog. Clifton, with a heavier rifle, which had been a burden, followed in the rear, keeping to high places, always watchful, true to the trust imposed in him. The other three dogs, older, marvelously trained, did not require to be ordered about. They knew their work. Seldom could a sheep straggle away from the main flock into the sage. When one did it was promptly chased back.

Grazing of sheep was slow, as far as travel was concerned. Clifton had to walk and stand and sit to suit their convenience. Over barren ground they were driven consistently until good grazing was again encountered.

On cold mornings like this one Clifton was hard put to it to keep from freezing. His blood was thin and apparently there was not much of it. The necessity of keeping continually in action was what had made it so desperately hard to stand up under this job. During the middle of sunny days, however, he could rest often. But back beneath the forbidding mountains there had been much cloudy and windy weather, which had been the greatest factor in breaking him down.

Around Gray Rocks there was ample feed. Clifton chose a high point and patrolled it, his eye ever alert for prowling beasts. Sometimes, despite the vigilance of the shepherds, a lamb would be snatched by a coyote and carried off. Usually, however, in daylight the dogs kept the flock condensed and safe from depredations.

He had a bitter few hours before the sun offered him a respite. Still he watched even while he rested, for at this season cottontail rabbits were wholesome eating and furnished welcome change from sheep meat. In fact a shepherd on that range developed into something of a hunter.

An hour's scanning of this apparently barren desert would have surprised an inexperienced traveler. Clifton espied a gray fox stepping through the sage, and several hungry, sneaking coyotes afar, jack rabbits in plenty, several cottontails, one of which he shot, packrats and gophers, and some skulking animal which he could not name. Hawks sailed by, and ravens croaked from the rocks. A flock of blackbirds winged irregular flight down the wash; a lonely gray speckled bird flitted through the sage.

These living creatures, and the various aspects of the desert, had begun to interest Clifton. It was an indication of release from himself, fragmentary at first, then more and more frequent.

At high noon he drew from his pocket a hard biscuit and some chops, well cooked and salted. These constituted his midday meal. He gnawed the bones with a relish, suddenly to be struck with the fact that he was nearly always hungry, and particularly so this day. In the past he had not cared for mutton. The tastes of a man varied according to his needs.

The sheep, however, did not linger in one place. They nibbled and nipped while passing on. Soon Clifton had to follow. He caught up with the flock, found a rock to sit on, and basked in the warm sun for a few moments. Many times he repeated this. As the afternoon began to wane Julio led back in a circle, and at sundown they were approaching camp. And by dark Clifton was through with work for the day, warming his palms over the coals, weary and dark-faced again, prone to the dejection that accompanied fatigue. Yet this night he did not crawl to bed.

Every desert day was a whole by itself; and the next was bleak, raw, windy, with flurries of snow. The sheep favored sheltered slopes and banks, and the beds of arroyos and the leeward of rocks. Clifton huddled in sheltered nooks to build little fires of dried sage and warm his numb hands and feet. It was a profitable day for the coyotes. More than once Clifton started up at an uproar from the dogs; and one well-aimed shot laid a coyote low. Julio skinned the dead beast and stretched the skin on a frame.

As the afternoon waned a lowering black cloud swooped across the desert, trailing a gray whirling pall of snow that whitened sage and ground, and quickly vanished. The squall passed away and the sun burst out, flushing the desert gold and red, with the promise of a better morrow.

The flock was laggard and difficult to drive back to camp in the face of wind. But for the faithful dogs it never could have been accomplished. Then for the shepherds the blessing of fire and food and rest!

The following morning while Clifton cooked breakfast Julio brought in the burros. The shepherds ate, packed, and with their flock headed south on the long trail. The morning was glorious. No wind! A bright sun tempered the nipping air. The cool fragrance of dry sage floated over the desert. The ridges were diamond white in frost, that quickly melted on the south slopes. Endless soft gray stretches led down to the purple landmarks above the horizon. Wild mustangs trooped to a rise of ground, there to stand and whistle, and then race away with manes and tails flying.

They had traveled six miles by sunset, and Clifton was not down at the finish. On warm days he lasted longer. They were now well over a hundred miles south of their own range.

One forenoon, several days later, the sheep crossed the last road which transversed that section of the desert. Clifton, following slowly, reached the road just as an automobile came by. He would have passed on, but the occupants of the car hailed him and stopped. He guessed the muddy old car belonged to a rancher and that the three were Westerners.

"Hey, Pedro, come over an' say hello!" called one. Then as Clifton approached closer he added: "Excuse me. I took you for a greaser."

"Howdy!" replied Clifton as he looked to see if he knew one or more of them.

"Fine bunch of sheep. Whose are they?" queried the eldest of the three.

"They belong to Don Lopez."

"Ahuh. I thought so. Lopez' last flock workin'

south. You must be young Forrest—Clay Forrest's son?"

"Yes, I am."

They appeared kindly, curious, and interested. "We heerd you got in a muss at Watrous some while back."

"I'm afraid I did," returned Clifton, reluctantly. "But as I left San Luis next day, I've never heard how bad the muss was. . . . I thought you might be a sheriff."

"Not much," laughed one, "we're glad to say. I reckon, though, you're worryin' fer nothin'. Mason wasn't bad hurt in thet scrap an' anyways you didn't shoot him."

"Wal, Forrest, there's not many people who're against you fer thet little cowhidin' stunt," added another of the three.

"I'm glad to hear it," rejoined Clifton.

"Whar you drivin'?"

"Guadaloupe Springs."

"Say, that's an all-winter job! Shore, you're goin' back?"

"No. I have only a boy with me. Lopez gave me the job and I'll stick. I'll drive back in the spring."

"Wal, excuse me, Forrest," said the elder man, feelingly. "It's shore your own bizness. But I want to give you a hunch. If you're hidin' out—it's all fer nothin'. There ain't any sheriff lookin' fer you."

"Thank you. That's a relief."

"But if I was you I'd chuck this herdin' job. Somebody in Watrous told me the other day thet Malpass was tryin' to buy Lopez out. Reckon it's only a rumor, but I wouldn't risk it."

"I've got to. Work is necessary, and jobs I can fill

are few. Lopez trusted me. I'll trust him. I don't think he'd sell without sending me word."

"Wal, Don Lopez is white, you can lay to thet. But Malpass has a hold over these greasers. Better throw your pack in the car hyar an' come with us."

"No. You're very good. But I'll go on."

"Are you well, Forrest? You look pretty worked out."

"I'm all right. It was hard at first—for a man in my shape. But I'll pull through."

"Ahuh.—Wal, good luck to you. Any message we can take back? We're goin' on to Kelsey's Ranch, then right back to town."

"If you meet anyone I know—tell them I'm all right," replied Clifton, haltingly. This was too sudden for him. He would have liked to be prepared for such a meeting.

"Shore will, an' go out of my way. . . . How're you off fer smokes?"

"I've quit. But my boy Julio—a pack of cigarettes would be most welcome."

"Hyar you are. . . . Bill, fork out. An' you too, Pedlar."

Three packages came flipping to Clifton's feet.

"Thanks. But I didn't mean to hold you up."

"So long, Forrest. Don't forgit. You're solid back thar."

"Wait!" called Clifton, as they were about to start. He stepped closer, suddenly gripped by awakening realization. "What's the talk—about me?"

"Not bad at all, Forrest," heartily returned the one who had been the most loquacious. "Most died out now. But it was some talk, believe me. An' the sum of it was thet you an' Miss Lundeen fell in love—which was quite proper—an' because of your parents hatin' each other you had to marry secret. Wal, Malpass, who was always sweet on Lundeen's gal, found it out an' had Hartwell fire you—insultin' your wife to boot. You jest beat hell out of Malpass, in accordance with Western ways. An' the dirty half-breed throwed his gun, near killin' poor old Jim Mason. Everybody is sorry you didn't use a gun yourself, instead of a whip. . . . Wal, then your respective fathers, sore as hell because you'd married, throwed you out. . . . I reckon thet's about all."

"Do you know—did you hear what became of—of Miss Lundeen?" queried Clifton, hoarsely.

"I'm sorry, Forrest, but I never heerd."

"Wal, I know," added the man called Bill, and he grinned happily. "I seen her get on the train thet very night. It was Number Four, goin' East, an' I was thar. She was dressed like one of them girls in the pictures, an' she shore looked white an' proud."

"Thar! She beat it, Forrest," declared the eldest man, with satisfaction. "Didn't you worry none about your wife! . . . So long now. Good luck."

They left Clifton standing beside the road, staring after the speeding car. It was long before he remembered the sheep, and longer before he could see to follow them.

Guadaloupe Springs lay four weeks' sheep travel from Gray Rocks. It was three thousand feet lower, and the winter climate was the perfect one of early autumn in high altitude, marred on rare occasions by a storm.

A vast bowl of uneven land held Guadaloupe Springs in its center, where many groves of cottonwoods and long wandering lines of willows marked the presence of the water that gave life to the desert. The trees lately touched by frost shone in a wondrous variety of greens and golds, strong contrast to the monotonous gray of wasteland.

From the height of the bowl, far over the broken red walls that rimmed it, could be seen the beginning of the arid zone of sand and stone and cactus, of that glimmering delusive region of the *Journado del Muerte*, which led on and on over the bad lands of the south and the border to Mexico.

From the beautiful valley, like an oasis, where Lopez' flock was to spend the winter months, no ghastly stretch or black butte of the southern desert could be seen. Only the slow-rising gray slopes, and the mounds of red rock, and the enclosing yellow walls, and the blue phantoms of peaks that resembled inverted cloud mountains in the sky, greeted the keen eyes of the sheep-herders.

Clifton was nine weeks out of San Luis. It seemed nine years. It was Julio who kept track of days. For the will that had upheld Clifton, the scorn of weakness and agony and death, the toil which dwarfed the trenches, the effort he owed himself, and the desert with its boundless horizons, its cruelty, its solitude, its lonely nights and solemn days, its piercing wind and cold and storm, its tormenting demand to be conquered—all these had worked upon Clifton's body and mind, to begin a transformation which, if completed, would be a miracle.

They pitched camp under a cottonwood that stormed Clifton's heart, so like was it to the one in the valley at home—the gnarled, low-branched old monarch which Virginia Lundeen had climbed as a bare-legged girl, and under which as a woman she had tempted him to make her his wife. No hope ever to forget her here!

A little clear stream babbled over rocks and left faint traces of white alkali along the sand. Rabbits and quail darted away into the green brush. Robins and larks and swamp blackbirds, on the way south, still lingered here, and a killdee sounded his piercing melancholy note.

At the head of the stream was a natural corral in a triangle of the rocks, where the bare ground, packed hard by countless thousands of tiny hoofs, attested to the shepherds' flocks of the past. Here Clifton and Julio drove their flock, shouting their gladness to be there, answering the barks of the dogs. The down journey was ended. In the spring the sheep would be fat and strong, and the return trip a reward of the months.

"Julio, your Virgin Saint spoke true. All is well," said Clifton.

"Eet es well, señor," replied the lad.

Clifton surveyed the fallen cottonwoods and willows, the driftwood that had come down the stream in flood, and smiled at the thought of luxurious camp fires during the winter. What had he ever known of cold? As the worth of a fire! It took the desert to teach a man.

Then, with trepidation of heart, he swung an ax. It strained him. It made him pant and sweat and labor. But he could swing it! A terrible, incomprehensible ecstasy assailed him. No man could ever tell what might happen. Life was sweet. Just to see and feel and smell! To be able to stand up like a man and work!

Love was not necessary. The affection and under-standing of a father could be dispensed with. The thought of mother must always be sad. No compensa-tion for her! Friends were nothing. It was just enough to feel life flowing back through the veins, hot, throb-bing, thrilling. To conquer physical obstacles—to be able to chop a log! In place of the God he imagined had failed him, he thanked Julio's Virgin Saint.

This vast shut-in basin was a desert paradise. There would be Indians and other sheep-herders, but they would not spoil the solitude, the long, long nights with the wind in the cottonwoods, the long, long days, solemn and still, empty of the hate and greed of men.

Julio came and stood in amaze to see him swing the ax, to watch with his soft dark eyes, and to cry out, "Ah, señor ez grande again!"

Clifton saw it through, and fell with the ax in his hands. He was weak. But how infinitely stronger than he had ever hoped to be! And as he lay there, panting, there was born in him an unutterable and ineffably passionate love for the raw, ruthless, flinty desert that had saved him.

SUNRISES of pale rose with fan rays, ice on the still pools that soon melted, lonesome full hours with the bleating sheep, sunsets of gold and red over the purple walls—so the days sped.

In January, one morning, Julio discovered a loss of sheep. At first Clifton believed they had strayed, but Julio shook his head, and soon he pointed to moccasin tracks in the sand. The sheep had been stolen.

"I will go fetch them back," said Clifton, with heat.

"No, señor. *Mucho malo*," returned the lad, and with impressive gesture indicated a flight far over the Guadaloupe walls, across the border into Mexico.

"But the sheep can't travel fast. I'll catch up with the thieves," protested Clifton.

"Mebbe no. Injuns shoot." Plain it was that Julio did not think the loss of a few sheep worth the risk. But Clifton did. The Mexican lad seemed to be trying to tell him that little thefts like this one were always happening at Guadaloupe, but he did not implicate the herders and Indians in the valley. The raiders came from far and were never trailed.

"I'll go," decided Clifton, with a zest. "They can't steal my sheep without a run for it."

He must travel light, and he sifted the necessities down to his rifle, with a box of shells, and a bag containing hard biscuits, meat and salt, and some parched corn. It would not be necessary to pack a canteen, because the Indians dared not go far from water on account of the sheep. He took matches, a small hand-ax, which he stuck in his belt, and set out.

The trail of the sheep was easy to follow, for their sharp little hoofs cut into even the baked adobe soil, but it took discerning eyes to find imprints of moccasins. He had never had experience enough on the range to become an expert tracker, which fortunately was not required in this instance.

The trail led east, toward the shortest way out of the basin. No doubt the raiders would turn south when they got through the walls. It took Clifton three hours of steady tramping to reach the walls. They loomed like mountains of smooth red walls, straight up, with rims weathered, broken, splintered into crags, turrets, crumbled ruins of rock, where green growths found lodgment in the niches.

Clifton had seen these irregular escarpments from a distance of twelve or fifteen miles, and therefore had underestimated their size. He passed through the break where the sheep tracks led, and found himself in an astounding world of walls, monuments, shafts, and rocks, all rising sheer out of level red ground, with aisles and lanes between, with hollows, caves, and caverns under the gigantic cliffs, water-worn perhaps, in an age when this region had been inundated. It was the most weird, colorful, and fascinating place he had ever visited. Guadaloupe Springs had not been an unknown name to Clifton, years before, but nothing had ever been told of these marvelous rock formations. They were scarcely three hundred miles from Las Vegas, south by west. It thrilled him to realize that many wonders and beauties of the desert were still unknown to all save a few wanderers.

A glamour of color and silence seemed to enfold the regions of these upstanding ledges of rock. The sunlight appeared to be a reflection of the dark red, almost purple hue of the walls, and the gold-green of the desert floor. There was no sound except the silken rustle of swallows, so swift in flight that Clifton could not see them until they had darted by.

He traveled cautiously, expecting to come in sight of the Indians around any corner. Between the great walls he sometimes had a glimpse of the open desert beyond, and the sight made him catch his breath. From the heights the land sloped away into a measureless and ghastly void of white and gray that seemed to have no end, that was lost in sky.

At last he got through the labyrinthine maze. Then far down the gradual incline he caught sight of moving dots. They were miles away, but he doubted not that they were his quarry. Clifton followed, moving out of a direct line toward a slight eminence, from which he hoped to sight the stolen sheep.

When he surmounted this vantage-point he made out a line of white specks that he instantly recognized as sheep, perhaps to the number of fifty. Behind moved the larger dots, dark in color. These were the

Indians on foot, and they were heading down and toward the west.

Clifton sat down to eat, and to ponder over the situation. He wanted only to recover the sheep, and that might not be easy unless he surprised the thieves. They were heading surely toward a dark green fringe, which probably marked a waterhole. If he could stalk them into camp, and fire a few shots to frighten them, the recovery of the sheep would present no great difficulty. On the other hand, however, if they sighted him in pursuit they might kill, or surely scatter the sheep, and probably ambush him.

Therefore he waited until they had passed on out of sight, and then completing his simple repast, he headed to the west, aiming to get back under the protection of the walls. In this manner he lost ground in the pursuit, but still did not sheer far from the general direction of the raiders.

By the middle of the afternoon Clifton had begun to tire. He had traveled far, at a rather brisk walk. Still he kept on, until he arrived at a point opposite the green patch that he believed the Indians were making for. Here he rested again and watched sharply for reappearance of the drivers and the sheep. They did not come in sight. Therefore, much concerned that he might have miscalculated, he pressed on straight down the slope.

At sundown he was within five miles of the patch of green, that proved to be trees, among which something pale caught the last light of the sun. It was water or sand.

A bulge of ground to Clifton's left had long concealed any extensive view of the lay of the desert in that direction. He devoted all his searching gaze there, and as the shadows thickened he grew bolder and trusted more to the sparse growths for cover. Suddenly he heard a sharp sound that brought him startled and crouching to his knees behind a bush. He listened. Presently it rang out again—the bark of a dog.

The Indians were probably just below the dip of ground ahead. He crawled noiselessly a few yards, then again listened. He thought he heard faint voices, but could not be certain. Presently he stole on farther, soon to attain a position where he could command the level below. And half a mile out he espied four Indians driving two score and more of sheep. He watched them. Just as the dusk was about to swallow them they entered the grove.

Clifton pressed on then, under cover of the gathering darkness, and in half an hour the line of trees showed black against the horizon, and low down flickered a camp fire. This afforded him much satisfaction, but the further problem was what to do, now that he had caught up with the thieves.

He had not noticed that they carried guns. But on the other hand this was probably their encampment, and there might be others. He circled, and entered the grove at its upper end, where trees stood far apart, yet the underbrush was thick. He slipped down into a dry wash, with sandy floor, and following it to a point he judged somewhat in proximity to the camp, he crawled up on the bank and under the bushes to reconnoiter.

He came abruptly upon a huge jumble of rocks, where he halted to listen. He heard running water, but no other sound. Even the leaves were still.

Whereupon he considered the situation. If he

could not light a fire he was in for an uncomfortable night. The four Indians he had seen did not present any great obstacle, and if they had not joined others at this camp, he thought it just as well to rout them at once, instead of waiting for daylight. He wanted to be certain, however, before he alarmed the dogs. He had heard one and there would certainly be more. So with extreme caution he set out to circle the rocks.

It struck him presently, however, that he could not have been any cooler. He remembered the excitement caused by disturbances with the Indians years before, when he was a boy. A situation approaching this would have stopped his heart. But he had done this sort of thing under cannon fire that was like terrific thunder. He had done it alone, and in company with hundreds of men.

This was vaguely amusing, but at length it roused him. The night, the desert loneliness, the presence of unseen Indians, the stalking as of big game, contributed to a quickening of pulse and a tightening of his skin. It was action that created excitement.

A break in the bank of rock afforded him a place to enter and climb up to where he could see a glow of fire. But there was brush or cover on the flat top, so he slipped down on the right side, and worked around that way.

Presently he saw the firelight and moving dark figures, more, he was sure, than those of the Indians he had tracked. Carefully picking the best covert from which to watch them, he stole stealthily on, sank to his hands and knees, and halted in shadow.

With the first clear look his grimness turned to amazement. There were a dozen figures, perhaps, before him, but not one of them was an Indian. They were Mexicans, and indeed a poor, ragged, starved lot. One woman held a baby to her breast, and it did not look many days old. They were cooking a sheep, which task was manifestly of profound importance. They jabbered gaily, and some of them performed antics not unlike dancing. The idea of pursuit was the remotest from their minds. Half a dozen gaunt dogs crouched before the fire. No doubt the only scent they could catch then was that of roast sheep.

They had no horses, Clifton could see, and only the most meager of camp equipment. If there was a gun in the party, Clifton could not spy it out. The dark lean faces, the wild eyes, and straggling black hair, the brown bodies showing through rents in their clothes, the mouths opening and shutting, the tiny baby and the tender mother who looked hungry as a wolf herself—these stirred Clifton to pity.

A few rifle-shots would have scattered that group like a fox running among a covey of quail. They were going to have a feast. Clifton felt that he would not lift a hand to prevent it. Silently he crawled back, and rising behind the brush to shoulder his rifle he strode away across the desert.

"Poor peons!" muttered Clifton. "I wonder if God knows how full the world is of misery. . . . Old Don Lopez can afford to lose those sheep. If he can't, I'll pay for them."

He headed for the dark walls that appeared to shed luster from the stars. Weary though he was, he did not slacken his pace until he was several miles up the slope, and then he chose a secluded spot rich in sage and hemmed round by outcropping rocks.

It amused Clifton to consider this protected nook, which would insure him comfort for part of the night at least, as a reward for his generous act. There was abundance of dead sage all around, which, broken into bits, would burn like coals. He collected a goodly supply, then built a little fire against a rock. He roasted pieces of meat on a sharpened stick, and did not fare ill. He fancied, though, that he would be thirsty on the morrow, before he found water.

With his hand-ax he cut enough live sage brush to make a soft bed. That done, he sat cross-legged before the little white-and-gold fire, and divided his gaze between that and the stars. Both were intimate tonight. He was no longer alone. He, who had been so utterly wretched a few months earlier, now experienced sweet sensations in extreme fatigue. He did not desire to be anywhere else. College, the war, government, friends, and family had all repudiated him, cast him out, like the mother fox the black cub in her litter. Bitterness had gone from his heart. There were things on the earth no one had ever dreamed of. What man needed was silence, loneliness, to be helpless in agony, to accept death while fighting for life, to be in contact with the earth and the elements. There was something infinite in the stars. Here the stars that once had been pitiless now spoke to him.

He put more fuel on the fire. How it sparkled, crackled, burst into tiny flames! He recalled a fire he had once sat over in a trench, with a stinking dead man lying on the ice a yard away. Fire, man, and ice had left him unmoved. Here, however, he was thankful in his soul. He had erected a temple.

The desert wind sprang up. It moaned over the tops of the rocks and the tips of the sage. He was snug there. He toasted his palms and heated the soles of his boots. Fire-worshiper by night, sun-worshiper by day! They gave birth to such beautiful thoughts. He marveled no more at Julio, who could sit all day and look, and be happy; nor at the range-rider who never forsook the range, nor the lonely prospector his hunt for gold. They could never lose. Because it was the seeing, the searching, that brought joy.

He lay down, and his heavy eyelids refused to open again. He fell asleep. When he awoke stars and sky had changed, dimmed, grayed over. His fire was dead ashes. He rebuilt it, and warmed himself again. The night was ghostly now, strange, with a wailing wind, and the coyotes seemed like lost spirits.

Once he nodded and fell asleep over the fire, and awakening with a start he stacked on all his store of wood, and stretched himself upon the sage.

In February the cottonwoods shed their leaves, carpeting the ground with gold. Clifton and Julio were returning from a visit to other shepherds in the valley. Some of these got supplies from the border, and readily shared them. Clifton carried two sacks, and Julio one. Clifton laughed when he reached camp. What was a heavy burden to him? Daily for two months he had packed logs of firewood to camp. He was stronger than ever before in his life. He gazed at his brown arms and hands as if they belonged to a stranger. He felt his powerful legs, hard as iron. The wounds he had sustained were as if they had never been.

What little winter Guadaloupe Springs ever knew in the run of the seasons had passed. The dawns were cold, crisp, but no longer did ice film over the still pools. Day by day the frost lessened, until that morning came when there was no glistening white on the logs.

It was getting time to think of the long return trip back to San Luis. The sheep were full and fat and lazy. Lambing season was near at hand, a little while after which, when the lambs were able to travel, the journey north would begin. Clifton was jubilant over prospects of a large number of lambs. How pleased old Don Lopez would be! He had predicted a poor season for reasons quite beyond Clifton.

More than once Clifton recalled the news given him by the three sheepmen who had told him Malpass was negotiating with Lopez for this flock of sheep. Whenever Clifton thought of this, it rankled. But somehow he had a conviction that he would never again clash with Malpass. Still many of his instincts had faded here in this red-walled solitude. Where was the crippled, embittered, hopeless, and atheistic soldier of last year? Clifton was confronted with the surety of a future, but he shirked the thought of it. He loved this nomad life. And upon his return to civilization, if he found the same things that he had contended with before his recovery, he would come back to life in the open. It was impossible now and then not to wonder about his mother, but he did not waste any feeling upon his other parent. Virginia had become a sad and beautiful memory, seldom recalled now. It had hurt to think of her, and gradually he had overcome the habit. By this time she would have divorced him.

Lambing season was late, but Clifton had the satisfaction of counting a thousand new sheep. What good business it would have been if he could have purchased this flock from Lopez.

"*Grande! grande!*" cried Julio, clapping his hands.

Clifton shared his enthusiasm, and he enjoyed the sight of the little lambs. It seemed absurd, but no two lambs looked alike. At least Julio claimed they did not. Clifton, however, would not have cared for the responsibility of the mothers in this regard. The lambs were some variety of white and brown and black. Wholly black ones were rare indeed in this family. A few days after birth they were as lively as crickets. Clifton never tired of playing with them. One evening in camp he had a number he had picked out. There was a black one, with only the tail white. There was a white one with a brown and a black ear, a brown one with white face, and another with black feet. Some of them looked as if they were painted, especially one with a brown leg, a white leg, a black leg, and all the rest of him a combination of the three colors.

Clifton lingered at Guadaloupe because he was loath to leave the beautiful lonely place, and because the longer he stayed the stronger the lambs would be. Fortunately, he did not need to worry about grass and water. At first he would travel a day and then camp a day.

This planning somehow seemed to break his tranquillity, for when he once turned his steps northward, every step would bring him nearer to San Luis, to home, and to Virginia Lundeen.

But soon now he must return. The long two-month journey would seem short. Clifton pondered whether or not to give up this sheep-herding for Lopez. He did not like the thought of driving sheep near

San Luis and Cottonwoods. On the other hand, however, he had grown to love both the flock and the free life in the open. At some future day he might accumulate a flock of his own.

The sheep range back of San Luis was open to automobilists and horsemen. He would always run the chance of meeting them, and that was not a pleasant anticipation. Clifton Forrest—returned soldier! One of the principals of the Lundeen-Forrest secret marriage! Cast off by his father! A herder of sheep! Divorced by Virginia Lundeen! He hated the idea of being the butt of such scandal. Especially the last! But for that certainty he might find the return bearable. Yet it was so utterly ridiculous for him to resent a divorce. What wild dreams he had entertained!

It was not conceivable that he could stay away permanently from his mother. Not during her lifetime! That was the strongest magnet to draw him back. So there was no use to deceive himself with false hopes of avoiding the embarrassment which would result. Sooner or later he would meet Malpass again; and he did not trust himself. He was now physically twice the man he had been when he went to war. He felt like flint charged with latent fire.

He had no illusions about Virginia's being permanently forbidden her father's house. As soon as Lundeen came to his senses and found out Virginia was her own mistress, then he would implore her to return to Cottonwoods. Nothing else was conceivable. To be sure, he would insist that Virginia divorce her undesirable husband. And Virginia could purchase freedom from persecution by breaking this marriage. Clifton could not think these thoughts without discovering that the ghost of his old self hung upon his steps like a shadow.

As he and Julio had been the last shepherds to come to Guadaloupe, so they were the last to leave. Julio became anxious and alarmed. "*Mucho malo!*" he would say, pointing to the sheep and the north.

"*Mañana,*" always replied Clifton, and at last realized he must start on the morrow.

That night there happened to be a full moon. The air was almost balmy, like spring at home. The valley was flooded with silver light. Clifton could only force himself to leave by promising himself that he would come back. He walked under the cottonwoods, listening to the soft ba-ba of the lambs and the tinkle of the bells, and the music of water flowing over the stones.

He tried to gauge the change, the growth in himself, the transformation that had been wrought. But it was impossible. He recalled the war with only pity for those who had caused it and for those who had endured it. His late ordeal of physical agony seemed like a hideous nightmare, gradually fading. He conceived that he might one day think of it without horror. He confessed to himself that it was love of Virginia Lundeen as much as the magic medicine of the desert that had worked a miracle. They were inseparable.

He seemed to feel himself more than human as he walked there in the lonely solitude. The earth, with its rocks, trees, sages, water, its strange leaven and strength, had gone into him. Moreover, there were also the beauty, the spirit, the nameless fulfillment of nature that forever forbade him mockery or revolt.

The moon soared white, and fleecy clouds crossed it, to make moving shadows on the valley. The sheep quieted down, and only the stream gave sound to the wilderness. How infinite and incomprehensible the heavens! How sweet, all-satisfying the sense of his presence completing that lonely scene! He asked no more of man or God.

15

ARLY in November Virginia returned to Las Vegas and took up her abode at the Castaneda. She had been so engrossed in her project to investigate the Padre Mine that she quite forgot circumstances likely to accrue when she arrived. It was a small town, and in half an hour everybody apparently had heard of her return. When she had answered the telephone a dozen or more times she realized that she had achieved a popularity that was almost notorious.

"Well, this is the limit," she said, resignedly, as she sat down by the window. "I ought to have let Ethel come with me. Where was my head, anyhow?"

When she answered the telephone the next time she heard a familiar gruff voice that made her jump with surprise.

"Hello! Is this you, Virginia?"

"Yes. Who's speaking, please?"

"Lundeen," came the answer.

"Who?"

"Your father. . . . Don't you know my voice?"

"Oh—father! Excuse me. I didn't credit my ears. How are you?"

"Not any too damn good," he growled.

"I always knew you weren't. . . . How is mother? Have you heard from mother lately?"

"Yes. An' I heah she's some better."

"That's good. I'm very glad. She was always in better health in Atlanta."

"An' how're you, Virginia?"

This was an amazing prelude to something, Virginia reasoned, and it sent a tingle over her.

"Me? Oh, I'm fine! Thank you for inquiring."

"Reckon I'll run down to see you," he replied.

"You needn't. I wouldn't see you if I bumped into you on the street."

"Ahuh! Wal, I sort of had a hunch you wouldn't. So I called you up."

"Pray, why should I?" inquired Virginia, with faint sarcasm.

"Virginia, I'm shore sorry aboot it all."

"Indeed! What a pity! But it's too late."

"Lass, I'm not gettin' any younger. An' mother's gone. She'll never come back. I've a hunch I'll never see her again. An' I'm sort of lonely."

"But you have your slick Señor Malpass," returned Virginia, cruelly.

She heard him curse under his breath.

"Virginia, I'll take you back if you'll divorce Forrest."

"Divorce Clifton!" she cried, as if in great amaze. "I couldn't think of that. How can you ask?"

"But you don't care for him!" expostulated Lundeen.

"Why, daddy darling, I just worship Clifton!" rejoined Virginia, tantalizingly.

"My Gawd! An' I've lived to heah a Lundeen say that!"

After a long pause Virginia continued: "Well, is there any more I can tell you? I'm very busy."

"Hold on. . . . Virginia, aren't you hard up for money?"

"Indeed I am! But don't let it worry you."

"Wal, it does worry me. You never knew the value of money. You'll be borrowing from the hotel, or the taxi-drivers—anybody."

"Oh, so you think anybody would lend me money?"

"Shore. I reckon you'd be good at the bank for what you wanted. But I don't like the idea, Virginia."

"So you want to save your face by sending me some?"

"Wal, if you put it that way."

"Dad, I'd starve before I'd take two bits from you. Presently I'll get a job here. Oh, I can do 'most anything from stenography to millinery. I might borrow some money and start a millinery store. But, if I'm not so much as I think I am, I could at least be a waitress. Reckon I'd be an attraction at the Harvey lunch-room here. Or——"

"Shut up! I'd buy the place an' close it. Do you think I'd stand for a Lundeen——"

"Listen, papa," interrupted Virginia, sweetly. "You forget I'm no longer a Lundeen. . . . I'm registered here at the hotel as Mrs. Clifton Forrest."

Crash! He had slammed up the receiver. Virginia

fell away from her end of the line breathless, excited, and exultant.

"That'll do him for a spell. . . . Poor dad!—ready to crawl! If I can get anything on Malpass——Oh! what can't I hope for?"

Virginia's task of unpacking suffered intervals of inaction when she stood idly gazing out of the window at the distant white-tipped range. Her father's appeal had given the situation an unexpected turn. Anything might be possible now. The overthrow of Malpass, which she was planning and which was all she hoped for, now seemed but the beginning of the crucial step in her career.

She caught a glimpse of her face in the mirror and stared aghast. There was a glow in her cheeks, a half smile on her lips, a radiant light in her eyes long a stranger there. And these persisted when later she went out. She had no particular errand in mind, but she wanted to walk. The November air was cold; the leaves were gone from the trees; she saw the range bare and yellow, and snow on the peaks. Before she reached the park she encountered Gwen Barclay, one of her friends. Gwen's greeting brought a blush to Virginia's cheek and further augmented her high spirits. They talked a moment, and then parted with agreement to meet later. Virginia continued her walk, and returning to the business section of town, she met another of her old friends, Richard Fenton, who happened to be coming out of the bank.

"Howdy, Dick!" she said, brightly.

"Virginia!—Well, of all people!" he exclaimed, in delight. "Wherever did you come from?"

"Denver. I got in this morning. Hadn't you heard? I might as well have had a brass band."

"No, I hadn't. But I'm sure glad. Say, Virginia, you just look wonderful."

"Thanks. It's the air. I looked like the devil in Denver."

"Impossible. You've been with Ethel. How is she?"

"Fine. Announced her engagement. Nice little chap."

"You don't say. Ethel! Well, that accounts. She certainly had something up her sleeve. . . . Where are you bound for, may I ask?"

"Back to the hotel."

"Suppose you have lunch with me there?"

"Thanks. It'll be jolly. You can tell me all the news. . . . But, Dick, hold on. I forgot. I'm a respectable married woman."

"By gosh! I forgot, too. Mrs. Clifton Forrest. . . . That lucky son-of-a-gun! But do you know, Virginia, as I couldn't have you myself, I was glad Clifton was the man? None of us could stomach Malpass. And believe me we were all scared stiff. We were afraid if Malpass didn't get you, some one of those Eastern galoots would. Clifton is Western and the real goods."

"Dick, I like you for that speech," returned Virginia, warmly. "Come, I'll take you to lunch."

It was only a step round the corner to the Castaneda, where Virginia presently found herself in the well-filled dining-room, sitting with Richard, and not unaware of the interest she roused.

"So you didn't go to Reno?" queried Fenton, with good humor, though he was curious.

"Reno! Why there, for goodness sake? Denver is bad enough."

"It was rumored you went to Reno to divorce Clifton. Pretty generally believed, Virginia."

"Well, there's absolutely no truth in it. I suppose I have father and Malpass to thank for that gossip. As if there weren't scandal enough!"

"Personally I didn't believe it," went on Fenton, after he had given the waitress an order. "Your friends were ready to gamble that if you married Clifton, even to get rid of Malpass, you'd stick to him."

"Dick, did they roast me for it?"

"I don't think so. Sure no one ever did to your friends. You've had us guessing, though. Spoiled the romance by leaving Clifton behind."

"Did I? . . . Dick, I'm ashamed to ask you.—Do you know anything about Clifton? Where he is—how he is?"

"Virginia, don't you know?" queried Fenton in surprise.

"I—I—haven't the least idea," replied Virginia, her voice trembling a little.

"By George! The story went that Clifton got fired out of his home the same day you got yours. He disappeared. Naturally we all thought you had it planned to meet somewhere."

"No. I didn't see Clifton that day."

"Then there was neither an elopement nor a divorce. . . . Virginia, I fear the tongues will begin to wag again."

"Let them wag. I'll give them some more to wag about, presently. . . . Dick, do you think I'll be able to borrow some money?"

"From me? I should smile. How much do you want?"

"Child, not from you. But the bank. You're supposed to work there."

"Well, I imagine you could knock down any reasonable sum."

"I haven't any security. Of course I have my jewelry, Dick. I had to pawn some diamonds in Denver. Ethel was furious. But I couldn't touch her."

"You can touch father all right, even if he is a hard-headed banker. He always had a soft spot for you. Shall I ask him, Virginia?"

"Yes, if you'll be so good. I don't need any money right now, but I will soon. . . . Dick, I'm afraid I never valued my friends."

"Better late than never," he rejoined, lightly; and then, after a more general conversation, they finished lunch and parted.

She entered the lobby and a bell-boy accosted her.

"Call for you, madam."

"Telephone?"

"No. There's a man here who says his business is too important to be phoned or told to bell-boys."

"Indeed! Where is he?"

"He's waitin' inside. I'll call him."

In a moment he returned, escorting an awkward rough-garbed man who bowed to her, embarrassed but earnest, and said:

"Are you Mrs. Clifton Forrest?"

"Yes," replied Virginia, annoyed that she blushed.

"My name is Smith. I'm a sheepman. Today I was in San Luis an' I had a talk with Don Lopez. An' jest now I happened to hear you was in the hotel, so I made bold to ask for you. I reckon I've somethin' interestin' to tell you, if you can spare me a minute."

"Certainly. Let us go inside where we can sit down."

She scanned his weatherbeaten face with the scrutiny of an eager and hopeful, yet fearful interrogator. He was middle-aged, and his coarse garments reeked of tobacco and sheep. His boots were muddy. He had great hairy hands, that rimmed his sombrero nervously. His strong chin had not come in contact with a razor for some time. He had keen blue eyes that met her gaze steadily.

"Malpass is dickerin' with Don Lopez to buy his big flock of sheep," said Smith, as if the matter was one of vital interest to her.

"Yes?" returned Virginia, encouragingly, though she had no glimmering how this circumstance could affect her.

"I heerd of this a month ago, an' when I got back I went over to see Lopez. He an' me have had lots in common, an' I was shore he'd tell me. Yes, he says, ever since young Forrest went south with the big flock, Malpass had been dickerin' to buy it. An' Lopez wouldn't sell because the offer was low. Malpass is a low bidder on my stock. He drives the Mexicans, but he could make it a go with Lopez. Wal, considerin' the market jest now, Lopez will sell, but not too low. Now my errand here is a tip to you. I'm advisin' you to forestall Malpass an' buy thet flock from Lopez pronto."

"And why do you advise me to do this?" inquired Virginia, too interested to be aloof.

"Wal, I was the last to see them sheep," resumed Smith. "It was some four weeks an' more ago, when I was goin' out to a ranch. We run across your husband an' a Mexican lad drivin' this flock south. I had a good look at the sheep, an' sheep is my business. I'm tellin' you thet flock will come back mebbe a third more in number. If you buy from Lopez now you'll not only beat Malpass to it, but make a big profit. It's a pretty big deal for me to swing, as I'm aboot as deep in as I want to get, but if you don't jump at it I'm goin' to see what I can do."

"You say—you saw my husband?" queried Virginia, trying to appear calm when she was very far from it.

"Yes, an' I talked with him. He looked pretty sick, an' I advised him to give up thet long drive to Guadaloupe Springs. I told him what Malpass was up to."

"What is that?"

"Wal, I had the idee when I first heerd Malpass was dickerin' for the sheep. An' today I shore nailed it. Malpass never overlooks a deal to make money, but you can bet his prime motive in buyin' them sheep is to send a couple of herders down there an' fire Forrest. Like as not turn him loose without grub or tent! An' as I was sayin', Forrest didn't look so well to me. I reckoned he took this job sheep-herdin' on account of his health, an' it was a blamed good idee. For if he doesn't kill himself on the way he'd shore get cured at Guadaloupe. It's jest the finest medicine in the world. . . . So, findin' you was here, I jest made bold to give you this hunch. It jest shot through me, strange-like an' I hope you see it my way."

"I do. You are very good and I thank you. How many sheep in this flock and what are they worth?"

"I watched them cross the road, an' me an' my pardners gambled on the count, as we always do. We didn't agree, natural-like. But there's around three thousand head. An' ten thousand dollars will buy them. They're worth a good deal more right now. In the spring after lambin' there'll be—wal, I won't risk a figger, but I'll say it's a big buy. An' Malpass will grab it pronto."

"We will beat him to it, as you say," declared Virginia, emphatically, and held out her hand. "I shall lose no time. And I'd like you to call on me again—to tell me more about my—my husband."

"Wal, I'd be most proud, Mrs. Forrest," he returned. "But I'm leavin' today, an' I don't know no more than I've told you. I'll gamble, though, if you block Malpass' deal, Forrest will come home in the spring as husky an' strong as any young fellar around. Why thet's the perfectest place in the world! The water an' the air—they'd fetch a dead man back to life, almost."

"Good-by, then, and don't forget you're a friend of the Cliff Forrests'," returned Virginia, earnestly.

Ten minutes later she sat facing Richard Fenton's father, president of the Las Vegas Bank.

"I want to borrow ten thousand dollars," she announced, after greetings had been exchanged.

"So Dick was telling me," replied the elder Fenton, smiling.

"But when I mentioned borrowing to him I had no idea I would come so soon or ask for so much."

"He guessed it, then. For he sure said ten thousand. May I ask, Virginia, what you want with so much money?"

Virginia told him briefly.

"That's different. You must forgive me, Virginia. I imagined you wanted it for your usual luxuries. This is good sound business, outside of your desire to help Clifton. I'll lend you the money. The sheep will be ample security. I'd like to make that buy for myself."

"Give me something to sign, then, and a certified check. And if you'll be so kind—a little advice about the purchase of these sheep."

"Take Dick with you. He's our attorney, and he'll draw up a bill of sale to protect you."

Fenton pressed a button on his desk, while looking kindly and thoughtfully at Virginia.

"There! The color has come back to your cheeks," he said. "You were white when you came in. I like the roses best, lass. Long ago, when you were a ragged school kid, I took a liking to you. Used to watch you and Dick and your kid schoolmates. And not so long ago I hoped you might make Dick the lucky boy. But life teaches we can't have all we want. Like Dick, I'm glad it was Clifton. . . . I hope and believe all will turn out happily for you."

That night Virginia was so fatigued by the rough ride to San Luis and so stirred by the success of her venture that she could not enjoy her dinner. And afterward she was beset by her friends. She was dead spent when she crawled into bed, almost asleep before she stretched out.

Next morning she awakened rested, cheerful, eager. At breakfast she found an item in the morning paper, on the front page, anent the return to Las Vegas of Mrs. Clifton Forrest, who aside from seeing many welcoming friends, had found time to run over to San Luis and buy from Don Lopez one of the largest flocks of sheep on the range.

It was not the news that caused Virginia's face to burn, but the name in print—Mrs. Clifton Forrest! It gave her the most unaccountable sensation of mingled shame, pride, and ache. Yet she had to confess she liked the look of it in print.

Not so long after breakfast the hotel clerk rang her room, and said: "Your father calling. Shall I send him up?"

"No. I'll come down," hastily replied Virginia, surprised into that much of an armistice. She had wit enough, even though flustered, to think that her father could not very well bully her in the hotel parlor. As she went downstairs, however, she decided if he did try that, or if he had Malpass with him, she would promptly beat a retreat. And with that in mind, and a freezing dignity, she swept into the parlor.

Lundeen was alone and rose at her entrance. Pity had been farthest from Virginia's emotions, but the instant she saw his altered face and manner she felt it. His greeting seemed less stilted than hers. Perhaps he was less aware that others were present.

"I thought I'd better run down an' see you," he said, motioning Virginia to be seated.

"Yes?" answered Virginia, interrogatively. She looked penetratingly to see what purpose hid behind this unfamiliar front. There was none. He seemed strange, but as composed as she forced herself to be.

"I'll come to that presently," he replied, with dark unfathomable eyes on her. "I reckon I never seen you look better. Like your mother when I met her. Only handsomer." He sighed, and then tapped the newspaper he held. "I see you're goin' in the sheep business."

"Yes. But I was as surprised as anyone to see that in print."

He scanned the page. "Mrs. Clifton Forrest!— Where'd you get the money, Virginia?"

"I borrowed it."

"How much?"

"Ten thousand."

"You're no fool, that's shore. But I reckon you weren't lookin' to make money. Why'd you buy them?"

Virginia told him bluntly. His astonishment was not feigned. Then his expression changed and she could not gauge him so well, but she divined something of resentment, either at her or Malpass. Next his troubled gaze sought the floor, and he twisted the newspaper in vise-like hands.

"Virginia, I can take a beatin'," he said.

"Can you? First I ever knew of it," she returned, with a laugh.

"Wal, I shore can. An' I reckon you've beat me aboot this young Forrest. Will you tell me a few things —honest?"

"Yes, dad, since you make such amazing statement as that last," returned Virginia, thawing in spite of herself.

"You didn't marry Forrest only just to fool me an' Malpass?"

"Indeed, no. But I couldn't truthfully say that wasn't included in my motive."

"You care real genuine for him?"

"Yes, dad."

"You love him like—like your mother did me?"

"I hope it's that well. Mother has loved you wondrously, dad. Infinitely more than you ever deserved."

"I reckon it makes a difference," he rejoined, ponderingly. "You see, I never had any idea you really loved Forrest. Not till yesterday. Somethin' you said on the phone. It got me. An' it struck me that I hated young Forrest only because of his father. . . . So I've come down to surrender. If you'll make up with me I'll take back my demand aboot the divorce."

"Oh, dad—you surprise me!" she exclaimed, gladly. "That's good of you. It's big. It makes me think better of you."

"Wal, it's not easy to come to. But that's my stand. Will you forgive me an' come home? This means for him, too."

She touched his hand, almost overcome. "I do forgive you, dad. And I will come home on one condition—that you break with Malpass."

He jerked as if he had been struck by a stinging whip.

"Reckon I feared just aboot that," he returned, his voice breaking a little. "Virginia, I can't do it."

"Why not? Even if you had to sacrifice money it would be better for you in the end."

"It's not money, lass, though I'd hate to let Malpass get any more of mine. But I'd sacrifice if that was enough. . . . Virginia, he hasn't ever given up expectin' to get you."

"The conceited jackass!" ejaculated Virginia, in angry amaze.

"So he'd hang on to me like grim death."

"But, father, he's crooked."

"Shore. An' there's the rub. He has made me crooked, too. I was easy to lead, though, an' can't brag. But if I'd break with him it'd be my ruin."

"Father, has it ever occurred to you that Malpass might have been crooked with you?"

"What you mean, girl?" he demanded, gruffly.

"Might he not have cheated *you*?"

"No. That never occurred to me. I'd swear by him."

"But suppose he had. Would that make any difference? Would you break with him then?"

"Ha! I'd not only break with him, but——" he growled, and rumbled the rest in his cavernous breast.

Virginia shivered, but she had committed herself to this supposition and would not heed a warning. He rose to glare sadly down at her.

"Wal, then we split on Malpass again, an' for good?"

"Dad, we don't split at all," she replied, rising to face him and to speak eloquently and low. "I can't come back to you yet, but I'll live in hopes. You've given me back something of respect for you—perhaps more. That means a great deal to me. I thank you for it. . . . Let's not split. Don't be angry with me any more. I'm sure I can help you. Oh, dad, I know it. . . . Let's be friends—until——"

"Wal, I'll think aboot it," he returned, and strode away.

*N*EXT day at an early hour Virginia telegraphed Jarvis, the mining expert, to come on at once. That done she anticipated calm, but she was in a fever of impatience, hope, and dread. What a step to take! But the plan had been conceived in cold, stern reasoning. She would abide by it, come what might. Her return home, all the news about Clifton Forrest, and her father's incredible capitulation had stormed her emotions.

It helped somewhat to write to Ethel—a letter she dared not read over for fear she would never sanction such raving. This act, however, was keeping faith with her staunch friend; and the mere expression of the facts, fancies, and fears occasioned by her return mitigated in some degree their dismaying power.

In the afternoon she went to see a motion picture. It happened to be a Western melodrama of ancient vintage, and in spite of a cherub-faced hero and a doll of a heroine, a plot that had no semblance to any possible life on the range, a villain who was a perfect counterfeit of Malpass, miraculous hairbreadth escapes from flood, fire, avalanche and the glass-eyed pursuer, it diverted her mind, amused, disgusted, and thrilled her.

Dinner was an ordeal, and to woo sleep seemed futile. Yet at length she dropped away and dreamed Clifton returned well and strong and handsome, but would have none of her. Helen Andrews, after the manner of dreams, appeared from nowhere, ravishingly lovely and mad about Clifton. Dispensing with the formality of marriage, they were building a marble palace above Cottonwoods when Virginia awakened to the blast of a factory whistle. "Whew!" she breathed, grateful for rationality. Her face was damp and her body cold. What fiendish power some dreams had! Weird, grotesque, impossible life seen through an opaque distorting veil, it was yet appallingly real.

Virginia was out before breakfast to meet the train from the east, and to her great satisfaction, Mr. Jarvis alighted from it.

She was not insensitive to the fact that every move of hers in Las Vegas was sure to be seen by somebody. She had become public property, and though she believed the populace championed her, it did not seem politic to invite speculation about this delicate venture.

The quiet-eyed Jarvis might have been a detective who saw all yet gave no sign. Virginia was spared the necessity of speaking to him obtrusively. He carried a grip which he set down before the newsstand. And presently Virginia found opportunity to address him.

"I've had breakfast," he said. "Can I change clothes out at the mine?"

"Yes. Meet me in ten minutes back of the station. I'll be in a car."

Those were all the words exchanged and these swiftly in passing. Virginia walked up town to a garage and engaged a car, in which she rode back to the station. When she opened the door, Jarvis appeared as if by magic and stepped in. With that, Virginia's tension relaxed. She was practically certain no possible observer would have reason to telephone out to Cottonwoods, and that contingency was all she feared. At her order the chauffeur speedily drove away. Jarvis gave her a knowing look, accompanied by a slight motion toward the driver.

"No fear now," she replied, in relief that was pleasant. "I was afraid some one might phone out home."

"How far is the place?" he asked.

"About twelve miles. The old road up the last hill has washed away in spots. We shall leave the car and walk up."

Outside of town the chauffeur slowed up where the road forked. "Which one?" he asked.

"Left hand. Then about five miles out take the road to the right. It's up hill and rough. Go slow."

Jarvis leaned toward her casually and whispered that it might be wise to talk about the range, or ranches, or anything but the Padre Mine. "It's just possible I'd require another day," he concluded.

Wherefore Virginia made conversation which, if the chauffeur overheard, would not be significant. And all the while she gazed out at the autumn hills and the fading cottonwoods, and southward over the range toward far-off Guadaloupe, with her heart in her eyes, with fists tight in her coat pockets and slow-rising excitement. Jarvis asked questions about ranches, sheep, Mexicans, water, everything about which an ordinary visitor might be interested.

The car was really traveling slowly, but to Virginia it seemed fast. All too soon they reached the old road that led up to the mine. And when the car had ascended the first hill to start across a wide, bare bench, Cottonwoods was in plain sight. Virginia had not counted on this and she was startled. Anyone at the ranch happening to look up would certainly espy the car. Soon, however, she was relieved of this worry, for the road cut into rough ground.

Then followed a bumpy, uncomfortable, uphill ride for several miles until further progress for the car was halted by washouts in the road.

"We'll have to walk," said Virginia. "It's not very far. . . . Driver, you back down the road till you can turn the car, then wait."

Jarvis looked up the slope with the appraising eye of long experience.

"I'm afraid you're not a judge of distance," he said, dryly. "It's both far and steep. But you look good for it. I'm glad you wore sensible outdoor clothes."

Presently the ascent prohibited conversation. It did not appear possible to Virginia that trucks and cars had ascended this road. It would have been a hard haul for horses. At length they came out on the west bank of a great ravine, at the head of which and on the opposite side lay the Padre Mine. Jarvis remarked that a good deal of earth had been dug out and dumped on the ugly slope.

A long gradual ascent led to a short steep one

which, when surmounted, landed them on the bench before the unsightly, weathered structures. What a hideous blot on that mountain slope! Approached from above it had not been so stark and tremendous, for the reason that a good deal of it was hidden.

"Oh, what—a climb!" panted Virginia, looking back at her companion.

"You're a Western girl all right," he returned. "Now let's step out a little way on that trestle."

From this vantage-point, which did not appear wholly safe, the slash in the mountain-side could be seen in its entirety.

"I don't know how many tunnels and shafts have been dug," said Virginia, when she had caught her breath. "But the big hole there, with the track coming out, is where my cowboy, Jake, went in and found the gold."

"That's our objective, then," replied Jarvis, his keen eyes snapping. "Most interesting place. There's been a tremendous lot of labor here. . . . I wonder what that big shaft was sunk for." He pointed to a black brush-lined hole. "Queer sort of mining. But there probably was silver here."

He surveyed the several apertures that led into the hillside, particularly the one Virginia designated, and the endless dump-heaps of clay and gravel and shale, the rotting trestles and the rusty pipes, the dilapidated smelter below, half buried in deposits that had washed down from above, the shacks with their brown galvanized iron roofs.

"Mistakes are easy to make in anything that pertains to mines," he said, seriously. "But all this does not have a legitimate look."

"You raise my hopes," rejoined Virginia, with an anxious smile. "Please hurry. I must know."

"You won't have to wait long. I suppose I can get in one of these shacks to put on my overalls."

"We'll try the office. It's up here a little way—the last house. When I was last here the door was open. . . . Seems to me not a soul has been here since."

"Desolated and decaying—the story of so many mines!" he returned. "Money is not the only thing sunk in mines."

They found the office building as Virginia had expected, the door half broken from rusted hinges, and her little boot-tracks still visible in the dust on the floor. After a curious peep inside Virginia withdrew to stroll up and down the hard gravel bench between the rude structures. What a desolate place! She peeped through cracks in boarded windows and doors. Usually all too easy was it for her to weave romance, but she could not here. Even the indefatigable Ethel would have failed. All concerning this ghastly place, in the past and now, was grim nude realism. Greed had fostered it. No wonder it had brought misfortune to her father. What would it bring to Malpass? Retribution and justice had prompted Virginia to this course, but now there loomed the possibility of somber tragedy which she could not dispel. Padre Mine seemed under its spell.

Jarvis came out to interrupt her meditations. He had on blue jeans much the worse for wear. He carried a small pick, a lantern, and other instruments which gave him a formidable look.

"Better go inside and wait for me," he advised. "There's a chair. You can't be seen by a chance rider above. I don't believe I'll be long."

"Take all the time needful. Don't hurry. It means so much to me."

"If I were a gambler I'd say you'd win this deal," he returned, a bright gleam in his eye. "But I'm a professional mining engineer and jealous of my reputation. So I can't make rash promises. Nevertheless, be patient and hopeful."

"Thank you, I will," responded Virginia, calmed by his kindly words. He was sure, but he wanted physical proofs. She watched him disappear down the bank and then she crossed to the office building and went in.

It was a single, large, bare room, well lighted by the open door and a broken window. The floor was thick with dust and dirt, and in one place where rain had entered there was caked mud. An old iron stove leaned crazily on its legs. Sections of stove pipe were missing, but one piece projected down from the ceiling. There were an old chair, which obviously Jarvis had cleaned off for her, and some rocks in a corner, pieces of wood scattered here and there, a closet, empty except for Jarvis' coat, a rude board table in the farthest corner, and lying on it a rusty iron poker, considerably bent.

Virginia walked round and round the room, trying to still her nervousness and to find occupation for her mind. But she was not very successful. Here in this interior stalked the same skeleton which haunted the rest of the Padre Mine.

As the moments passed she grew more nervous, and scarcely could resist the desire to look at her watch. Yet every moment surely was helping to prove her contention. She sat down for a while, but only to rise and peep out, and begin again her restless pace to and fro. At last in desperation she surrendered to the one state of consciousness that could always annihilate the hours—dreaming of Clifton. It was a dangerous luxury which she seldom allowed herself, and then never for long. This case, however, seemed justifiable. If she did not yield to it, presently she would be tagging after Jarvis, to dirty her clothes, to risk being seen or hurting herself.

Where was Clifton this bleak November day? Tramping along behind his flock, a shepherd of the range. There seemed to be something uplifting and beautiful about all he undertook. Surely he was again torturing his poor maimed limbs. But how blessed the sheep-herder Smith, who claimed the desert would cure Clifton! Soon, surely, the period of pain would be past and he would begin to mend. She prayed for it. Then he would grow straight and strong again, with body in harmony with his fine mind and soul. How often did he think of her? She was his wife. Could he remember that and be indifferent? Would he always be so modest and blind as to believe she had not cared? Would he not be sorry she too had been turned from home, like him? Perhaps he had never heard of it. If the desert had magical properties to make him well, would it not also teach him love? Virginia trembled inwardly with that longing. Sooner or later they were bound to meet. Then what! Could she conceal her love—would she want to? If he did not take her in his arms and kiss her as she yearned to be kissed, she would fall at his feet.

Suddenly Virginia's sweet trance had a rude awakening. She had heard something in the direction of the slope. Jarvis had not gone that way. She listened—heard the thumping of her heart. Then thud of hoofs!

Violently she started up, to sink back in the chair, cold as ice, quivering in every muscle. Some one was coming on a horse. She tried to still her heart. A rider or a hunter presented no obstacle to her enterprise. Perhaps he would ride by. She could not be seen through the door, unless the horseman dismounted. She grew perfectly rigid in her fear—recognizing a fatality in the moment.

But the hoof thuds passed on by. Virginia breathed again, and relaxed. Then the thuds slowed—stopped. Every function within her except that of listening ears seemed deadlocked.

The horse started back toward the house. Virginia heard a low exclamation, then the solid footfalls of a man dismounting hurriedly. Her vital being surged with the rush of blood back to her heart, to leave her body dry and frozen like ice.

Quick sharp footsteps on the porch. A shadow entered. Following it a man crossed the threshold. Malpass! She could have shrieked at her infernal luck. When he saw her sitting there he halted dead short with a half step, one foot in the air. It dropped, to scrape on the floor. Upon entering, he looked for an instant as she had seen him a thousand times. The moment he espied her the transformation was immense and indescribable.

"For God's—sake! . . . Virginia!"

She kept her seat because she did not have strength to rise. But with certainty upon her, the icy inward clamp was released and she burned.

"What are you doing here?" he shouted, almost incoherent in a staggering amaze.

"That's no—concern of yours," she found voice to reply. Her mind grasped at straws.

"You're on my land. What do you mean? . . . You're up to something."

"Your land! That's another of your lies," she returned, and with scorn and rising battle she strengthened. He must be deceived and, if not that, held off as long as possible. Jarvis would return, perhaps was on his way now.

"Have you made up with your father?" he demanded, as if suddenly accounting for her presence and her apparent assurance.

"Yes. And this property is as good as mine."

It was a falsehood, but served its purpose. Malpass turned from red to white, and cursed Lundeen in impotent fury. Virginia gathered that all had not been so well between her father and this usurper. It gave her more nerve and cunning. Anything to blind him!

"So that's the trick? I've been double-crossed, eh?" he burst out, at the conclusion of his profane tirade.

"We are the ones who have been double-crossed, Señor Malpass."

"We?" he snarled, but he was again struck to astonishment.

"Yes. My father and I—and others interested in Cottonwoods."

"Your sheep-herder husband included. To hell with him! . . . I want to know what you're doing here."

"I told you—none of your business," retorted Virginia.

"I'll make it mine."

"You can't do it, Señor Malpass."

"Cut that señor stuff," he flashed, his black eyes

hellish. "I told you once before. If you call me that again I'll slap your impudent face."

"Evidently it fits you well—señor," she returned, contemptuously.

He fairly bounded at her, and cuffed her sharply across the lips. Virginia realized her blunder. She had overdone her part. She realized, also, that the blow roused the Lundeen in her.

"That will cost you something," she said, rising with her handkerchief to her lips, which were stained with blood.

"This deal is liable to cost *you* something," he rejoined, with a menacing glance at her that no woman could mistake. "Are you alone?"

"Certainly not. Do you imagine I'd come here without protection?"

His glance was one of doubt and suspicion. "Who's with you?"

"I advise you not to wait and see."

"You came in that car I saw below?"

"Did you see only one?" she countered.

He was no match for her in finesse and he gave that up in disgust. He peered out of the window, surveying all the ground possible. Then he went to the door to do likewise. Following this he began to scrutinize the dust on the floor of the porch, and like a hound he trailed Jarvis' footprints into the room. When he raised his eyes Virginia recoiled.

"Liar! You've got only one man with you."

"I have two men. But one would be enough," retorted Virginia.

"Some Las Vegas masher. He'd better steer clear of me. Are you going to tell me what you're up to?"

"Padre Mine has always had romance for me. Don't you think it natural I'd like to see it again?"

"Anything would be natural to you," he growled, his gimlet eyes boring into her. Manifestly he could not satisfy himself either with her speech or her look. Suddenly his roving gaze caught sight of the coat hanging in the closet. Leaping forward, he pounced upon it, shook it, and searched the pockets, pulling out letters and a notebook. Avidly he scrutinized them.

"George Jarvis, Mining Engineer, Denver, Colorado," he read aloud. *"Mining engineer!"*

When he wheeled to Virginia he was livid green. "You—you . . . Is that the man you fetched here?"

"I didn't say so," returned Virginia, coolly. His reaction to this name seemed damning evidence of his guilt.

"You meddling hussy! Talk, or I'll choke it out of you."

"Stand back!" cried Virginia. "If you dare to lay your vile hands on me——"

"You proud white trash!" he hissed, and the half-breed in him showed, as he backed her across the room until the table stopped her. "I'll do more than lay my hand on you. Tell me your business here."

"If I had any I wouldn't tell it."

She saw that he could hardly restrain himself from seizing her. And primitive fear mounted in her, equaling her anger. All of a sudden he snatched at her, over her raised arms, and catching her with iron clutch he let out a savage cry. Virginia screamed for help. Wrestling with him, she saw Jarvis run into the room. He halted stockstill to stare in utter consternation. Then he seemed to comprehend.

"Let go that woman," he shouted, and ran at them.

Malpass whirled like a wolf at bay, releasing Virginia and reaching a hand for his hip pocket. Virginia in a flash caught his arm. Then Jarvis was upon him, punched him in the face, tore him free, and swung him against the wall. Malpass' body, but not his head, struck so solidly that the jar floored him. Not to stun him, however, for he scrambled erect, facing Jarvis, his eyes deadly with the evil of a snake.

"Oh—Mr. Jarvis—look out!" panted Virginia, noting that Malpass sidled round between them and the door. "It's Malpass."

"Malpass, eh? I thought as much," replied Jarvis, wrathfully. "Explain your attack on this girl."

"So you're Jarvis?" rejoined Malpass, low and harsh.

"Yes, I am," flashed Jarvis, slowly edging toward him. Then as Malpass stood like a sullen statue he half turned to Virginia. "If he meant ill by you I'll beat him to a pulp. Tell me."

"He wanted—to know—why I came here," returned Virginia. "Swore he'd choke it out of me."

"That's what," snapped Malpass, curtly. He had made up his mind. "You tell it, Mr. Mining Engineer."

"You know damn well why she fetched me here," retorted Jarvis, not in the least influenced by Malpass' subtle change. "It was to have a look at your crooked work in this mine. And you can bet I found it. Of all the clumsy fool jobs of planting a mine this is the worst."

"The hell you say!" exclaimed Malpass, with the insolence of one who knew he commanded the situation. The look of him made Virginia's blood run cold, but it only the more angered Jarvis.

"Malpass, I've got the goods on you. You or your tools planted this mine with every grain of gold that has been taken out. The silver mining was a bluff. There was silver ore here once, but it played out long ago. . . . You're a cheat, a thief—if you're not worse, and I can prove it."

"You could, but you won't," replied Malpass, bitingly cold, and pulling an automatic gun he deliberately leveled it at Jarvis.

He shot three times in quick succession. Virginia heard the bullets strike something, the last with a soft sickening spat.

"My God! he's shot me!" huskily whispered Jarvis, in immense surprise. His hand fell away from his breast dripping with blood. His face changed, and then he crumpled in a heap on the floor.

Terror-stricken and mute, Virginia wrenched her starting gaze from Jarvis to Malpass. He was in the act of pocketing the smoking gun. Striding to the door, he guardedly looked out, to left and right. He stood there a moment, and nodded, as if to convince himself that Jarvis was the only man about the mine; then like a cat in his movements, he made again at Virginia.

"Murderer!" What her voice lacked in strength it made up in horror. She extended shaking hands at full length to ward him off.

"Do you want me to kill you, too?" he demanded, halting before her, his face pasty white, his eyes inhuman.

"Merciful God! . . . Would you—murder me, too?"

"I'll do worse unless you swear you'll hide what's happened here."

"Worse!" she echoed, and live fire seemed to touch her every raw nerve.

"You know what I mean," he rejoined, thick with passion, as he tore his tight collar loose from a black bulging neck.

Virginia understood him. The man stood revealed in all his monstrous baseness. The very hideousness of him probably was the one thing alone which could have shocked her from horror into savage and hot hate, into the spirit of self-preservation that was the most powerful instinct in her.

"Malpass, you'll have to kill me!" she cried, her voice rising.

"No, by God!" he shot at her. "I'll treat you like a peon slave! . . . You'll never lift your face again! . . . Then I'll make your father believe this Jarvis did it— and *I* killed him—because of that!"

"Insane monster!" flamed Virginia, and then she screamed with all the power of her lungs—a piercing sound that rent the air.

As Malpass lunged she darted away from the table, but too late to escape him, for he caught the sleeve of her coat. Whirling out of the coat, she left it in his grasp and ran for the door. She reached it, too, and the porch before he pounced upon her and dragged her back.

Virginia saved her breath. No use to scream again! If no one had heard the last, she could not hope another would bring succor. She had to fight for life and more than life. His intent and his soiling hands had made a frenzied woman of her, a tigress who would rend and tear.

But she eluded him. She got the stove between him and her. She preferred flight to fight, for she believed if she got out she could run away from him, at least down the road far enough to alarm the chauffeur.

Malpass kicked the stove down and leaped over it. He got her, but could not keep his hold. She left part of her waist in his grasp. She ran, with him close after her, always between her and the door.

His reaching hand clutched her shoulder, checking her, dragging her off her balance. Then like a beast he had her again. A terrific struggle ensued. She was as strong as he, and actuated by a passion as great. She came out of that struggle with her upper clothing torn to shreds, her bare arms bleeding from scratches, her white shoulders blackened by his sweating, dust-begrimed hands.

"You—hellcat!" he hissed. "The more you fight—the more joy I'll get—out of you."

Virginia was past words. She was in the grip of something terrible. No fear of this beast! No more flight! She awaited his next attack, panting, disheveled, crouching, like a cornered tigress.

He came on, and as ever, his intent was to hold, to weaken, to master her. And she beat and clawed at his face, and kicked. But Malpass broke through this rain and closed with her. His arms folded her back on the table and his weight augmented his advantage.

Virginia did not surrender or lose her wits. She was momentarily at a disadvantage. She ceased her struggles. Then her assailant, with a hoarse utterance, fell to kissing her face. He thought she was beaten.

She took that vile unguarded moment to fasten both hands in his hair, and dragged with all the strength left her. Like a dog he howled. Her right hand, the stronger, came away full of hair.

Then the table collapsed, letting them down and breaking his hold. Virginia rolled out of his reach. She had heard the ring of the iron poker on the floor. If she could get her hand on that!

But as she bounded up Malpass grasped her leg, tripped her, pulled her down into his arms. It had been his weight, however, that had handicapped her. Without that he simply could not master her. The whistle of his breath told that he was more winded than she. Not for nothing had Virginia taken those long climbs in Colorado! She fought more fiercely, and while her arms were free, with tight pounding fists. Then when he got her head down under his arm, pressing her helpless, choking her, she opened her mouth and like a wolf at bay she fastened her teeth in it.

Cursing horribly, he released her and she dropped to the floor. She rolled away. She felt the poker. Swift as light she snatched it. Leaped up! Malpass was on his knees. Bloody, bedraggled, dirty, holding the arm she had bitten, with distorted face expressing a fiend's defeat, with basilisk eyes betraying murder now, where before they had burned only with lust, he roused all that was virile and primal in Virginia.

She swung the poker. He ducked, but she hit him a glancing blow that rang off his skull. He toppled over with a thump that jarred the house.

Virginia heard other thumps. Heavy boots on the porch! In vain she tried to scream, but only a dry, thin sound issued from her lips.

A huge frame hurled itself into the room.

Lundeen! Like a black-maned lion he glared. Vir-

ginia staggered back. The wall stopped her. And with
legs buckling she slid to the floor. Her sight almost
failed.

"GOD ALMIGHTY!" thundered her father.

CHAPTER
17

VIRGINIA by supreme effort fought off faintness.

Lundeen stamped into the middle of the room. It appeared to the girl then that the squirming, groaning Jarvis halted her father. Jarvis was not dead.

"Who's this man?" boomed Lundeen, his great eyes popping half out of his head. "Virginia! . . . Malpass! . . . What the hell?"

Slowly Virginia gathered what force was left her. Deliverance had come, but the reaction of it gave her a deathly sickness, a sense that her flesh wanted to succumb and a consciousness that her spirit refused.

Malpass rose to his feet, a spectacle to make any observer blink. But he was not in as bad bodily shape as he looked. He moved easily, warily. He was thinking hard. Trapped, he still seemed to have latent power. His eyes narrowed to black daggers.

"Answer me," commanded Lundeen. "What's come off? Who shot this man?"

"I did," replied Malpass.

"He's dyin'. Why'd you do it?"

"I caught him trying to outrage Virginia."

"Huh?" ejaculated Lundeen, in blank stupidity.

Malpass repeated his assertion in stronger terms. Lundeen's jaw dropped as he stared at his partner, and then at Virginia.

"How come?" he asked, hoarsely.

Virginia bided her time. She would let Malpass have his say and then destroy him.

Malpass swallowed hard, and that part of his face not bloody or black showed ghastly white. He was at the end of his rope.

"I saw a car from town crossing the bench below," he said, hurriedly. "I jumped my horse and rode up here . . . found Virginia wrestling this man. Think he'd got the best of her! . . . He—he beat me up before I could pull my gun, but finally I shot him."

Suddenly Jarvis sat up quickly as if propelled, like a corpse revived to life, his eyes awful to behold.

"He lies!" The gasping voice was just distinguishable. "I caught him—assaulting her." He fell back and seemed to expire.

"Crazed by a bullet," said Malpass through ashen lips. "I've seen men act like that."

"More'n one crazy heah," muttered Lundeen, gropingly. The fact that he stepped so as to place his bulk before the door attested to the gradual trend of his thought.

"I tell you that's what happened," went on Malpass, sharply. "I'm all bunged up. . . . I want to get out of here—to a doctor."

He made as if to pass Lundeen, but was thrust violently backward.

"Stand back!" roared Lundeen. "Are you shore it's a doctor you need?"

"Lundeen, you'll cross me for the last time," returned Malpass, with threat in tone and mien.

"If I do, you can bet it will be the last time! Malpass, this heah deal looks queer. Keep your loud mouth shut or I'll knock your white teeth down your throat."

Malpass sank against the wall, quivering all over.

"Daughter, come heah," went on Lundeen.

"Dad, I can't. I'm too weak. And I'm torn to pieces."

"Ahuh. So I see. Wal, you're able to talk. . . . Are you hurt—the way he said?"

"No. He lied. I'm beaten and bruised, but I'm all right otherwise."

"Who stripped you half naked—an' blackened an' bloodied you up this heah way?"

"Señor Malpass," declared Virginia, ringingly. She saw her father's huge form swell, but he kept himself well in hand.

"How come?"

"Dad, last summer my cowboy, Jake, found signs of a salted mine here," replied Virginia, swiftly flowing to this denunciation she had prayed for. "When I went to Denver I consulted a mining engineer, an expert. Mr. Jarvis . . . Oh, I fear I've been his death! . . . Upon my return I wired for him. This morning he arrived. We drove out at once. Left the car below. We——"

"All a damned lie," interrupted Malpass, wildly.

Lundeen made a threatening gesture. "If you

don't shut up I'll fix you so you won't heah nothin'. Didn't you have your say? Let her have hers."

Virginia rushed on. "We climbed up here. Mr. Jarvis went to investigate the mine while I waited. . . . Presently Malpass rode up. He came in. He was astonished and scared. He had reason to be. I refused to answer his questions. He grew furious—tried to choke me into explaining. . . . Then Mr. Jarvis came back—caught Malpass mauling me—knocked him down. . . . He told Malpass the mine had been planted. That every grain of gold coming out of there had been planted before! The clumsiest cheat Jarvis had ever seen. . . . Then Malpass shot him! . . . After that he tried to frighten me into lying to protect him. Then, dad, on my honor, Malpass swore he'd degrade me—blame it on to Jarvis—give that as an excuse for shooting him. . . . Then we fought. Oh, I fought him. I wasn't afraid of him. He would have had to kill me. . . . But, dad, he couldn't master me. . . . He gave up that . . . he meant more murder. . . . I hit—him with—the poker! . . . And then—you came."

Lundeen gradually crouched, as a huge bat that meant to spring. His bushy hair rose upon his head. His arms lifted and bowed—his large hands crooked like claws.

"You—*planted*—THAT—MINE!" he bellowed in slow-swelling, awful voice. "YOU MANHANDLED MY DAUGHTER!"

"Yes, and I'll plant you!" Malpass thrust out the gun. It was steady. He had accepted the issue. There was only one way out. And the little gun began to crack—crack—crack spitefully.

But the bullets, though staggering Lundeen, did not stop him. Like a bull, lowering and blood-lustful, he plunged on. Malpass shot again, missing for the very reason that he aimed at Lundeen's head. One sweep of Lundeen's giant arm sent him spinning. But up he sprang, cat-like, to fire again. This bullet rang off Lundeen's skull to thud into the ceiling.

Virginia's ears filled with her father's mad roar. She saw him sway, beating the air, and fall with a crash. Malpass stepped over his body toward the door. Then Lundeen kicked with terrific force, knocking Malpass' legs from under him, and when he struck the floor the gun went flying across the room. Lundeen hunched himself with spasmodic full-length hops toward the gun, but Malpass beat him to it. And he shot again as Lundeen half rose to clutch his arm. There came a snapping of bones—an awful cry of agony.

Consciousness gradually faded from Virginia. But though her sight was dark, that horror filled her ears and beat upon her brain, until she fainted.

When she came to, the combatants were gone from the room. Jarvis lay with suggestive limpness. What had happened? She was too weak to rise. Had it all been a fearful nightmare? No—there was the man who had befriended her, prone on the floor.

From outside came sounds of scuffling—then again her father's roar, hoarser now, strangling in his throat.

Virginia crawled across the room and out on the porch, and fell flat as if she had been deprived of movement. Yet she could still see what had paralyzed her.

They were out on the trestle. Malpass' right arm hung broken. In his left hand he held a short club which he was swinging ineffectually on Lundeen's head, shouting maledictions in Spanish. Lundeen was not only being dragged, but he held on to Malpass like the grim death he meant and would not relinquish.

There was a branch trestle leading across the ravine. Not improbably Malpass had sought to escape by this. His struggles indicated that. When he reached it, however, he could not shake Lundeen off. He beat frantically, weakly with the club, until it bounced off Lundeen's head and flew out of his hand.

Then they wrestled and fought all the way to the tottering end of the trestle. It was broken there. The floor consisted of a few beams on rickety poles. It shook and rattled under them.

Malpass' fighting ceased, all his efforts bent to escape. His shrill wild cries attested to the doom he realized. Lundeen dragged him down, like a wolf at a crippled deer, on the swaying verge of the trestle. He knelt on him, and bent his head back over a beam—farther—until there came sudden, horrible break in that stiff strain.

Then Lundeen let go. Malpass slipped off the rafters and turned over to fall a hundred feet and thud soddenly on the rocks below.

Lundeen peered down. His shaggy head bowed, his broad shoulders sagged and sank, and his legs flopped over the beam that sustained them. He slipped and it appeared he would follow his adversary. But the weight of his upper body held him there.

Virginia got to her knees—then to her feet. Yes—he still hung there. How long had she watched? She held desperately to the porch post. They had destroyed one another. Awful retribution! She must keep on her feet—think of something to do. A gray cloud filmed her eyes—cleared away. There was an icy gnawing at the pit of her stomach. She could not un-rivet her gaze from that still form on the trestle, hang-ing limp. What was the thin, shiny, dark stream drop-ping, wavering at the will of the wind?

A groan freed her—quickened her. Jarvis must still be alive. She staggered back into the house—to the prostrate form—knelt beside it. He was living—conscious. He knew her. His lips moved, but no sound came. She thought he wanted water. His life might yet be saved. That thought lifted Virginia out of the abyss that had weighted her down.

She picked up her coat, and putting it on, started out, needing the support of wall and door and the porch posts. Leaving them for the open road, she fell, but got up again. Action responded to her spirit. She could make it down to the car. And she dragged her-self on.

She was crawling again, dragging herself round a bend in the road, when the chauffeur's cry roused her failing senses.

"My Heavens, Miss, what's happened?"

"Murder!—But I'm all right," she whispered. "Go quick. . . . Up the road. . . . Take water—whisky if you have it. . . . The last—house—door open—one man—still alive——"

Then she slipped into darkness.

*I*T WAS a rare and remarkable phenomenon of nature that definitely decided Clifton Forrest to spend his life on the desert.

At least this singular experience had clinched the matter. The process by which he had developed to such decision had been a long and gradual one, covering an extraordinary range of consciousness, from supreme agony of body to supreme ecstasy of soul. But it was sight of a comet or bursting falling star that at last won him forever to the desert and the lonely, free life of a shepherd.

The incident happened on the night of the thirty-sixth day—according to Julio's count—of their return trip from Guadaloupe Valley. Spring had come to the higher range, for this was in late April. They had reached the one dangerous stretch for sheep on all the long trail—a twelve-mile arid belt of lava, rock, and cactus, with only one waterhole, and that situated about halfway.

Clifton and Julio had arrived there at sundown, after a continuous drive on a day as hot as any in summer. If it had been a wind-blowing, sand-and-dust-storm day, many sheep would have perished. But it chanced to be still.

There had been no grazing that day, and for this reason the sheep were difficult to move. They strayed in search of something to nibble, and in that desolate region seldom found anything green which was not either poisonous or sharp. They bleated incessantly. The lambs also slowed the day's journey. They tired early. Through all the hot hours Clifton and Julio had packed a lamb, and often two lambs, to give them a little rest. Some puny and exhausted ones they had to kill. It was hard, but the lambs could not be left behind alive, nor could the flock wait. The shepherds would carry this one, then that one, put it down to take up one weaker. So that when they reached the end of this most trying link of the whole long chain of days it was not a moment too soon.

The thirsty, parched sheep baa-baaed and drank; the lambs tumbled into the water. Then many rested while the others went to grazing. The place was a wide hollow in black lava, through which a stream ran during the rains, and in dry weather clear pools remained in the deeper holes. There were grass and weeds enough for the sheep, but they had to be ranged for far and wide. The region was infested with coyotes, foxes, wildcats, which collected around a waterhole because of easy prey. There would be no sleep for the shepherds and their dogs that night.

After supper Clifton had taken one side of the

wide wash and Julio the other. The dogs were down among the sheep. Well those shepherd dogs knew their responsibility! The larger danger would be during the early hours of the evening, when beasts of prey were prowling about and sheep were ravenous. Ever and anon there would come a tiny bleat, wild and sharp on the air, suddenly quenched. That told a tragic story. One or the other of the shepherds always fired his rifle on these occasions.

Clifton's beat was a high wall of black lava, broken in many sections, resembling huge blocks of granite, mostly rough and difficult to walk over. He had to keep going all the time and maintain a vigilant lookout. A mile or more to the eastward this hollow closed, and here under the cliff there was always water, even during the *anno seco* of the Mexicans. Feed, however, did not flourish hereabout, because there was very little soil. The sheep would work up as far as this, and turn back, one bunch after another. Westward the hollow spread out into the bleak bare desert. Here was the greatest danger of losing sheep at night, because the opening was wide and rough.

On the whole the shepherds were very fortunate, for the reason that the bad hours passed with little loss, and toward midnight the sheep, weary and sleepy, and fairly well fed, massed in an open spot.

Clifton perched on a high section of the broken wall, in a seat he had occupied on the trip down. It resembled an armchair, and the only drawback was that it induced slumber. Julio was down among the flock with his dogs. Clifton could see the slight dark figure moving to and fro, seldom resting. Clifton had learned to love Julio. The taint of peon blood did not signify anything to Clifton. The lad was honest, simple, true; he loved the sheep and he loved the life. Many and many a time Clifton had caught him absorbed in contemplation of the heavens.

Clifton had long ago learned to study them himself. But seldom indeed did he have opportunity at midnight.

The night or the hour seemed portentous. There was no wind, yet Clifton heard a faint moan out of any direction to which he turned a keen ear. The rocks and blocks of lava still held the heat of the day's sun. For some occult reason the desert coolness had not set in. Clifton's brow was moist; he did not wear his sombrero, and he sat on his coat. The metal of his rifle was hot to the touch.

It seemed to him that the air was drying up. League-long strips of black cloud, strangely weird, lined the sky; and between them wan, pale stars shone. All objects near at hand looked opaque. There was an invisible mantle over the desert, and upon it pressed the sultry atmosphere.

The season was early for heat lightning, yet far to the north, where the range heaved, fitful flares lighted the bold black horizon, and faded away, leaving an impression of the vastness of the desert and the infinity beyond.

Suddenly Clifton became aware that the darkness was lessening. It amazed him. There was no moon. The clouds had not moved away across the sky to leave it open. Yet there was light all around. He heard Julio cry out to his saints.

Then came a sound like the low rush of wind in high grass. It increased. So did the light. Clifton whirled to see the approach of a comet or a falling star. He sat transfixed, with all functions but that of sight in abeyance.

How inconceivably swift its flight, its brightening radiance, its strange increasing roar! All in a second the desert became whiter than a noon of the clearest day. The rushing body crackled like particles of dry splintering ice. It passed by, a blue-white streak like the air-blown molten iron in a blast furnace, leaving a diminishing tail as long as the distance it had come. Suddenly it exploded into immense blue-white stars that fell, faded, vanished. The long tail, like that left by a rocket, lived for a moment, paled and died.

It was when Clifton recovered from this spectacle that his decision to remain on the desert crystallized.

After the decision came his brooding, pondering thought. The desert had made him a thinker. Solitude and loneliness inspired the mind. Cities, people, noise were inimical to the harvest of quiet thinking.

From midnight to dawn Clifton thought—of his boyhood, his early family life, his school days, his brief college career with its misadventure, the war. Of his travail, his love of mother, father, Virginia and his fight for their sake, of catastrophe—and then the desert!

What he might be at this moment, of course, he owed to all that had happened; nevertheless, the desert and its thousandfold mysteries had been his salvation. He could never become a normal useful member of society as the thing was taught in school and business, and harangued from pulpits, from benches and editors' chairs.

He needed to sit down alone with the elements. What he had gone through had left no bitterness now, no hate, no unrest, no scorn for the selfish, the ignorant, the brutal. He had seen behind a veil, caught just a glimpse of the infinite from which man had come and where he must go.

Clifton watched the gray dawn lighten. A rose bloomed over the eastern ramparts of the desert. Wisps of clouds grew shell-pink and burned to silver. Then a glory of red and gold stole over the lifeless reaches of the naked earth. He had eyes to see and a mind to think; and there the sheep bleated and the wide trail wound away. When he slid down from his perch he was whistling. It was good to be grateful, to have chosen irrevocably.

On the march northward that day he saw Old Baldy stick a white, round dome up over the rim of the world. It had the unreality of a mirage—the illusion that it seemed soon attainable. But for days the strange blue medium between Clifton and the peak that loomed over his home remained the same. It was distance on the desert, and it had never deceived him.

The closer Clifton came to San Luis the more proof he had of his tranquillity. Far back along the sheep-herders' trail he had left that phantom of himself—the frail, suffering, tormented past. He had rebuilt his soul on the rocks of the desert.

About the 1st of May the shepherds reached their permanent camp on the range behind Don Lopez' ranch, a few miles back of San Luis.

Julio had missed count of days, so that Clifton could only guess at the date. However, the cottonwoods said it was spring on the uplands and summer below. Clifton found cactus blooming and bunches of daisies. The sage appeared gray and forlorn after the long winter and needed rain that would come soon.

The summer range for Lopez' sheep consisted of valleys and ridges as far from Sycamore as the herders could graze the flock and get back the same day. Since the decline and almost total failure of cattle this range had been a boon to sheepmen. There had been snow during the winter, and the grass was coming out fresh and green.

Sycamore was the name of the camp at the head of one of the large bottle-necked valleys characteristic of this region. Water flowed from a narrow gorge. A few distorted old sycamore trees, pale white and brown, with many dead branches, and green leaves just starting, gave the spot its name.

The sheep knew they were home. Almost they rolled in the green grass. But they avoided the corrals and long chutes that led to the dipping-troughs. All except the lambs, and they had yet to learn of sheep-dip.

Clifton liked the place well. Years before, with boys from town, he had come here to shoot rabbits. Cottontails were more plentiful now than then, which was owing to the depletion of foxes and coyotes.

It was in Clifton's mind to start a flock of his own, however small it might be. Lopez, after the manner of sheepmen, would sell that fall. Clifton had seven months' pay coming, which, little as it was, would purchase a few sheep. He laughed at his wardrobe, which was on his back, a patchwork of his own mending. He would require a new outfit, for Sycamore was far removed from Guadaloupe. It would be fun, however, to let his mother—and anyone else, for that matter—see him in his present shepherd's garb.

Julio went singing away across the valley, taking the trail to San Luis. He was to stop at the ranch and report to Lopez, then go on to San Luis to see his people and return with supplies.

Clifton remained with the sheep. They had made Sycamore early in the afternoon, and Clifton, meaning this camp to be his home during the summer, pitched his tent with an idea of permanence. Up the gorge there was abundance of cedar brush, some of which he cut for his bed. He built a fireplace, and packed down a quantity of wood. His tasks this day, however, were broken by desultory spells, in which he gazed raptly over the hill. Three miles from San Luis—five from home—six from Cottonwoods! Incredible! He could not keep from wondering, longing, hoping. These were emotions which must abide with him the rest of his life. He wondered about those he loved, he longed to see them, he hoped for their well-being and happiness.

All afternoon he alternated between long periods of labor and short ones of idle speculation. But the sum of his work resulted in a most comfortable, picturesque camp.

Sunset and evening star! Always different, always the same! He ate supper beside his lonely camp fire. Always the sheep-herder would be lonely, no matter where. The lambs were bleating, but the dogs were quiet. All was well with the flock. And with him.

He went to bed early. The cedar fragrance in his tent was sweet, and he thought how pleasant it was to stretch out and lie still. He was not haunted by the proximity of kith and kin. And when, with the closing of his eyes, he dropped to sleep, it was not to be untroubled by dreams. Nor did the sheep-herder who walked all day in the open, in sun and wind, wake before the dawn.

While Clifton ate breakfast, which was an apology for a meal, and later than usual that morning, the dogs set up a clamorous barking, so unusual that it startled him.

He espied Don Lopez riding across the green flat toward his camp. Then a rush of blood throbbed to Clifton's temples, which, slowly receding, left him cold. He had been absent seven months. A long time in the life of elderly people! Fateful and mutable lapse of days for a girl in her twenties!

"Don Lopez!" he murmured, gladly, yet with reluctance. "He will tell me everything—if only I can understand him!"

19

*T*HE selfsame hour that Clifton Forrest arrived at Sycamore that golden early May day, Virginia rushed out of the house, possessed by she knew not what. Indeed, she had been possessed ever since she had taken up her abode in the old home where as a girl she had played and wept and dreamed her girlhood away.

She could not stay indoors, despite the work that had fallen to her hands. The day was gorgeous, lovely, like one of the amber-tinted, white-clouded, pageanted June days in the East. The cottonwoods, fresh and thinly green with their new leaves, called to her in an unknown potent tongue. There was something in the air, beyond her ken.

Virginia had been distraught for long, waiting for him she called her shepherd to come home. But it had been a wholesome counter-irritant. Only lately had the aftermath of the tragedy of her father's end left her to take up the threads of the future she prayed for and dreamed of. Sorrow would always abide with her, and remorse. For though her father had been the tool of an unscrupulous villain, he had at the last been true to the blood of the Lundeens.

Every day had been a little easier to bear. Summer was coming. It would not be long now until——
And she would try to still her aching, throbbing heart. Ethel would be coming soon—after what seemed ages of separation.

She wandered restlessly under the cottonwoods, catching at the white thistledown cotton that floated from above, as if it bore hopes to clasp to her bosom. She kept out of sight of Jake and Con, who were working round the barn. She did not even glance out into the green valley where the last and best of her horses grazed. She sat by the irrigation ditch and trailed her hand in the cool clay-colored water that came sliding and gurgling along under the grassy banks. A few violets lifted wistful purple faces out of the green. She could not linger there long; the music of the water and the melody of birds grew unbearable. She dared not venture back into the garden, to that secluded corner by the broken wall where she had lured Clifton to ask her to marry him. She had gone there only once since coming to live here.

She strolled away. She stood watching the white sails in the sky. Her hands drooped idly. She saw nothing—heard nothing. Then the cloud-rimmed mountain peaks gave her a pang. She must go up to her shrine at Emerald Lake. There would be strength in the solitude and sublimity of the heights. But she could not go until——

The beauty and mystery of the day stung her. Of

what avail to live, to be young, healthy, handsome, longing—to look back at sadness, and fear a gray uncertainty of future?

It had been only of late, though, Virginia reflected, that she could find no peace, no occupation. There had been incalculable happiness, upon her return from Georgia, in deeding Cottonwoods to its rightful owners—the Forrests. That had been no easy task—not for her to surrender, but for Clay Forrest to accept. In the end she had won him. "You girl—you Lundeen," he had said, brokenly. "First my son—then his mother! An' now I, too, must love you!"

With hatred overcome, and the recovery of his beloved Cottonwoods, Forrest became a transformed man. The years of his exile were as if they had never been. To do him full justice, though, Virginia had been compelled, and gladly, to admit she could never have won him to accept her sacrifice had she not told him that the estate in the south left by Lundeen had enriched her far beyond and outside Cottonwoods. It had been her whim to bind Forrest to secrecy for the present.

She had gone back to the old adobe home in the cottonwood grove, and asked no more than for Clifton to seek her out there. But would he? How endlessly long these last weeks! Was he dead? Her prophetic and loving heart could not abide that possibility. She knew, and the torture was only fear that he might not want her. Where had gone the old vain coquetries and audacities?

Virginia dragged herself back into the house, to try to take interest in the work of creating beauty and comfort there. For a while she shared the efforts of her two Mexican women servants, but soon she grew listless again. Her little room claimed her for hours by day as well as by night. It had been Clifton's room, too. The few things he had left there had never been moved, or touched, except with reverence, for they were relics of his boyhood, his brief days at college, and of the war. She had made no change in this room. She trembled whenever she lay down on that old bed. The hard hair mattress had the same sag in the middle as when she was a girl. It used to hurt her back. As long as she could remember it had been there. And Clifton had lain there night after night, his mother had told her, sleepless and racked with pain, staring into the blackness, listening to the patter of the leaves outside and the murmuring water.

"I'll be all right when he's back, even if he doesn't come to see me," she sighed, and clenched her hands, and gazed up at the blank, dark wall.

And next day, Jake, returning from an errand to San Luis, informed Virginia that Clifton Forrest had come back with her sheep.

"My sheep!" cried Virginia, in rapture, and silent gratitude to God. But she was thinking of her shepherd.

"Eight hundred lambs, ole Lopez said," went on Jake, grinning. "He shore was sore for sellin'. Thet was a plumb good buy of yours, lady. An' with sheep jumpin' on the market you're settin' pretty."

"Did—did Lopez say how—how Clifton was?" asked Virginia, tremulously.

"Never nuthin'. Lopez is a talky ole cuss, too, but he was shore stumped about them eight hundred lambs."

Virginia rushed away to the green covert of the cottonwoods, where she felt unseen even by the eyes of birds. And there she wept for joy, and raged at her weakness, and paced the walled aisle, and whispered to herself, and at the sound of her voice betrayed herself utterly.

"Oh, he's back—he's back! Thank God! . . . It was time. I'd soon have died. . . . He must be well again. Seven months on the desert! Alone! Ill and weak when he left! O God! Poor brave boy! And I could not help him!—Oh, how I love him! He must know! . . . But if he doesn't know—if he doesn't want me—his wife!—what can I do? I can't crawl to him, like a dog to lick his feet. But I want to—I want to."

She felt the better for her outburst, for the facing of her soul. That he was alive—strong enough to toil as a sheep-herder for over half a year—that he had come home—was near her—only a few short miles across the hills!—these facts mastered her selfish longings and stilled the troubled depths of her.

Virginia decided there was no understanding human nature. First she had prayed that if only Clifton would live, she would be forever grateful and satisfied. Then it was for his return. And now that he was home, she yearned irresistibly to see him. How little she divined the complexities of love! What would she want—nay, more terrifying, what would she do when she met him?

The following morning she drove to Las Vegas to meet Ethel, who was coming on the early train, and timed her arrival so that she would have but few moments to wait at the station. Since her return from Atlanta, and the change in her fortunes, she had avoided town and people as much as possible. There had been many a nine days' wonder over the Lun-

deen-Forrest feud, but her relinquishing of Cottonwoods had made her the subject of endless gossip.
She did not care to run the gauntlet of acquaintances
just yet.

When the train pulled in, Virginia scanned the
Pullman vestibules with eager eyes. Soon she saw
Ethel appear on the step, trim, dainty, like a butterfly
in her spring finery. She looked anxiously up and
down the platform, and did not espy Virginia coming
toward her from the parking place. There were other
passengers, trainmen, and loungers present. Ethel
pointed out her several pieces of baggage to the porter, which momentary lapse enabled Virginia to slip
up behind her and put both hands over her eyes. She
felt Ethel shake and whirl. Otherwise the meeting was
the only solemn one they had ever had.

After the porter lifted the baggage into the back
of the car Ethel, still holding to Virginia and piercing
her with hungry eyes, opened the dammed gateway of
her speech.

"Oh! . . . you perfectly stunning Virginia!" she
burst out. "You lovely marble thing! . . . Where's
your old tan—and the red of your cheeks? You're pale.
You've thinned out. And that's all you needed to beat
Helen Andrews two ways for Sunday. . . . But your
sad, sad eyes! Poor darling! if you haven't had the
rottenest deal! . . . Oh, Virginia, I'm so glad to see
you, I'll cry my eyes out."

"So will I, honey, but let's wait till we get out
home," replied Virginia, conscious of a sudden sweet
and wonderful warmth. It had not occurred to her that
Ethel would be the best medicine in the world. Now
she knew it. She took her seat in at the wheel, and
Ethel got in beside her.

"Just one word, darling, and a question," said Ethel, "after that it's all you."

"I think I can guess," replied Virginia.

"But you're not smiling. . . . Virginia, I'm to be married in June."

"Marvelous! I congratulate you. I'll be happy with you."

"Will you come to my wedding?"

"I surely will. How could you be married without me?"

"I couldn't. That's why you've had me guessing. Virginia, do you know I've had only two letters and one telegram from you in seven months? . . . Seven months!"

"But, honey, how could I write, even to you?" implored Virginia.

"It would have been better for you. But you always were a strange, close-mouthed creature. I think I understand and I forgive you."

Virginia drove out of town on the San Luis road, which was far from being a thoroughfare.

"I'll make up for my neglect," returned Virginia, humbly. "I'll talk you deaf and dumb and blind."

"I had your letters, as I said, and of course I read what was in the papers. You need not rake up that horrible——"

"But I shall," interrupted Virginia as her friend hesitated. "It will do me good to talk."

"I met Mr. Jarvis yesterday. He asked all about you. I told him I didn't know much, but I would soon."

"How is he now?"

"Oh, he's completely recovered."

"I am very glad," said Virginia.

"Virginia, were you hurt in—in that fight?" asked Ethel, anxiously.

"I should say I was. Scratched—beaten black and blue! He even bit me! Uggh! . . . I'll tell you all about it some day."

Virginia could see that her faithful friend was repressing all kinds of explosives in consideration for her feelings. But Virginia would not have minded anything now. The ice was broken. She had been too long choked by her own inhibitions.

"Say, this is a swell road, if you don't know it. Where are we going?" remarked Ethel.

"Home."

"But this isn't the way to Cottonwoods."

"I don't live at Cottonwoods any longer."

"Oh, I see!" rejoined Ethel, bursting with curiosity. "Is your mother with you?"

"No. I left her in Atlanta."

"How is she?"

"Pretty well. I spent three months with her. I don't think she will ever come back to the West. She likes her old home best and has better health there. My grandfather and grandmother have a fine plantation just out of Atlanta. I like it there, too—for a visit. But give me the desert."

"Well, dearie, it's better news than I expected. I was afraid your mother would sink under that calamity."

"No, she didn't. Of course she never heard any but the barest details."

When they crossed the lower end of the valley below San Luis the whole wonderful triangle of green led up beautifully to the impressive white-and-red mansion on the bluff. Cottonwoods shone clear and

stately in the sunlight. Virginia saw it without a pang.
She had never been happy there.

"It's so lovely—everything, I mean," murmured
Ethel. "I don't blame you, though, for not living at
Cottonwoods just yet."

"I gave Cottonwoods back to the Forrests," said
Virginia, quite casually.

"*Virginia!*" cried Ethel, and with a flop sank back
in her seat. She had been prepared for revelations, but
this was too much. For the time being she was
crushed by the catastrophe.

They drove out of the valley, through the sleepy
little town of San Luis, past the spot where the blackened walls of Clifton's store still stood, and up the
shaded, dusty country road where nothing had
changed. And at length under the old weatherbeaten
Spanish gate and into the green-gold grove where the
vine-covered adobe house stood, surely in Ethel's
eyes memorable of Clifton Forrest and inseparable
from his story. Virginia's heart was full. It was
strangely sweet to bring her dearest friend here. Ethel
was pale, her eyes were wide and brimming with
tears.

"You live here?"

"Yes, honey."

"Alone?"

"I have two servants. Jake and Con have a cabin
below."

"It is—lovely," concluded Ethel, with trembling
lips.

"I like it better than Cottonwoods. Come. We can
carry your bags in. You take the lighter ones."

The room into which Virginia led Ethel had once
been her mother's and later Mrs. Forrest's. It was light

and fairly large. Virginia had furnished it most comfortably, in harmony with the old-fashioned walls and beams, the open fireplace and the Spanish windows.

"One wouldn't think it was so nice—from the outside," murmured Ethel, as she divested herself of gloves and hat, and fussed with her pretty blond hair before the mirror, significantly keeping her back to Virginia. Presently she turned a convulsed little face and eyes streaming with tears.

"Gin—ia, I'm going—to bawl."

"So am—I," choked Virginia, and spread wide her arms.

A little while later, after donning comfortable clothes, in fact the same in which they had run and romped and climbed in Colorado, they went outdoors.

"I'm from Missouri," said Ethel, slangily. "You gotta show me. How big is this jungle?"

"About ten acres of grove, some valley meadowland, and fifty acres running up over the range."

"Not so poor, for Bertha, the Sewing-machine Girl."

Eventually they wound up tired and hot and happy on a shady knoll under a giant cottonwood that spread its wide branches on the edge of the valley. The view was open and the mountains stood out splendidly and close. But Cottonwoods could not be seen for trees. The irrigation ditch flowed down here, and by reason of the little slope, made swift gurgling sound. There were innumerable bees humming over the stream, among the blossoms of a flowery vine.

Ethel gazed out over the meadow at the graceful, glistening horses. "Oh, what horses! You must take me riding every day. I miss riding so much at home in

Denver. Sure we're Western, but a horse is rare these days. . . . There's Calliope and Moses and Calamity. . . . Oh, I see your grand black Sirius. Some horse! If only I could straddle that stallion! . . . And there's Dumpy—the little pinto that threw me, darn his dusty hide! . . . Virginia, you can't be so awful poor, or you couldn't take care of those horses."

"I'm not so *very* poor that I can't give you a ride occasionally—and a wedding present in June," returned Virginia.

"You darling! Now if you go blow yourself on me I'll never forgive you. But it seems strange for you to be poor at all." Ethel fell back with a sigh, her head in Virginia's lap. "Tell me your story backward."

"You mean from present to past? . . . Well, to begin with—Clifton is back," rejoined Virginia, averting her face.

"Back? Where'd he go?"

"When his father turned him out he became a sheep-herder."

"What! Cliff Forrest a sheep-herder? You mean a shepherd?"

"Yes," replied Virginia, dreamily.

"But isn't that a poor job for a white man—a college man—a soldier?"

"Poor, yes, in a matter of wages. But Cliff had no choice, and besides I think he went for his health."

"Say, angel-face, turn round here and look at me," said Ethel.

Virginia complied.

"Oh," cried Ethel, "then all is not well between you and Cliff?"

"It is—for my part. But I've never seen him since that time—nor heard from him. He drove the sheep south. . . . Upon my return from visiting you, I heard that Malpass was dickering with Don Lopez to buy the flock Clifton was driving. Malpass' motive was not solely a business one. He wanted to acquire possession of Lopez's flock so he could send a herder out to Guadaloupe and throw Cliff out of his job. Leave him all that distance to come back alone and without supplies."

Ethel swore. "I'm sure going to get a kick out of your story of how your dad killed that *hombre*."

"It was horrible!" said Virginia, her flesh creeping and tears coming into her eyes. "Malpass shot father I don't recall how many times. Five bullet holes, I think, the inquest reported. . . . But father broke Malpass' arm—nearly tore it off—and then cracked his neck . . . dropped him off the high trestle."

"Served him right," replied Ethel, fiercely. "But never mind that now. Tell me more about Cliff."

"There's very little more. I borrowed money and bought the sheep from Lopez. And Cliff drove on to Guadaloupe never knowing."

"You amazing girl!—All the time, then—for it was early last fall when you left me—Cliff has been working for you?"

"Yes. It's funny."

"Funny! It's great. Shepherd of his wife's flock! And never knowing. Say, if that isn't a romance, I don't know the real thing. . . . Say, darling, sure you raised his wages?"

"Don't giggle," entreated Virginia. "I'm scared to death. . . . You see, Clifton has just come back. He must know now that all the winter—seven months— he has worked for me. . . . Sheep-herders are poor.

He'll need his wages. And if he doesn't come for them —what on earth shall I do?"

"Goose! Take them to him."

"Ethel, I absolutely couldn't do that," expostulated Virginia. Then she felt a tender hand stealing up her arm, along her neck to her cheek.

"Look down at me, dearest," said Ethel, softly.

Virginia surrendered then and betrayed herself to the wide, shrewd, loving eyes of her friend.

"You love Cliff still?"

"Still! What do you think I am?"

"I think you're an angel. . . . Then you love him more?"

"I don't know how much it *was*, but it's killing me now."

"*Virginia!*—Why, for Heaven's sake? You ought to be tickled pink! It's something to be able to love a man these modern days. Ask *me*. . . . Dear, are you concealing more from me?"

"I don't think so. Anyway, if I am it'll come out soon. You'd get blood out of a stone. . . . I'm just scared, Ethel. . . . It has been a long agony for me, since last fall. I'm all right now, except—I—he—oh, well, I want him, I *want* him—and if he doesn't want *me*—I—I'll drown myself in the ditch here."

"It's a cinch," yelped Ethel, ecstatically.

Virginia wiped the dimness from her eyes and stared down at this galvanizing scion of modern feminism.

"Cinch?" she echoed, stupidly.

"That's what I said, Desdemona. You're so modest you make me sick. Good Heavens! Girl, I'll bet he went off on that sheep-herder job just to think and dream about you. Of course you never had the nerve to give him a hint you loved him."

"I was so afraid I would—it made me queer, cold. . . . But I led him on. And he asked me to marry him because he thought I wanted to use him as a convenience. To save me from father's machinations with Malpass. . . . No, poor fellow, he never dreamed I was crazy to be his wife."

Ethel let out a peal of silvery, happy laughter. "Oh, it's rich! I'd love to be in your boots. Think of how glorious it'll be to *tell* him! I'd have had it done by now."

"Oh, you—you callous girl! How can I tell him?" cried Virginia.

"You've got eyes, arms, hands—and lips, everything, all about as perfect as nature bestows upon a woman."

"That's nonsense. But suppose I have?"

"Use them. You darned fool! Didn't you fight Malpass?—Well, fight Cliff in another way. It's a woman's prerogative. We're no longer vassals of men. We don't have to wait. But since we're so soft—since we have to love a man—since we must be mothers, it's self-preservation or destruction."

"Ethel, I sent for you to help me—not drive me mad," replied Virginia, piteously.

"Now, dearest Virginia, I am in dead earnest," returned Ethel, suddenly starting up. "I wouldn't hurt your feelings for the world. I'm just taking an extreme view of your trouble. I don't really believe it's bad at all. I honestly think Cliff is as much in love with you as you are with him. And you bet I'll know after I see him."

"See him? Are you going to?"

"I am. Or I should say *we* are."

Virginia covered her face with her hands. "Let us wait a little. He might come—to me. That would help so. . . . Ethel, you don't know all about it."

"Ahuh! I thought so.—How can I help you when I don't know anything?"

"I am disgustingly rich," confessed Virginia. "Father's holdings in the south brought a great deal of money. And there's more to come. No one here except Mr. Forrest knows it. I made him swear not to give me away. I took this place in exchange for Cottonwoods. I kept a few horses, a car, and some help just so I wouldn't look too awfully poor. But that Payne ranch at Watrous is mine. All the rest of my horses are there. And there's other property in the estate. I simply can't conceal it for long. That's another thing that scares me."

"Mrs. Clifton Forrest, may I inquire why in the name of Heaven that should scare you?"

"Clifton once said he could never take anything from me. And when he finds out I'm not poor—that I've barrels of money, he'll not want me."

"Then he'll be a darned queer *genus homo*."

"But, Ethel, you don't know Cliff."

"He belongs to the male species of our generation. You're his wife. You're a lovely thing—perfectly dippy about him. Considering these facts, I hardly think he'll cast you off when he finds you've got barrels of coin. Men are not that way. Do you want to know what my sweetie would do in such a case?"

"What?" asked Virginia, dubiously.

"He'd proceed to blow some of it pronto."

"Cliff won't," replied Virginia, dejectedly. "I'd be in the seventh heaven if he would."

"Very well, Melancholy Mag," said Ethel, with wise resignation. "We'll proceed from your angle. We'll get good and serious. We'll plan to win Clifton. But we'll go slow. Consider the whole matter from Clifton's point of view. You can rely on little sister to dig that up. If he doesn't come to see us soon, then I'll plan to see him—quite by accident. After all, it's a matter of love. We're not trying to put over any crooked stuff. We'll think always of his pride, his sensitiveness, his suffering. Now, old Owl-eyes, how does that suit you?"

"It's better," said Virginia, coming out of her trance.

"Thanks, Pollyanna. Meanwhile we must do things. We'll ride and climb and drive. Have a perfectly spiffy time."

"But suppose I—we would be absent if—if Cliff came," faltered Virginia.

"Help! Help! . . . Virginia Lundeen Forrest, I tell you I've got to pull this off my own way or have a lunatic on my hands."

A *STEP* on the dry cottonwood leaves startled Virginia, and even before she moved a familiar voice thrilled her:

"Howdy, daughter!"

Leaping up, blushing scarlet, she saw Clifton's father right upon them.

"Oh, Mr. Forrest, you—you gave me a scare."

"Wal, I'm sorry. The cowboys steered me down here. I sort of hated buttin' up your pretty little party, but it's kind of important."

"Ethel, this is Clifton's father . . . my friend, Miss Wayne, from Denver."

"Think I once met you before, Miss, but I'm shore glad to meet you again," replied the rancher. "Suppose we—all set down. It's nice here."

"Virginia, if you'll excuse me——" began Ethel.

"Don't run off, young lady. I reckon, judgin' by

your looks, you'd make a handy helpmeet. An' I'm shore goin' to need one."

"Very well. You're a good judge of character, Mr. Forrest," said Virginia, with a laugh. "Ethel, you're elected to stay."

Forrest sat down with his broad back to the tree, and he laid his hat aside. Virginia had never seen him look so well. He was ten years younger. The somber shade had gone from the dark hazel eyes that were so poignantly like Clifton's. He was clean-shaven and neatly garbed.

"Wal, it shore ain't easy to begin this confab," he said, with a smile that made him winning. "But I reckon I've got to."

"I am all curiosity, Mr. Forrest," returned Virginia, who was thrilling all over. "Not to say sympathetic."

"Lass, I've been out to see Cliff," he announced, tragically.

Virginia's hand flashed to her breast, and her eyes and lips must have added to that gesture.

"Aw, don't look scared. Cliff's all right," he added, hastily. "Fact is I had the jar of my life. I never was so surprised. He's well!—He's a strappin' big fellow, dark as an Indian. I just couldn't get over it. . . . Now, Virginia, for that good news you shore ought to call me dad, shouldn't you?"

"I—surely should—dad," replied Virginia, huskily. She could have kissed him, and probably would have but for the tight hold Ethel had on her.

"Good! That will tickle mother. Do you know, Virginia, I'm like to grow jealous of you. . . . Wal, Cliff wasn't surprised at all to see me. He was as nice an' kind as if I'd—as if nothin' had never happened between us. Asked all about mother, an' shore wanted to see her bad. But he can't leave the sheep just now. An' I reckon mother will have to go over to Sycamore."

"Oh, I hope she goes soon," burst out Virginia.

"Huh! Trust that little lady. Wal, I was pretty gingerly about tacklin' Cliff. You see, he had me buffaloed. There's sure been a vast change in that boy. So I beat around the bush, talkin' a lot, to get my wind."

"Did you speak—of me?" queried Virginia, breathlessly.

"I should smile. You were my best bet. First I told him you owned the sheep he'd been drivin'. He said Lopez had told him. An' then Cliff said it wasn't so good for him, as he needed his wages an' shore couldn't take money from you."

"Oh!" cried Virginia, poignantly, clinging to Ethel's comforting hand.

"An' I told him that was just as well, 'cause you was now a poor girl. He looked blank. Then he laughed. But I knocked him open-mouthed by tellin' him you had deeded Cottonwoods back to me. He cussed me, an' wanted to know how that could be. He'd never heard of your father killin' Malpass, an' then dyin' from gun-shots. That made him sober. He whispered, 'Poor Virginia!' An' then he wanted to know what had become of you. I told him how you'd gone to live where we used to. That you had a few horses, an old car, an' not much money. You'd have to sell the sheep presently. I could see he was sick about it, an' shore mad at me, but he didn't cuss me again. He set there on the stump an' thought. Finally he looked up with the saddest eyes I ever seen an' said. . . . What do you think he said?"

"I can't imagine. Hurry!" whispered Virginia. In the excitement of the story Ethel had arisen from her elbows to get an arm around her, to hold her tight, a support she surely needed.

" 'When did she divorce me?' he asked. I told him you hadn't divorced him at all. . . . 'My Gawd!' he said, an' showed me a letter some months old that he hadn't got till his shepherd lad fetched it out from San Luis. It was not signed, but I recognized Malpass' handwritin'. The letter told of Virginia divorcin' you an' marryin' Malpass. . . . What a skunk an' greaser he was!"

"Oh, despicable! That's—the worst!" panted Virginia.

"Wal, it was good Cliff didn't get that letter way out on the desert, months ago. 'Cause it shore would have killed him."

"You—you think—Cliff cared?" asked Virginia, as if strangling to force utterance.

"Cared? My Heaven! Lass, the boy worshiped you. I saw that long ago, right after he first came back. Mother put me on to it. . . . I hated you because of that very thing. I accused him of it. All the time I could see his heart in his eyes. . . . Wal, it shore hurts me to think of that now—for Cliff's love for you saved his life."

"Oh, it couldn't be!" cried Virginia, wildly.

"Don't take on so, lass. Shore you must let me tell you. Most of all, let me ask help of you."

"But you mustn't make such rash statements. I can't believe them. But I—I might. And then how could I bear——"

"Child, I'm tellin' you the truth," expostulated Forrest.

"Oh, how can you say that?"

"Cliff told me. Told me right out, just as cool an'

calm as could be. He said: 'You needn't tell her, dad. No use to distress her further. Her heart is big, an' I don't want her sorry for me.' . . . Wal, then I——"

"You—you——" gasped Virginia, who divined what was coming.

"Shore. I told him plumb straight that it wasn't all to get free of Malpass you married him."

Virginia, in default of vocal powers, squeezed Ethel into asking, "And then what did Cliff say?"

" 'Wal, dad,' he said, cool an' easy, 'you never was very strong in the head. An' I'll thank you not to talk that way. Especially to anyone else.' It shore flabbergasted me, so I shut up. But I was deep stirred an' I asked him to forgive me for disgracin' him an' turnin' him out when he was ill an' crippled. . . . My Gawd! it hurt me to ask. That was damnin' me black. But once I got it out I felt better."

"Did he forgive you?" asked Virginia.

Forrest showed emotion. "Never a harsh word, lass. He told me, yes, an' that it made him happy to have everything straightened out. But he added that he expected me to forgive you, too. An' I said I had done that long ago. Wal, that nerved me for the last, an' I begged him to come home to Cottonwoods!"

"He refused," divined Virginia.

" 'No, dad,' he said, simply, 'I can't do that. I'll see mother often when I'm here, an' you too, if you want, but my home is the desert henceforth.' I wanted to rave an' swear. A sheep-herder! My son Clifton! A sheep-herder like those peons! . . . But somethin' about him nailed my lips. You'll feel it when you see him."

"See Clifton!—I'll never have the courage now," moaned Virginia.

Forrest's face fell. "Lass, you love him, don't you?"

She made a hopeless, helpless gesture, more eloquent than any affirmation.

"You're my last card, Virginia," he went on. "If you can't persuade Cliff to come back to us—mother an' you an' me, I'm ruined, an' it'll finish mother."

"I would persuade with the last drop of my heart's blood," flashed Virginia, passionately, "if it would be of use. But I know Clifton Forrest. He is beyond us."

"Lass, I felt that, too. But you ain't takin' into account the one big factor. If he learns you love him—from your own lips—he will come back to us. But at that, I think he'll stick to the sheep an' the desert. I'll never forget him when he said, 'I'm a sheep-herder.' You'd think he thought he was President. . . . Wal, lass, I've laid my cards on the table, an' you've got the ace. Will you play it for us?"

"I'll do anything," answered Virginia, feeling herself abandoned to the fates, now aloft on the pinnacle of hope and again lost in the depths of despair.

Forrest kissed her hand with quaint old courtesy.

"A man ought to be grateful an' humble. *Quíen sabe?* Who knows, as the Mexicans have it? I once showed you my door—insulted you—to my endless shame an' regret. Today nothin' could do me more honor—make me happier—than to have you cross my threshold again as the wife of my son."

Barely had he disappeared among the trees when Ethel hugged Virginia within an inch of her life. Her rapture was infectious.

"Oh, I want to yell—to sing—to dance—to pray!"

cried Virginia. "He loves me—he loves me! . . . Years ago, Ethel, I used to pull the petals off the daisies and say, 'Clifton loves me—he loves me not.' . . . Oh, indeed, who knows what may happen? Only God! Surely way out there on the desert He heard Clifton's cry."

"Say, come down out of the clouds," quoth the practical Ethel, quickly recovering. "We gotta get our heads together. I'm not quite so stuck on myself as I was. For that 'I'm a sheep-herder' stuff of Cliff's has got my goat."

But Virginia was hopeless for the balance of that day, and Ethel had to do all the intriguing herself. Virginia soared back to the zenith; she could not hear, she did not talk, she was not hungry, and she would not sleep for hours.

Next morning she felt herself to have some semblance to a rational being, and reinstated herself in Ethel's intellectual regard. Both of them, however, were disrupted out of a possible even tenor by a message from Helen Andrews, which was brought in by Jake. Helen, on the way to Phoenix to visit her brother, had stopped off at Las Vegas to see Virginia. She had sent the message to Cottonwoods, whence it had been relayed to Virginia.

"Isn't that perfectly dear of her?" exclaimed Ethel.

"Indeed it is! . . . . I forgot to write her."

"Virginia, you were a jealous cat. But that girl was true blue."

"I really loved her. Only, Ethel, in my trouble I forgot everybody save you. . . . Hurry and dress. We'll drive in to town."

And this was how it came about that Virginia, late

in the day of friendship, though not too late, found another loving and steadfast heart.

The following morning Helen motored out in her riding-clothes, as planned, and the three had a glorious run on the horses. After luncheon Virginia's guests mysteriously disappeared.

It set Virginia to pondering. When they did not come back soon she went out to look for them. Nowhere in the grove! She fled to the barn, to confront Jake and Con at work on the horses that had been ridden.

"Jake, have the girls been here?" she queried.

Now to Virginia's knowledge no cowboy was a good liar. She saw through Jack in a second, and as for honest Con, he could not lie.

"What horses did you saddle?"

"Wal, Mrs. Forrest——"

"Don't call me that," flashed Virginia, not because she did not love the name, but for the reason that when she heard it she became a scarlet-faced schoolgirl.

"Tell me," she commanded.

"Shore, Miss Virginia, I reckoned somethin' was wrong," explained Jake, very contritely. "But not quick enough. Why, those girls could do anythin' with a man. I shore let them have Dumpy an' Calamity Jane without your orders. Honest to Gawd, though, I thought you was goin' to. Not till they rode off like mad did I take a tumble."

"Which—way did they—go?" asked Virginia, very weakly.

He pointed. "First they asked how to find Sycamore, an' I told them. They rode out the lane an' up the hill."

After the first shock had passed, Virginia realized that it was due only to her supercharged emotional capacity these trying days. Before she got back to the welcome shade trees she was divided between elation and gloom. Trust that sharp-eyed little Wayne lady! That was the terror of the thing, because after Ethel had seen Clifton there would never again be any doubts as to his status as a lover and husband.

If she had been on a rack of the Spaniards she could have held herself quieter than on this interminable fiendish afternoon. She had been warped out of her orbit. She fluttered like a leaf of an aspen tree. But at last they came.

Virginia had not been able to breathe inside the house. She had carried blanket and pillow out under the cottonwood where Clifton's father had told his story. But never until she espied the girls coming through the grove from the barn had she sat down, and then her legs gave way under her.

How slowly they came! Guilty wretches! But Ethel was radiant and Helen resembled the glorious Helen of ancient romance. The panic of dread, at least, stilled in Virginia's breast. They could not be so callous as to look so marvelously mysterious and angelic if they had bad news. Nevertheless, Virginia fixed on them terrible accusing eyes.

Helen threw sombrero, gloves, and whip to the turf, and she dropped on her knees before Virginia. Never had she looked so beautiful. Her face had the tint of a golden pearl and her eyes the sweetness of violets. Virginia had not before seen this Eastern woman under the influence of powerful emotion. Her

classic beauty had never lacked soul, but now it `ore
the glow of grave wonder and joy, of a woman's divi
understanding of what life or death meant to her
friend.

"He loves you, Virginia. You have been blessed by
the gods," she said, softly.

Virginia had not fortified herself for such a statement from Helen. Anything from the dynamic Ethel!
But Helen Andrews was patrician. In such an hour
rash or false words would have been impossible. Virginia lost her fierce strain of body and her consciousness succumbed to this attack. There was nothing she
could say. Ethel plumped down on her knees beside
Helen, sweetly serious for once. These two were
leagued against Virginia. She surrendered and never
before had she loved them as in that moment.

"We found Clifton a wondrously changed man,"
said Helen, speaking with the solemn gladness of one
who had been exalted by deeper insight into human
life, or confounded by a spiritual transformation. "I
pray that your desert can do as much for my brother
Jack. I have faith that it can. But far more than recovery of health and strength has come to Clifton. He has
seen through death, Virginia. I felt so slight before
him. No one could ever tell what he has gone through.
But you know he has conquered self, cast out evil,
seen the pitiful frailty of men and women, of our fleeting time here, of the unknown future. He is like the
Shepherd we read of in our childhood. . . . I felt
ashamed to be deceitful before him—to probe at his
heart, as this merciless Ethel wanted me to do and did
herself. . . . Just the mention of your name—Virginia
—betrayed him to me. How you have wronged him
not to know! All women are loved some time or other,

or often, or once, anyway. But this soldier—this sheep-herder—has surrounded you with his soul. . . . I think I understand men. My sweetheart went to war, the same as Clifton. He went a rollicking happy-go-lucky chap. But the war changed him. His letters over a period of months told of tremendous cataclysm of mind and heart, of spirit and faith. These letters have sustained me to bear his loss. . . . I felt in Clifton something of what Richard wrote me. These men stand apart. We can never understand them wholly. But the war built or it destroyed. Mostly the latter, alas! . . . I don't understand the desert. But so long as I live I shall never forget Clifton Forrest."

Virginia, almost blinded, clasped Helen in an unutterably grateful embrace, passionate and eloquent.

"You, too, Ethel," she said, presently, when she could speak. And it was reproachful acceptance of more just crucifixion.

But Ethel, despite the gravity of the occasion, in her excitement reverted to type.

"That heavy stuff of Helen's is beautiful, but it is bunk," she began. "Just listen to me a minute, will you? Clifton could cut out my fellow in two winks of a cat's eye. Do you get that, Virginia, old dear?"

"Yes, I get it, Ethel. I know how you'd exaggerate and lie and swear false witness to heaven itself to spare me. But don't spare me. I am dizzy with the ecstasy Helen inspired in me. But tell me honestly what you thought."

Ethel showed plainly that she was touched deeply, though not deflected from her natural trend. Or else she was deep as the sea!

"That Sycamore is sure a swell place," she went

on. "How come you never took us riding out there? It's not far. Clifton has the prettiest camp, as you'll agree. He has an eye for things. Camp all spick and span. Pots and pans clean. Everything orderly. I peeped into his tent. Gee! but I had a thrill. No girl ever had a room so sweet and comfortable as the inside of that tent. Soft woolly sheepskin rugs. Cedar boughs under his bed. Pure white sand. Indian paintbrush in a——"

"Child, tell me of him!" burst out Virginia.

"I didn't know him when he came up out of the gorge," returned Ethel, swiftly. "I didn't, yet I did. He appeared tall, but maybe that was because he walked erect. His color was a shiny dark gold. Face, arms, neck all bare. He might as well not have had a shirt at all, it was so ragged. And his trousers had a thousand patches, all kinds and shapes, some of them sheepskin. He wore a belt with a knife, and he carried a long stick, a shepherd's crook. . . . Well, he knew us both. Wasn't surprised even a little. 'Howdy, girls!' as glad and kind as you'd want to see. I let out a whoop and made for him—and well—dare I tell her, Helen?"

"I think it will be safe," replied Helen, with a smile that would have mitigated much.

"I just had to kiss him. Afterward I had the queerest feeling I ever had when I'd——Ahem! Well, I did. But Clifton took it fine. Made it easy for me in his gentle understanding way. All the same I won't be so fresh again, Virginia dear. . . . He asked why you didn't come, just as cool and natural-like. I wonder how much his father salved it on us in his story. Anyway, Cliff was just like your brother who hadn't seen you for a long time."

"So he asked for me!" murmured Virginia, and closed her eyes for a moment.

"Don't faint, honey. You know I can't stand indifference or aloofness from *any* man. And for you I was not standing it, either. Cliff was exactly that. He was just different. And I went after him. . . . Virginia, he has the purest, clearest eyes, the most eagle-like look, the finest face I ever saw on a man. Almost he is beautiful. But the cold flint is there—the desert. . . . I told him about your sufferings since that tragedy which freed you from tyranny. Of your sacrifice to his father. I lied like a trooper about your poverty. But, however he may have satisfied our Helen here, he sure didn't me till I told him—well, never mind what I told him, but he came across with what I wanted."

"And that?" whispered Virginia.

"I had to see where we stood in this deal. . . . Virginia, if you look at that fellow once *now*—and touch him with your little finger—he'll grab you in his arms and eat you up and——"

"Oh, hush!" cried Virginia, faintly. "Dear friends, don't tell me any more. I believe. I will do what you tell me. . . . And if you're wrong you can drape me like Elaine and lay me to rest here under this old cottonwood."

Ethel screamed her glee and hugged them both singly and together. "You glum darlings. Oh, how you make me laugh! All the time I knew. Leave it to me. There'll be nothing to it. Poor Cliff hasn't a show on earth, or on the desert, either. War is hell, and the desert may be a lot I don't savvy, but I'm telling you the little feminine genders rule the world."

"Then it is settled," returned Helen, rising, flushed and happy. "I shall leave for Phoenix in the morning. Let us all plan to forgather next June in Denver, when this precocious madcap gives her promise for better or worse—to learn men have always been the masters and ever will be. I shall fetch my brother. Find him a Western girl half as good and true as either of you, and I shall have further reason to love you."

"That's a cinch," laughed Ethel. "And, oh, Helen Andrews, how I'd love to land you for the West!"

"Thank you! That's a compliment I shall cherish. . . . Perhaps you can find me another sheep-herder!"

So in the golden sunset light under the cottonwoods they passed on arm in arm to the house.

Like one in a dream Virginia rode out on the range, captive of Ethel, blind and tumultuous in her faith. Sirius was not a horse to ride with her mind steeped in enchantment. He required an iron hand which he did not feel in this hour. But the trail led uphill and wore off his restive edge.

Many a day had Virginia ridden this range, but today was a stranger to all the past. She could look up to the notch between the mountains and see the gray flat crag with its pines—her shrine above Emerald Lake. It was best to look up. She was humble and longing. Introspection and philosophy and resolve were mere thoughts. She was motivated now by the simplest and sublimest of emotions.

How the range shone under the westering sun! Far away sloped the gray desert, dim and obscure, retreating toward the west. Northward heaved the bronze mountain barrier. But both range and mountain lost to their rival—this strange empty colorful desolate void called desert. It had saved her lover. She must learn how and why, and forever reverence it as a manifestation of God. Some day she might ride far across it, down and down toward that purple haze, to Guadaloupe.

"We will ride up under cover of the cedars there," said Ethel, bringing Virginia back to reality. "Then we can peek down into Sycamore and see the sheep grazing. Some class of a picture, old dear."

Presently, then, Virginia was gazing down into a wide beautiful valley, mostly green, but ribbed with amber bars, and rendered pastoral by a long straggling white flock of sheep. Her flock! But where was her shepherd?

"Come. I've called you twice," said Ethel. "We must go back of the hill and round to the head of that draw. There we can hide our horses. The sheep are working up to the camp. We've no time to lose, if we're to beat Cliff to it. Come, you old white-faced coward."

It seemed an age, though it was scarcely a quarter of an hour, when Virginia followed on Ethel's swift heels, through fragrant sage and among gray boulders, into a narrow defile, and through that to an open high bench graced by old sycamores, under one of which a white teepee tent gleamed red-gold in the sunset glow.

"Good!" whispered Ethel, in high exultation. How her eyes shone! "The coast is clear. I'll hide here and watch. Go now."

"Where to?" queried Virginia, abjectly.

"Anywhere to surprise Cliff," retorted Ethel. "Haven't I coached you a hundred times. Pop out of the earth. Drop out of the sky. Anything to get the first blow in. Personally, if it were I, I'd hide in his tent—

pretend to be asleep—let him find me there. And I'd sure——"

"I haven't the nerve."

"Beat it!" went on Ethel, sternly. "I hear the dogs. They'll eat you up if they see you. Hurry to get in his tent. . . . Virginia, you're his wife. . . . Beat it now."

She gave Virginia a hasty hug and warm kiss and then a shove.

Virginia looked around to find she was alone. She ran, her heart in her throat. The action lent wings to a thousand thrills. From somewhere deep in her came courage, too. She must hide from Clifton, and for the moment it was not the thought of surprising him that dominated. Still Ethel's suggestion landed her at the door of the little tent. She slipped in, panting.

She had a picture in her mind of this interior, precisely as she found it. Only the reality had the fragrance of fresh sage and cedar and the potency of intimacy. There was his bed, neatly made, though it consisted only of sheepskins on boughs, with a blanket folded back. She touched them, and it was as if she had been caressed.

Dogs barked outside. She heard the bleating of sheep, the pattering of many tiny feet. But she could not see either dogs or sheep.

Suddenly a tall form hove in sight, coming up over the bench. The sunset light shone brightly on the man—a shepherd, stalking bareheaded, with a staff in his hand. He had a ragged, wild look. Virginia's eyes devoured him. How lithe and dark! How queer the patched trousers of many hues. He strode nearer—up to the camp, to lean his crooked staff against a tree. Then he turned so the light fell upon his face. Clifton!

But transformed, as he had seemed in her dreams. She fell upon his bed, but not from pretense.

Suddenly the quivering of her body ceased. Too late! His step sounded close. Blood and nerve and muscle became inert. The canvas whipped.

"Santa Maria!" he exclaimed, aghast.

A silence ensued. Virginia lay on her side, face to the tent wall, and she did not breathe.

"Are you ill, lady, that you . . . Who are you?"

The voice was Clifton's and it unlocked her petrified functions. His hand fell upon her shoulder. With the contact every nerve and vein in her leaped to stinging, pulsing life. As he rolled her over her hands flew instinctively to hide her face.

"Who are you?"

"It's your—wife!" She had been coached and driven to that infantile speech. How idiotic! She longed for a hole to open in the ground to swallow her.

Strong hands exposed her face, lifted her to her knees—and she saw Clifton perilously close, the radiant sunset light upon him. For a moment the mother in her dominated, and her hand tenderly touched his cheek, that appeared dusky yet strangely pale, and then slipped to his clustering hair.

"It is you! Changed beyond belief. But I know you . . . Clifton, well and strong! Oh, thank God!"

His arm slipped round her waist and clasped tight to draw her close, while his free hand, under her chin, tilted up her head.

How stern his eyes! Clear, hazel, eagle-keen, with a blaze in their depths. She could only stare at him, fascinated, fearing it could not be true, shamed yet thrilled in the embrace of a man who was Clifton and a stranger.

"*Virginia*?" he asked, hoarsely.

"Yes. Don't you know me?"

"What does this mean?—My father comes to prate of you. . . . Then these friends of yours. And now you!"

"Aren't you glad to see me?"

"My God, woman! Would you play with fire?"

"Oh, Clifton, indeed I would, if——"

"You never freed yourself?"

"Never—and never will."

"Virginia Lundeen!"

"No. My last name is Forrest."

"Still my wife!"

"Yes, Cliff."

"I am in a maze. . . . Virginia, you married me to escape that half-breed Malpass."

"Yes, but that was not my main reason."

"What was?" he asked, incredulously.

"I just wanted to—to belong to you."

"You—you—Oh, I cannot say it!" he cried, huskily.

"Yes, Cliff, all my life, mostly. Since I was a girl. . . . At least since you kissed me that time."

He uttered a cry of commingled rapture and incredulity and fear.

"On the ship? On the train? That day in the store? And that night on the trail when you found me crawling, almost dead?"

"Yes, yes. Then, and the night I led you to propose to me—and the night you married me. Yes, and every day and every night since then I've loved you with all my mind and soul and heart and body."

"You glorious girl! . . . O God! I have fought and lived for this!" It was then Ethel's prediction was verified. He seemed fire and ice, savage and man all at once. The breath was crushed out of her body, and every mad longing she had ever had for his kisses was satisfied. They left her limp and numb. But she felt that he had spent himself, though he held her still. Gradually she sank with him to a seat on the bed, and when she recovered sufficiently to see and understand it seemed that Clifton was staring at the setting sun as a man to whom heaven had opened.

"But you've not told me," she whispered.

"Virginia, I love you," he replied, divining her hunger.

"Oh, Cliff! Oh, Cliff! . . . You don't have to propose to me—do you?"

"No? Why don't I?"

"Because I'm your wife."

"So you are," he replied, marveling, while his arm tightened. "I can't realize."

"Dearest, it is true. And at last I am happy. . . . Clifton, do not look so dazed. I will be guided by you. I am a woman who will obey. I do not ask you to give up your desert and your sheep. They are yours because they are mine, and all I have is yours. I shall love what you love. Your life and religion shall be mine."

"You will let me divide my time between the desert and home?"

"Let you? I implore you to. Your father and mother need you. They are growing old. So little will make them happy now."

"Virginia, don't shame me. I will do it."

She kissed his cheek. "You must teach me to love the desert. I understand a little the terror life has been to you. And how the naked earth, the elements, solitude and privation, have worked this miracle. Perhaps these things are God. Anyway, I reverence them."

She got to her knees again and slipped her arms round his neck and kissed him again and again.

"Ethel's way, darling," she whispered, with a shaky laugh. "She is wise. She sent me here. God bless her! . . . Cliff, I've a confession."

"Don't make it. Let me dream on. I am at Guadaloupe and you are with me."

"Will you take me there some day?"

"Child, you could never walk that long, long trail."

"But I could ride. Promise me." And she bent to his lips again, and would not desist until he promised.

"Cliff, I'm an impostor."

"Are you? Explain."

"You believe me poor white trash now?"

"Virginia, such a question!"

"Well, at least they told you I was poor, didn't they?"

"Yes."

"It's a lie. I am rich. I returned Cottonwoods and more to your father. Then I went to live in your—our old home. I love it there. I meant to pretend to be poor. But I can't lie to you. Father's estate was cleared and came to me. It was in father's will. I paid every claim I could find, and some that were surely questionable. Yet still there was a fortune left. . . . What do you think about it?"

"I hardly know," he returned in perplexity.

"Do you love me any the less because I'm not the poor ragged bare-legged Virginia Lundeen who used to waylay you?"

"I couldn't love you less because of anything."

"You'll let me keep it, then?" she queried, gravely.

"Let you, child? I'm very glad you have it. Could I support you in luxury on a few cents a day? Buy you exquisite clothes? Take care of your horses?"

"No, indeed, you couldn't. Then that is settled. Oh, how it worried me!"

From outside the tent rose a high sweet trilling laughter, wild and gay and exultant on the night air.

"Ethel—the little devil!" ejaculated Virginia, aghast. "She was with me. She's slipped up and listened."

"Let her," he replied, happily, and he spoke louder. "She was at considerable pains to let me know how poor you were. . . . That laugh now! . . . Well, Virginia Lundeen Forrest, you can buy me all the flocks on the range and I'll glory in driving them for you."

Virginia's modesty went into eclipse and she leaned to him, murmuring, "My shepherd!"

Zane Grey, author of over 80 books, was born in Ohio in 1872. His writing career spanned over 35 years until his death in 1939. Estimates of Zane Grey's audience exceed 250 million readers.